LET ME TELL YOU A STORY. . . .

"I'm very disappointed in these grades, Stephanie," Miss Fenton said. "This time, though, I'm afraid you're in deeper trouble. It's nearly the end of the semester, and thanks to these grades several of your averages are slipping into D territory."

That made me sit up fast, let me tell you. I may not be a straight-A student, but it didn't take me long to catch on to the real problem here. All Pine Hollow riders have to maintain at least a C average, or no riding until their grades come up. Summer is just weeks away, and if I finish below the cutoff, Max'll cut *me* off—and that means no riding ALL SUMMER!

Miss Fenton told me that she got all my teachers to agree to let me make up the worst of my bad grades. But there was more. "I'm adding a makeup assignment of my own as well, Stephanie."

Then she hit me with it. I have to write a report for her, explaining exactly why the work didn't get done right the first time.

"Don't look so alarmed," she said. "You're a creative girl. I'm sure you'll have no trouble completing this assignment. I'd like it on my desk first thing Monday morning. And I'll expect something very interesting."

Other books you will enjoy

THE SADDLE CLUB

STEVIE: THE INSIDE STORY

BONNIE BRYANT

A SKYLARK BOOK
NEW YORK • TORONTO • LONDON • SYDNEY • AUCKLAND

Special thanks to Sir "B" Farms
and Laura and Vinnie Marino

RL 5, 009-012

STEVIE: THE INSIDE STORY

A Bantam Skylark Book / February 1999

*I would like to express my special thanks
to Catherine Hapka for her help
in the writing of this book.*

Dinah Slattery
124 Mountain View Lane
Sugarbush, Vermont

Dear Dinah,

   Aren't you surprised to get an actual letter from me—me, Stevie Lake, who once told a teacher I was allergic to pencils to try to get out of taking an essay test? Join the club. I can hardly believe it myself. But Dad wouldn't let me call you on the phone. For one thing, he said Mom is waiting for some client to call; but of course he also started squawking about how much it costs to call Vermont from Virginia, and how when I get a job and pay the bills I can make long-distance phone calls whenever I want. Typical parent stuff.

Of course, that begs the question—why don't I just e-mail you? Here's the short answer: Brothers stink. And now the long answer. The Loser Posse, also known as my brothers, has been hogging the computer all week, ever since the three of them pooled their money and bought this idiotic new computer game called—get this—Awesome Jawsome. The hero is some stupid shark-headed mutant named Jawbone. I'm not sure what the point of the game is, but an awful lot of it seems to involve chomping on innocent bystanders and trying to rack up incisor points. You heard me. Incisor points. Don't ask me what it means—I think it has something to do with teeth. Leave it to Chad, Alex, and Michael to get hooked on the world's most ridiculous game! Mom and Dad have already warned them about a million times that they're not supposed to play more than two hours a week until school lets out for the summer, but they haven't let that stop them (especially when Mom and Dad are too busy chasing me away from the phone to notice what the three dorkateers are doing).

Anyway, I guess that means I'm stuck with snail mail, because if I have to wait another second to tell someone about what happened to me today I'll probably scream. And even if Mom would let me near the phone, I can't call Carole or Lisa. Lisa's at that ballet class her mom makes her take, and Carole's out making the rounds with Judy Barker, the vet who takes care of the horses at Pine Hollow. (Oh, wait, scratch that last explanation—I just remembered that Judy started coming to Pine Hollow before you moved away, so you know who she is.) Remind me to tell you about Carole's new job with Judy sometime. Anyway, I figured you were the best person to write to, since you're sort of involved in what I need to talk about. Well, indirectly, anyway. Actually, in a way, you could say you started the whole thing.

It all began this morning in homeroom. I was just sitting there, minding my own business and hardly talking at all during morning announcements. Then, out of the blue, I heard my name blaring out over the PA system. It was Miss Fenton, of course.

"What was that?" I asked the girl next to me—it was Betsy Cavanaugh, you probably remember her from when you went to Fenton Hall. She's that tall blond girl who's always trying to suck up to the Snob Queen (Veronica diAngelo, in case you've forgotten—as if anyone could actually forget the girl who once refused to eat the cafeteria's grilled cheese sandwiches because the cheese wasn't imported!).

Betsy gave me a sort of snotty look and said, "It was Miss Fenton. You know, our headmistress." And she stressed "headmistress."

It was kind of a weird thing to say, even for Betsy, but after half a second I figured it out. I remembered that when Betsy first moved to Willow Creek and started going to Fenton Hall, you and I convinced her that a headmistress was sort of the same as a janitor. And so Betsy asked Miss Fenton to throw away her banana peel for her. Remember that? Miss Fenton looked as surprised as if one of the students had asked her to stand on her head and sing the national anthem. Anyway, then I remembered Betsy is mad at me because I convinced her last week in math class that a denominator is the name of a character from an action movie. So when Ms. Snyder wanted us to find the denominator in a fraction problem, Betsy started giggling really loudly and couldn't stop. The whole class thought she was crazy—especially when she tried to explain. Naturally, I innocently pretended not to know what she was talking about. I guess that was why she looked kind of annoyed with me today, even though it happened three whole days ago. I mean, she'd had the whole weekend to get over it. Some people have no sense of humor!

I didn't have time to worry about that, though. "What did she want?" I asked Betsy with infinite patience. (Did you get that? <u>Infinite patience.</u> Pretty cool phrase, huh? Mom uses it all the time.)

"She wants you to come to her office right now," Betsy said. She looked pretty happy about that, and I guess she thought I was going to get in trouble.

She was right. When I got to the office, I recognized the expression on Miss Fenton's face right away.

"Sit down, Stephanie," she said in her super-serious voice.

One good thing you can say for Miss Fenton—she doesn't waste time beating around the bush. My rear had hardly touched the seat when she started telling me why I was there. It was my grades. Namely, my English test on <u>To Kill a Mocking-bird</u>—remember, I brought the book along when I came to visit you over spring break?—and a big math test I took a couple of weeks ago, and my last history paper (it was about Paul Revere), and maybe one or two other assignments...The point is, I guess I hadn't done very well on any of them. You know me. Grades don't always sink in if I'm busy thinking about something more important, so I guess I hadn't really noticed until I saw them all in front of me in black and white (well, red and white, mostly, except for the one from my English teacher, who writes all her grades in purple) just how many not-so-great ones I'd been getting lately. I mean, I hadn't actually <u>failed</u> anything, except the math test. But you get the idea.

"I'm very disappointed in these grades, Stephanie," Miss Fenton said. "I'm sure you are, too. You're a much smarter girl than these marks indicate." She kind of sighed then and took her

4

glasses off so she could rub her eyes, sort of like Mom does when she gets a headache (usually after my dopey brothers have been fighting). "I've never understood why a student who is perfectly capable of making straight As is satisfied to scrape by with a C-plus average most of the time."

"I don't understand it, either," I said. I wasn't sure what she was expecting me to say. It also didn't seem like the ideal time to point out that my average for the first half of the year was a solid B. Anyway, she just gave me a look and continued.

"This time, though, I'm afraid you're in deeper trouble," she went on. "It's nearly the end of the semester, and thanks to these grades several of your averages are slipping into D territory."

That made me sit up fast, let me tell you. I may not be a straight-A student (duh!), but it didn't take me long to catch on to the real problem here. You know Max's rule. All Pine Hollow riders have to maintain at least a C average, or no riding until their grades come up. That's scary enough most of the time. But the timing right now really stinks. Summer is just weeks away, and if I finish below the cutoff, he'll cut _me_ off—and that means no riding ALL SUMMER! You know how tough Max can be about stuff like that. So I was practically shaking in my boots. (Did I mention? My brothers poured molasses in my sneakers yesterday and Mom's still trying to get them clean, so I actually did wear my low riding boots to school today. Let me tell you, those boots may be nice and comfy when I'm in the saddle, but just try walking around on those hard tile floors all day long and see how comfy they are by the final bell!)

I started to talk then, trying to explain what had happened. How I had been really busy with totally important stuff that I couldn't possibly have missed, and how I had really, really meant to do a better job on those assignments.

5

She waved her hand to shut me up, looking sort of, I don't know, <u>weary</u> or something. I kept trying to explain, but it was no use. She didn't want to hear it.

But don't worry. There's some good news, too. Well, sort of. You see, Miss Fenton went on to tell me that she got all my teachers to agree to let me make up the worst of my bad grades. I thought that was pretty cool, even though it means I'll have to waste even more gorgeous spring afternoons studying and writing boring papers about Paul Revere. Still, it seemed like a small price to pay for a relaxing summer of riding every day.

But there was more. "I'm adding a makeup assignment of my own as well, Stephanie," Miss F said, looking at me over the tops of her glasses—you know, like she always does when she's about to say something really serious and wants to make sure you're hanging on every word.

Then she hit me with it. I have to write a report for her, explaining exactly why the work didn't get done right the first time and "offering ideas for preventing such problems in the future." That's a direct quote, I think. Anyway, it sounds like her, doesn't it? So I'm sure it was something like that.

I guess I must have gasped when she told me, because she smiled a little.

"Don't look so alarmed, Stephanie," she said. "You're a creative girl. I'm sure you'll have no trouble completing this assignment. I'd like it on my desk first thing Monday morning, exactly two weeks from today. And I'll expect something very interesting."

<u>Interesting</u>? That's a joke. Teachers sometimes say they want you to be interesting, but what they really want is for you to be quiet and boring and obedient. Definitely <u>not</u> interesting. So I know I'm not in for much of an <u>interesting</u> time with this report.

6

Still, I know I can't afford to mess this up. You remember Miss Fenton—she looks kind of meek and nice, but underneath she's tough. And I'm probably pretty lucky she's giving me a chance to save my riding privileges at all. She didn't have to do that. Of course, even if I'm grateful, that doesn't mean I'm not still bummed about having to sit around writing some boring report when I could be out riding or whatever. Especially since I'll probably have to spend hours and hours working on it to make sure it's good enough—"interesting" enough—to satisfy Miss Fenton and save my grades. Lisa might not mind that kind of work, but hey, I'm not Lisa! For once I almost wish I were, though. Having a little of Lisa's talent for schoolwork would make me feel a lot more confident about this report, and a lot more certain that I'm not going to mess it up—and mess up my whole summer along with it! If I can't ride at Pine Hollow, there's no way Mom and Dad will let me go to riding camp. So Carole and Lisa will go without me, and I'll be stuck here at home with my Jawboneheaded brothers for three solid months without even being able to escape to the stable.... Ugh! It would be a total nightmare.

So I guess that means I'd better start figuring out what Miss F is expecting. I already have some ideas. You know—lots of boring junk about <u>responsibility</u>, her favorite word. With plenty of dull examples about how important it is to do the right thing, do your homework, blah blah blah.

She'll probably also expect me to say it would have been better if I'd concentrated more on my schoolwork and less on whatever it was I was doing instead. If she only knew all the stuff I was doing instead! There's no way I would have missed out on any of it, not for <u>To Kill a Mockingbird</u> or a bunch of stupid fractions or anything else. I mean, how could I have wasted even one second of my Vermont trip thinking about Paul Revere when we were doing such interesting stuff? If my teachers cared more about sugaring-off season in Vermont and less about denominators and mockingbirds, I wouldn't have to worry about my grades at all. Then when I got home there was all that excitement with Pepper and Dorothy DeSoto that I wrote you about, not to mention meeting a real live racehorse and watching her run! And of course, I've spent most of the past few weeks thinking about nothing but foxhunting....

Speaking of the fox hunt, I almost forgot to tell you something. My hand is about to fall off from all this writing, but this is important—Veronica diAngelo is acting really weird.

Okay, okay, I know what you're thinking. The Snob Queen always acts weird. But this goes beyond her usual blabbing about her rich family and expensive clothes and all that stuff. Her behavior is getting downright bizarre. At first all I noticed was that she was walking around with a strange expression on her face—sort of frowny and spaced out. I just assumed she was only looking at me that way because she was still mad about what happened at the fox hunt.

But there has to be more to it than that. She missed school twice last week, and not only did she not look sick, but she also didn't brag about skipping to go to some fancy spa or anything like that. And here's the really strange thing. As I was leaving Miss Fenton's office today, I would have sworn I heard Miss F tell her secretary to call "Miss diAngelo" in next. Could Little Miss Perfect actually be getting herself in trouble? I have no idea, but you know me—I definitely plan to find out! And I promise to keep you updated.

Anyway, I'd better sign off and mail this letter before my hand cramps so much I can't even pick up the reins (or type my re-

8

port—ugh!). I'll be sure to let you know what happens, with my report and the rest of it....

Your incredibly responsible friend,
Stevie

RESPONSIBILITY
A Report by Stephanie Lake

It is very important for every person to take responsibility for the things that they do. If we all don't take responsibility, then the lack of responsibility will make the world a less responsible place.

For example, if a doctor isn't responsible, he or she might miss an important symptom that might help to diagnose and cure a patient. A lawyer has to be responsible so that criminals will get punished and innocent people won't. The owner of a riding stable must be responsible for taking care of the horses there and making sure the riders learn what they're supposed to learn so that they can ride safely and responsibly.

Students like me must be responsible, too. Responsibility isn't something that starts when you get old and grown up. It is important for students to do their assignments and study for tests, and

AAARGH!!! THIS STUPID REPORT IS SO BORING ALREADY THAT I'M GOING TO KILL MYSELF IF I HAVE TO WRITE ONE MORE WORD!!!!!!!

Hi, Dinah! Okay, I know you probably didn't get my letter yet, since I just sent it the day before yesterday. But it should come soon, and then this e-mail will make a lot more sense, I promise! :-)

I was so worn out from writing you that long letter (you'll be impressed when you get it, just wait and see!) that I decided to wait and sleep on it before I started writing my report. So I sat down yesterday right after school—well, okay, make that right after my Tuesday riding class—to get started. Mom even chased my Jawbone-obsessed brothers away from the computer for me. (I may have forgotten to mention it in the letter, but Miss Fenton called my parents about the assignment, and naturally they weren't exactly thrilled about the state of my grades. They grounded me for the next two weeks so that I'll have "plenty of time to make this report good," as Mom put it. Luckily they're still letting me go to riding lessons, though, since they already paid this month.)

And so I sat there staring at the blank computer screen. For about an hour. Every time I thought of something to write, it sounded incredibly lame and boring.

Finally I decided I just had to do it. Maybe Miss Fenton would actually like lame and boring. So I started typing, trying to work in all that stuff she likes, especially stuff about responsibility. I got a few paragraphs into it, but then I couldn't take it anymore. It all sounded so fake and stupid, not like me at all. But I wasn't sure what else to try. So I told Mom I had a headache and she let me go to bed early.

I was worried about my report all day at school, especially when Miss Fenton stopped me in the hall to ask how it was going. I just mumbled something and escaped, and made sure I avoided her for the rest of the day. At that point I was sure my school career—and my riding career—were doomed.

Despite being grounded, I decided to swing by Pine Hollow right after school. I figured that if I was going to be banned from the stable soon, I might as well spend a little time there while I still could. (Plus, I knew both Mom and Dad had late meetings today and wouldn't be home until almost dinnertime.)

It turned out to be one of the best decisions I ever made. As usual, just being at Pine Hollow made me feel a little bit better. I gave Topside a good grooming and tried to convince myself to go back to the report I had started and keep going. But I still wasn't sure I could do it. I figured I needed a new angle. But what?

Then Carole and Lisa helped me come up with the answer. We were doing a few chores in the tack room and talking as we worked. All I could think about was my stupid report, so that was what we were talking about. (Mostly, anyway—Carole kept drifting off to other topics, like Starlight's training, Starlight's feeding schedule, Starlight's new horseshoes . . . Hey, but you remember Carole, right? The phrase "one-track mind" was practically invented for her. Not to mention the phrase "horse-crazy.")

So when she wasn't talking about Starlight, Carole kept saying how Miss Fenton couldn't possibly understand why I had been so distracted unless she understood how I feel about horses. And I guess that's true, since a lot of my distractions lately have had a lot to do with horses and riding. Although if Carole went to Fenton Hall, she would realize that Miss F can have a pretty one-track mind herself when it comes to grades. . . .

Anyway, Carole's point was that she thought my report should be all about horses. She even volunteered to let me use her favorite photo of the three of us (me, Carole, and Lisa, that is) on horseback. It's a really good picture—Carole's dad took it a few months ago at one of our Horse Wise meetings. (Horse Wise is the name of our Pony Club, in case I never told you that.) Carole thought the picture would make a perfect cover for my report.

Lisa wasn't convinced about the horse thing. She kept saying I should make sure my report is very well written and complete, because she thinks teachers usually care just as much about *how* you write something as *what* you write. That doesn't make much sense to me, but I guess Lisa should know. After all, she's the straight-A student, beloved by every teacher she's ever met. It's a good thing she goes to the public school instead of to Fenton Hall, or Miss Fenton would probably give up on me altogether!

But the point is, talking with my friends actually inspired

a fantastic brainstorm. (The Saddle Club works that way a lot—the three of us seem totally different, but we can make each other think in ways we wouldn't otherwise.) Carole's idea about including the horse photo made me realize that a report doesn't have to be just boring words. Lisa's suggestions reminded me of some of the things Miss Fenton said to me and made me see that she would probably be wowed by any extra creative effort I put into this project, no matter what it is. (I hope so, anyway.)

So here it is: I'm going to turn my boring report into a THRILLING MULTIMEDIA PRESENTATION! If Miss Fenton can totally relive the past month or two of my life—every exciting detail, every bit of action and fun—through my report, she can't help loving it. For one thing, she'll be impressed by my thoroughness (as you may recall, that's another obsession of hers). But also, she might even understand what I tried to tell her the other day—namely, exactly why I've been so busy lately and how much I learned that I couldn't possibly have learned in school even if I studied for a million years. And how only having such a creative and interesting life could prepare me for writing such a creative and interesting paper—I mean multimedia presentation.

Okay, I'd better send this and get to work. If Mom and Dad catch me e-mailing you instead of writing my report, they'll flip out. Not to mention what my brothers would do. They've been skulking around all afternoon, peeking in here every two seconds to see if I'm finished yet.

Anyway, I know I can make this the most incredible assignment any Fenton Hall student has ever done. It will have it all—action, adventure, excitement, emotions, bravery, and thrills galore.

I just hope Miss Fenton is evolved enough to appreciate it!

Welcome to My Life!
A Multimedia Presentation by Stephanie Lake

Step right up, ladies and gentlemen! You're in for a thrilling, fascinating, and rare peek into the life of yours truly, Stevie Lake. Miss Fenton, you asked me to explain exactly why my schoolwork has slipped lately, and explain it I will. I'm not trying to make excuses for my less-than-wonderful grades. I only want to show you the real reasons for them. It isn't that I'm not smart enough to do better or that I didn't take the assignments seriously enough. It was simply that the whirlwind of action, mystery, intrigue, and drama that is Life consumed so much of my time that I wasn't able to give my schoolwork the full attention it deserved.

It all started with spring break. I was ready to spend the week reading *To Kill a Mockingbird* and studying fractions when fate intervened. Little did I know how much excitement, learning, even danger, was in store for me. But first . . .
Personality Profile: Dinah Slattery
(Miss Fenton, I know you know Dinah, because she used to go to Fenton Hall. But I thought it might be helpful to in-

14

clude this, just in case you don't remember her well enough, since she's pretty important to this part of my story.)

Dinah Slattery was born in Maryland, but her family moved to Willow Creek, Virginia, when she was seven. She attended Fenton Hall, and she took riding lessons at Willow Creek's own Pine Hollow Stables from age eight. While at Pine Hollow, Dinah rode a horse named Barq, a spirited Arabian whose name means "lightning" in Arabic. Dinah was a fine student at Pine Hollow, though she often had trouble remembering to keep her heels down. But she always loved horses. I remember that Max Regnery, owner of Pine Hollow, would often comment on how "enthusiastic" Dinah always was in riding class. Dinah is also good at lots of other things, like drawing and telling jokes. She was a terrific friend and a wonderful student at Fenton Hall, and I know I'm not the only one who missed her when she moved to Vermont the year before last. But Dinah and I have kept in touch through letters and e-mails, so we're still good friends. And she still has that enthusiastic spirit and sense of adventure that always made hanging out with her so much fun, as you will see.

And now, on with our story . . . It was the week before spring break, and I couldn't wait. I was looking forward to spending a lot of time at the stable, riding and hanging out with my friends. And of course, I was raring to start reading *To Kill a Mockingbird*, which I was sure must be a very fasci-

15

nating book, especially since I've always been interested in birds and other animals.

Then I got Dinah's letter inviting me to Vermont. An excerpt from her letter follows:

Every year around spring break, we have sugaring off. That's when we collect the sap from the maple trees and make syrup and sugar. We make up teams of three and I just learned that my team is one person short. Naturally, I thought of you. It's a whole week full of fun. We do it the old-fashioned way, using horse-drawn sleighs and everything. You're going to love it, Stevie. It's a great time of year here, and I promise we won't spend a minute of it in the principal's office!

NOTE: Dinah's reference to the principal's office was just a joke. You may recall, Miss Fenton, that Dinah and I occasionally let our natural exuberance get the better of us so that we would have to come to you and explain ourselves. But of course, we were both much more mature than that by this time, so she was just kidding. She certainly didn't intend for us to get into any trouble on this trip. Little did she know . . . But you'll just have to continue reading to find out about the exciting and unexpected things that happened to us.

Naturally, I was excited about the trip, even though it meant missing a very important meeting at Cross County Stables and having to give up many trail rides with my fellow members of The Saddle Club. Which brings us to . . .

Close-up on: The Saddle Club

The Saddle Club plays an important role in my story, so I'd like to introduce it here. It's a club I started with my two

16

best friends, Carole Hanson and Lisa Atwood. We all ride together at Pine Hollow, and we've been best friends ever since Lisa started taking lessons there. Carole and Lisa both attend the public school in Willow Creek, so I'll give you a brief idea of what each of them is like, since they'll be appearing frequently in this report.

Carole has been riding for practically her entire life, and she loves it more than anything. She's the best junior rider at Pine Hollow, and she lives, eats, sleeps, and breathes horses. Every inch of her room is plastered with photos, posters, and drawings of horses, especially her own horse, Starlight, who was a Christmas gift from her father. Carole already knows she wants to work with horses somehow when she grows up, although she changes her mind every other day about exactly what she wants to do—competitive rider, trainer, breeder, vet, or who knows what else. Personally, I'm not sure she'll ever be able to decide. She just might have to do them all! Carole has lived in Willow Creek for a few years, but before that she lived all over the country on different military bases because her father, Colonel Hanson, is in the Marine Corps. Her mother died of cancer a couple of years ago, and Carole still misses her, but she has a great relationship with her dad, who's a pretty cool guy. In addition to her horse, Starlight, Carole has a cat named Snowball. She loves country and western music, making Rice Krispies treats, and watching funny movies, and she hates green peppers.

Then there's Lisa. She's the newest rider of the three of

17

us, even though she's a year older than Carole and me. But she's almost as good as we are because she's such a fast learner. And not just in riding—Lisa can do almost anything once she sets her smart, totally logical mind to it. Her grades are perfect, she plays about five instruments, takes ballet, and used to take art classes and tennis lessons. She even knows how to play chess and golf! Mostly it's her mother who makes her learn all that stuff—Mrs. Atwood worries a lot about making Lisa into a proper young lady. But even without her mother bugging her, Lisa would probably still be a perfectionist. That's just the way she is. Don't ask me to explain it. At Pine Hollow, she used to ride a sweet, gentle horse named Pepper . . . but more on that later. Lisa has an older brother who's studying in Europe, and a Lhasa apso named Dolly who can balance a Ping-Pong ball on her nose (I taught her that trick). Lisa loves studying, grooming Pepper, mashed potatoes, and writing in her diary; she hates being late and forgetting things.

Despite our different personalities, the three of us get along great. That's partly because we all love horses so much. Being horse-crazy is the first requirement for being admitted to The Saddle Club.

The second requirement is also very important: All members must be willing to help each other out, no matter what. In the past, this has included standing by each other when we have problems with school or family or other things. Lisa and I are always ready to help Carole when she feels sad about her mother or is worried about some horse-related

18

problem. Carole and Lisa are always willing to give me advice when I get a little too competitive with my boyfriend, Phil Marsten. Carole and I were even able to help Lisa survive her first and last date with my older brother, Chad. (And if we can do that, we can do anything—ha ha! Just a little report humor!)

But the helpfulness of The Saddle Club goes beyond helping each other. We also love to help all kinds of other people whenever we can. For instance, we once helped Max Regnery get more business for his stable when we thought he might be having money troubles. We worked hard to run a festival fund-raiser for the children's hospital. (You may remember that, Miss Fenton, since we held it at the same time as Fenton Hall's spring fair.) We helped Skye Ransom, the famous teenage actor, learn to ride and thereby saved his film career. We pitched in to save the barn at our riding camp from a big fire. We threw a cool party for Colonel Hanson's fortieth birthday. We even helped one of Pine Hollow's mares, Delilah, give birth to her foal, Samson!

As you can see from the above examples, The Saddle Club is more than just a group of friends who like to ride, just as the Red Cross is more than just a gang of doctors and the Supreme Court is more than a bunch of people who wear robes. The Saddle Club could be considered a service organization of the highest order, and we take our responsibilities—to ourselves, to each other, to the community, and the world at large—very seriously indeed.

FROM:	Steviethegreat
TO:	LAtwood; HorseGal
SUBJECT:	Surprise!
MESSAGE:	

Hey, Lisa and Carole, guess what? Forget it, you'll never guess. Remember that report I was complaining about earlier today? Well, I think I've really got it this time. I'm ready to write the greatest report in the history of the world! I don't have much time—Dad just called Michael to set the table for dinner—so I'll try to sum it up quickly. I'm going to try to really express to Miss Fenton what my life has been like lately. That might convince her that I have a good excuse for my bad grades—especially if she can see how much I learned about other stuff (like sugaring off, avalanches, horse racing, life and death, foxhunting, even elephants!). Also, instead of calling it an essay or something boring like that, I'm calling it a "multimedia presentation." What that means is that I won't be limiting myself to dull, dry words like in normal essays. I can do anything necessary to show her what it's really like to be me!

I won't say I'm not a little nervous about this. After all, my entire summer is riding on this assignment (ha ha—*riding* on it—get it?). And Miss Fenton can be kind of serious sometimes, so I'm not a hundred percent sure she'll appreciate what I'm trying to do. But I do know I couldn't possibly finish the boring report I started yesterday, so I guess this is my only chance to redeem myself. (See Lisa? I was listening when you were talking today. I just hope I spelled "redeem" right!) And to be honest, I'm pretty pumped up about this whole assignment now. Finally, I'll have my chance to explain what really prevented me from doing my homework. It might even be fun!

I already wrote the whole introduction, including some stuff about The Saddle Club that I thought you guys might want to see. So I'm attaching the file with this e-mail so you can read it.

Let me know what you think!

FROM: HorseGal
TO: Steviethegreat
SUBJECT: Pigs fly in Willow Creek
MESSAGE:

Who are you, and what have you done with Stevie?

Hee hee, just kidding. It's great that you're excited about your report. Although Miss Fenton and your teachers would probably die of shock if they found out that you were excited about *any* schoolwork. . . .

Seriously, though, what you wrote so far is really great. I don't know Miss Fenton that well, but I don't see how she could help liking it.

I hope you don't mind me putting my two cents in, but I have one tiny suggestion about how to make it even better.

21

I noticed that you haven't mentioned Topside yet, or most of the other horses at Pine Hollow, either (except Starlight, Barq, and Pepper, but even them you only mention briefly). You're probably already planning to do that next. Maybe you could do a personality profile for some of the important horses like you did for Dinah and The Saddle Club, but you may want to consider going farther than that. Like I was saying this afternoon, I think the most important thing for your paper (especially now, with your new direction) is to make Miss Fenton understand about the horses.

I've been thinking as I type this, and I have a few ideas about how you could do it. For instance, how about this for a new opening line:

Topside is his name, and he's the most talented, gorgeous, athletic horse I have ever known. . . .

Or maybe . . . *the most wonderful, obedient, lovable horse on four hooves.*

If you don't like that approach, what about this as an opening paragraph:

Pine Hollow Stables is nestled among the rolling hills of Virginia, and it's the most special place on earth. The owner, Max Regnery, takes good care of his horses and riders, and they love him for it. I love every horse in the stable, but most of all I love ~~Starlight~~ *Topside. He's a Thoroughbred gelding who used to belong to the famous competitive rider Dorothy DeSoto, and he's the most talented, gorgeous, athletic horse I have ever known. His story and mine are inextricably intertwined, and it all begins at the wide double doorway of Pine Hollow's main building. . . .*

What do you think? The exact wording probably needs

some work, but I think something along those lines would really draw Miss Fenton in and get her excited about the report right away. Just a friendly suggestion . . .

FROM: LAtwood
TO: Steviethegreat
SUBJECT: Congratulations!
MESSAGE:

I'm glad you're psyched about your new report! It's really well written and exciting. I just have a few comments you may want to think about.

For instance, you sort of switch your point of view around in the first paragraph. First you address "Ladies and gentlemen," then you address Miss Fenton specifically. You might want to change that. Also, where you mention your "less-than-wonderful grades," I think you should change the phrasing to something less slangy. Maybe your "poor grades" or "inferior grades" or "disappointing grades."

There are a few other minor grammatical issues, but if you want, I can wait and read the whole paper for you before you turn it in. Basically, like I said, it sounds great. You just might want to keep in mind that it is a paper for school, so it should probably sound a little more formal from now on. Teachers don't like too much slang and casual language.

By the way, I don't think you have to worry about Miss Fenton. (You know, like you were talking about earlier when

23

you thought your summer was doomed.) I have to admit, I was a little worried myself when I heard about your assignment. It would really stink if you couldn't come to riding camp with us; and it would stink even more if you couldn't ride for the entire summer. But now that you're so enthusiastic about your report, I'm not worried at all. Didn't you tell me once that Miss Fenton admitted she thinks you're clever? You said she said it's your saving grace, I think. So I'm sure she'll like the new direction of your report—IF you really take it seriously and make it solid and substantial.

I have some ideas about how you can do that. While you're talking about everything you did in Vermont, you could include some specific information about sugaring off. For one thing, it's interesting; and for another thing, teachers like it when you show that you've learned a lot about a topic. Besides that, you told me once that Miss Fenton likes a lot of detail. (I think the way you put it was that she's obsessed with details, especially when she wants to know why you're late for homeroom!) So I'm sure she would love it if you included a lot about sugaring off. You could probably work in the information most easily in the form of footnotes. Teachers LOVE footnotes, and I just learned how to format them on the computer. I can show you how if you want.

By the way, another thought: Didn't you also mention that Miss Fenton's favorite word is "responsibility"? Maybe you should throw that in once or twice near the beginning—you know, just so she knows you remember this is all connected to homework somehow. . . .

Steviethegreat
DSlattVT
My nutty friends

Okay, so I finish dinner and come back to the computer to get back to work on my report, and what do I find waiting for me? E-mails from Carole and Lisa. You see, I e-mailed them about the new direction of my report just before dinner and sent them a copy to read. They both read it, and they both said they liked it. But they both also had an awful lot of "comments" and "ideas" and "suggestions" about how to change it.

Get this: Lisa wants me to add footnotes! I can't believe it. I would never hurt her feelings by telling her this, but footnotes would totally defeat the whole purpose of this paper. It would turn my cool, exciting, fun idea into something dry and dull and scholarly and, well, Lisa-like. I know you've never even met Lisa, since she started riding at Pine Hollow after you moved away, but I'm sure I've told you enough about her to understand what I'm talking about. She can sometimes be a little too serious and thoughtful for her own good. Especially when it comes to stuff like schoolwork.

Then there's Carole. (You *do* know her, so I'm sure what I'm about to say won't surprise you one bit!) She wanted me to make the entire project about horses. Of course, it will be partly about horses anyway. But leave it to Carole to forget that there's anything else to life! Ninety-nine percent of the time I don't mind at all when she goes on and on about horses. Actually, I usually think it's sort of cute—you know, just what makes Carole be Carole. But this is one of those one-percent times when I wish she could focus on something else for a change, like what my idea is really all about. I mean, if I were writing this report for Max, it would make sense to concentrate almost totally on horses. But somehow I don't think Miss Fenton would be interested in reading the entire personal history of every horse I've ever met.

Whew! I feel better now that I got that off my chest. Plus, as I was reading over my friends' e-mails again, I realized that maybe they do have some good ideas after all. Maybe the new opening lines Carole suggested for my paper were a little silly, but she does have a point when she says I've hardly mentioned horses at all so far. It couldn't hurt to stress that angle more, especially since Miss Fenton already knows how serious I am about riding. It might impress her more if she thinks a lot of my distractions were horse-related (instead of, say, TV-related or shopping-related or Awesome Jawsome–related—ha ha!) And Lisa's idea about adding lots of detail about sugaring off is a good one, even if I would rather close my hand in the car door than put the info in footnotes. Maybe she even has a point when she reminds me to keep the homework connection in mind (though leave it to her to bring it up).

Okay, so while I still think they kind of missed the point, I have to admit that the two of them have come through for me yet again. (Though not in quite the way they thought they were.) From now on I'm going to try to sort of mix in their good ideas as I write, working all that horse and sugaring-off and homework stuff right into the course of the story. I'll try to make it all seem so natural that my report can be chockful of facts and information and details and it will still be more like reading an exciting book or watching a great movie than plowing through some deadly dull term paper.

You know, I just thought of something. If all those textbook writers out there would do exactly what I'm planning to do, maybe I wouldn't be in this situation at all. Maybe I would have been so caught up in the story of the American Revolution that I would have been dying to learn everything there was to know about Paul Revere. (Though I'm not sure *anything* could make fractions seem exciting . . .)

By the way, I'm attaching the file of what I've written so far. I thought you might like to see the personality profile I wrote about you. I've included part of that letter you wrote inviting me to Vermont. Do you mind? Don't worry, I explained that comment you made about the principal's office—I even managed to work in that phrase Miss Fenton always used when she was scolding us. Remember? She always blamed most of what we did on our "natural exuberance." (I looked it up to make sure I spelled it right.) Plus, that gave me a perfect chance to write in a suspenseful reference to what happens later on in the story, just like you always see in books and movies.

I'd better sign off and get back to work. But let me know what you think of my report. Also, could you send me any info you can think of about sugaring off that I can use? I remember a lot of stuff, but I want to make sure I get everything exactly right. And you know a lot more about it than I do. If you can think of anything else I can use, send that too—you know, like the names of the horses at your stable, facts about the weather in Vermont, stuff like that. You know how Miss Fenton feels about details, especially useless or boring ones. Thanks!

Welcome to My Life . . .

I spent almost every second of the next week looking forward to my trip to Vermont. Finally the big day arrived. I packed my suitcase (which had plenty of room for my math book and *To Kill a Mockingbird*, along with the warm winter clothes I would need in Vermont's northern climate), and my dad drove me to the airport in Washington, D.C., and made sure I got on the right plane. While I waited for the other passengers to board, I had a chance to think about my first trip to Vermont, which is known as the Green Mountain State. Actually, that's what its name means—the *Ver* part means "green," and the *mont* means "mountain." That's because there are lots of mountains there, and lots of green—except in the winter, when most of the green (and the mountains, for that matter) are covered in a layer of white snow.

My seatmate was one of the last people aboard. He was

a middle-aged man wearing a business suit. He smiled and said hello as he stuck his briefcase under the seat and sat down, so I said hello back. "Are you going to Vermont?" I asked him. Okay, I know that doesn't sound like a very intelligent question, since obviously the whole plane was going to Vermont. But I was just trying to be friendly.

"Yes, I am," he said. "I'm going to an office supply manufacturers' conference."

I controlled my urge to wrinkle my nose at that. It sounded pretty dull. I was afraid he might start going into more detail about staplers or whatever and put me to sleep, so I decided to change the subject. "I'm going to visit my friend Dinah," I told him as the plane started taxiing down the runway. I turned to look out the window, wanting to see the city disappear beneath us. My mother always tells me it's polite to look at someone when you're speaking to them, but I figured this must be an exception. My seatmate probably wouldn't mind if I kept an eye on the scenery while I talked.

I don't remember exactly what I said, but basically I explained all about Dinah's invitation for me to be a part of this year's sugaring off. I figured the businessman probably knew a lot more about three-hole punches and pencil sharpeners than he did about making maple syrup, so I told him everything I had found out about it. For instance, I explained that the sap that becomes maple syrup comes from a tree called the sugar maple, or *Acer saccharum*, which grows best in temperate places where it's really cold in the winter, like Vermont. I also discussed how we would be driving horse-drawn sleighs to collect the sap from the maples, and some of the ways that driving a horse pulling a cart or sleigh is different from riding in a saddle.

Everything I was saying was so interesting that I hardly even noticed the flight. I guess it took a few hours to get from Washington to Vermont, but it felt like just a few minutes. I felt the plane begin its descent, and through the window I watched as we broke through a bank of fluffy white clouds and the land below us came into view. I watched in silence for a minute or two, amazed by the difference between the kind of landscape I was used to and this hilly, snow-covered place. Then, feeling guilty, I quickly summed up what I had been talking about so that my seatmate wouldn't be left in suspense. "So," I explained, "the most important part seems to be keeping an even tension on the long reins."

I could see little figures on the ground below as our plane aimed for a long, straight runway that seemed to be the only thing that wasn't covered with snow. Suddenly I realized that I was really here—in Vermont, about to see Dinah, ready to throw myself into the cool new experience of sugaring off. The excitement sort of overwhelmed me for a second so that I thought I wouldn't be able to stand it.

"We're almost here!" I cried.

My seatmate sat up straighter. "In Vermont already?" he said, rubbing his eyes and peering past me toward the window. "I had a great nap. I always sleep well on planes. Now, what was it you said you were coming up here to do?"

I couldn't believe it. He had slept through my entire fascinating lecture on sugaring off and sleigh driving! For a second I felt really annoyed and considered telling the man exactly what I thought of his manners. I mean, looking out the window while you're talking is one thing. Falling asleep while someone else is talking—especially when she's talking about something interesting—is something else!

Then I had a better idea. I smiled at him politely. "I said I'm going deep-sea diving as part of an archaeological exploration of the underwater caves that housed the early Viking settlers who actually turned out to be first cousins of Kublai Khan's publicity people and who gave the recipe for spaghetti to Marco Polo. We want to find the part of the recipe that includes the sauce. You may think I'm too young to be involved in something like that, but I'm actually forty-three years old."

The man gave me a really weird look, then cleared his throat and leaned over and started fiddling with his briefcase, even though the pilot had just said that we shouldn't take out our under-seat baggage until the seat belt sign went off. I just shrugged and returned my attention to the window. I had better things to think about.

I was excited about seeing Dinah and about learning to drive a sleigh. I was also interested in learning more about sugaring off. It was sure to be a vacation I would never forget. But I had no idea at that moment exactly how memorable it was going to turn out to be. . . .

I had no trouble spotting Dinah in the airport. She and her father were waiting just outside the gate. As soon as I saw her, it was as if she had never moved away. She was grinning and waving and jumping up and down, and as soon as I got through the gate, we raced up to each other for a good long hug.

In the car on the way to the Slatterys' house, Dinah told me a lot more about sugaring off. She said they could only do it at that time of year because it had to be when the days were warm enough for the sap to flow and the nights cold enough to freeze it.

"Sounds perfectly logical to me," I told her, "only I can't figure out where the spigot is. What do we do? Twist off a branch?"

I thought that was pretty amusing, but Dinah just rolled her eyes. "Very funny," she said. "No, what we do is make a hole." She went on to explain. We would drill a hole in the trunk of the tree, then put a spile (that's sort of like a spigot) into the hole. After that we'd hang a bucket from the spile. The spile directs the sap out of the tree and into the bucket.

Of course, back then I didn't know as much about the whole process as I do now. "That's all there is to maple syrup?" I asked. "We just go get it from the tree?"

"No way!" Dinah told me. "What we get from the tree is sap. That's like very watery syrup. In fact, you can taste it and you'll hardly be able to figure out what it is. No, what we do then is boil it. And boil it. And boil it." You see, it turns out that it can take fifty gallons of sap to make one gallon of maple syrup! It takes even more boiling to turn the maple syrup into maple sugar. But Dinah in-

32

sisted that all that work was definitely worth it—and now that I've learned so much about the whole process, I can say that I agree with her. Maple syrup and sugar are the best!

But I still hadn't learned that yet. In fact, I was so busy thinking about how I had to remember to read *To Kill a Mockingbird* while I was there that I almost missed what Dinah said next. Luckily I tuned in just in time, because it was very interesting and informative. She was explaining the connection between sugaring off and her riding class (since she had mentioned in her letter that her riding class would be doing the sap collecting). She said that the owner of her stable, Mr. Daviet, bought the land the stable is on without even realizing that it was just packed with sugar maples. When he figured it out, he decided to start the Sugar Hut as an offshoot business. He even named the place Sugarbush Stables, both after the closest town and, of course, because of the whole maple sugar connection. Pretty fascinating detail, huh?

Anyway, Dinah also told me about the contest we would be taking part in. Mr. Daviet's students had divided up into teams of three. The team that collected the most sap (and helped turn it into the most syrup) would win the grand prize.

"What's the grand prize?" I asked her. For a second I imagined things like a trip to Hawaii, a million dollars, a fancy house. . . . But I figured it wasn't really anything like that.

Still, I was surprised when Dinah told me what the real

prize was. "The winning team will always have first pick of riding horses at classes all next summer," she said.

"Outstanding!" I said, and I meant it. Maybe someone who doesn't ride wouldn't understand, but being able to ride your favorite horse in every class is truly a terrific prize.

I was ready to get started right away, and so was Dinah. She said the weather was perfect for setting out the buckets. "You can meet Betsy Hale, our teammate for the competition," she said, "and then we can get started."

"Today?" I asked.

Dinah grinned. "No time like the present!"

I grinned back. I hadn't seen Dinah for a long time, but if I had ever forgotten why we were such good friends (I hadn't), I remembered now. We think the same way. Neither of us likes to sit around and wait for the fun to start. We like to get out there and start it ourselves! I guess you could chalk that up to our natural exuberance.

We stopped at Dinah's house long enough to drop off my stuff and change clothes. Then we headed to the Sugar Hut. I'd like to take a moment right here to give you an idea about what the Sugar Hut is like and how I felt when I first saw it.

WHAT IS THE SUGAR HUT?
Let me spell it out . . .

S is for small—the Sugar Hut really is little more than a hut

U is for the unfinished, rough-hewn logs that form the walls

34

G is for the gorgeous drifts of snow that nestle around the tiny building

A is for the aroma of sweet-smelling wood-smoke from the fireplace

R is for the red-painted front door

H is for the humble look of the central stone chimney

U is for unbelievable—I still couldn't believe I was really there!

T is for terrific—which is how I felt when I realized I was in for a whole lot of fun! And educational learning.

We actually didn't spend much time at the Sugar Hut that day. We had other things to do. The first order of business was for me to meet Betsy Hale, the third member of our team. She has dark brown curly hair and a really cool smile that makes deep dimples in her round cheeks. I liked her right away. She was that kind of person.

"Are we ready to start?" Dinah asked her after Betsy and I had met.

"Mr. Daviet has been sending out teams on snowshoes," Betsy said.

They explained that we were all supposed to go out on snowshoes when we first put in the spiles. It sounded like slow going to me, especially since I'd never used snowshoes before. As it turned out, Betsy agreed. When I glanced at her, she had a mischievous sparkle in her eyes.

"Everybody but us has to go out on snowshoes," she said. "See, I explained to Mr. Daviet about this friend you had visiting, and I told him all about the fact that she was somewhat lame . . ."

I caught on right away. I slung one arm over Dinah's shoulders and pretended to have suddenly developed a limp in my right leg. "What's the matter with me?" I asked Betsy.

Betsy giggled. "That's what Mr. Daviet asked. I had to think fast. The first thing that came into my head was that you'd thrown a shoe, but I knew he wouldn't fall for that. I just told him you were recovering from surgery. It seemed to sort of cover everything."

The point of all this, as it turned out, was that we didn't have to use snowshoes after all. We got to use a horse-drawn sleigh!

NOTE OF EXPLANATION: Why this wasn't really cheating

It would be easy to look at our behavior and think we were just lying to get ahead of everyone else. But if you think about it, that isn't really true. You see, we were getting a later start than most of the other teams because of the time my plane got in. Also, everyone on the other teams lived in Vermont. They all knew their way around the woods (on snowshoes or otherwise) and how to work the sap-collecting equipment. I, however, was a visitor from the South, with much less experience with snow and none whatsoever with maple syrup (except on my pancakes). So we were really just evening things out.

Betsy explained that her sister, Jodi, would be there any minute with the sleigh. Jodi worked at Sugarbush Stables. Dinah told me that Jodi was a really great rider.

"She's not all that great," Betsy interrupted.

"Well, she's better than we are," Dinah said, "and she gets to spend all her time at the stable—"

"Except for the time she *says* she's at the stable, when she's really with a boyfriend," Betsy finished for her.

"And she helps in class and she can ride whenever she wants to and she told me that she'd take me on the Rocky Road Trail one of these days," Dinah said.

I could tell even then that Dinah and Betsy were similar in a lot of ways and agreed about most things. The big exception was Betsy's sister, Jodi. Having several siblings myself, I could sort of see where Betsy was coming from. Maybe to her having an older sister seemed just as unnecessary to a full and satisfactory life as having three annoying brothers did to me.

I didn't think too much about that just then, though, because I heard a wonderful sound floating toward us at that moment. It was a sound I had only heard once before—on the Starlight Ride at Pine Hollow on Christmas Eve, when Max rode through the fields in a horse-drawn sleigh. It was the sound of sleigh bells!

I turned and saw a sleigh coming toward us on the packed

snow of the wooded road. A large workhorse was pulling it, and the bells on the reins chimed merrily every time the girl who was driving moved her hands.

All of a sudden I had the weird but wonderful feeling that I hadn't just traveled up the East Coast from Virginia to Vermont. No, I had also traveled backward in time a century or two. It was a magical moment, and the only thing that could have made it even more perfect was if Carole and Lisa had been there to share it with me.

The older girl pulled the sleigh to a stop in front of us, then hopped down and tossed the long reins to Dinah, making the bells ring crazily all at once. "Here, you take the reins," she said.

"Me?" Dinah said.

"Yeah." That was all the older girl said in reply. Without so much as glancing at Betsy or me, she walked back the way she had come.

"That was Jodi," Betsy told me, rolling her eyes a little. "My older sister."

"She's usually friendlier," Dinah said quickly. "I guess she wasn't crazy about having to hitch up the sleigh for us. That must be why she hurried off. Anyway, you'll meet her again while you're here. I'm sure you'll like her."

"I'm sure I will," I agreed. But I only said it to be polite. I wasn't too sure at all—not after the way Jodi had acted.

But I didn't think about her for long. We were all eager to get started. Dinah and Betsy started talking about their favorite horses at the stable—the ones they would get to

38

ride all summer long if we won. Dinah's was named Goldie, and Betsy's was Mister.

We went into the Sugar Hut and collected all the equipment we would need—two large hand drills, a bunch of spiles, and an equal number of buckets. The rules of the contest stated that we had to set out every bucket we took with us. For each one we brought back empty, we would have to forfeit a bucket of sap to the other teams. So we were careful to take only as many buckets as we thought we could use. We loaded everything into the sleigh, then climbed aboard.

Then, finally, we were on our way!

Betsy drove first. She was sitting between Dinah and me on the long wooden bench-type seat. Actually, she wasn't sitting so much as standing, with her feet braced against a board at the front edge of the sleigh.

Driving a sleigh is a very interesting process, full of educational details. For instance, I noticed that Betsy was holding one rein in each hand. When we were ready to start, she flicked the reins so that they slapped the horse's rump lightly, and at the same time she made a sort of clicking sound with her tongue. At first I could feel every lumbering step the big horse took, because it tugged at the sleigh with each one. But once the horse picked up its pace and the runners started sliding smoothly over the snow, all I felt was an easy, gliding forward motion.

"Wow," I said. "Now I really feel like I've traveled back in time a few hundred years."

"Wait until we get to work," Betsy said. "You're going to wish for the twentieth century again!"

I wasn't sure exactly what she meant by that, but she and Dinah both seemed to find it awfully funny.

As we drove, I learned that driving a sleigh is more complicated than it looks in at least one interesting way. When you want to make a tight turn, you have to make sure the horse moves in the opposite direction first. For instance, to make a quick right, you first have to tug on the left rein so that the horse will shift a few steps to the left. Then the sleigh will move way over to the left side of the path, and it can make the turn to the right without pushing its shafts— those are the long wooden pieces that stick out from the sleigh on either side of the horse—into the horse's body.

Luckily, Betsy knew exactly how to manage the trick. So we made good time on the snowy, wooded paths.

I was still having a hard time believing I was really there. The landscape looked as though it had been painted for the front of a greeting card or something. It was really beautiful. As we drove along through the peaceful, snow-blanketed forest, I turned to count the buckets in the back of the sleigh once more. That reminded me of the fraction problems I had waiting for me back in my suitcase. But I knew I would have to worry about that later. Because now we had work to do.

I don't like to brag, but I caught on to the tree-tapping process really fast. It didn't hurt that Betsy and Dinah were such good teachers. They taught me all kinds of interesting things, like how to tell the sugar maples from the other trees (they're marked with a little maple leaf, which is painted on in the summer when it's easier to tell the trees apart) and how to decide where to place the spile (it's usually a good idea to tap right under a big branch, since the tree sends lots of sap to branches that are growing fast).

We tapped tree after tree, drilling holes, inserting spiles, and hanging buckets. After a while, I started to think we would never finish, that we could never possibly use up all the buckets we had brought in the sleigh. I was also starting to understand what Betsy had meant when she said I'd be wishing for a return to the twentieth century!

We kept at it until it started to get dark. By that time, we still had two buckets left. None of us liked the thought of returning empty buckets, but we knew we had to hurry if we were going to find two more sugar maples. We also realized the trees would have to be easy to find, or we might forget where they were.

We decided to look on our way back to the Sugar Hut. It was Dinah's turn to drive.

"Mr. Daviet thinks it's important for all of us to learn to drive a horse on a wagon or sleigh," Dinah told me as she picked up the reins and got started. After a minute or two, she offered to let me try driving for a few minutes. I said yes, of course. It looked like fun, and I had never driven anything except a tiny pony cart back at Pine Hollow.

It took me a moment to get used to the feel of the long reins. They were much heavier in my hands than normal reins, which made sense—after all, they were more than ten feet long! I quickly realized that they would also be harder on the horse's mouth than shorter reins, so just a bit of pressure would be enough to signal the horse clearly. It was exciting to drive, even just a few yards, and I was determined to learn more about driving sometime soon. I just love learning!

Soon I gave the reins back to Dinah, and we continued on our way through the woods. We were all scanning the trees around us, looking for those maple-leaf marks so that we could use our last two buckets.

"There's one!" Dinah declared. She pulled the sleigh to a halt.

"I see it," Betsy said. In a flash, she was out of the sleigh and hard at work tapping the tree. Then we were off again, keeping a close watch for that one last tree we needed.

"There must be one, there must be one," Dinah said, almost chanting.

My eyes were getting tired of squinting for tiny painted maple leaves, especially in the fading light. But suddenly I spotted what we were looking for. "There it is!" I shouted, pointing to the right.

They saw it, too. "Let's get it!" Dinah cried, flicking the reins to send the horse toward the sugar maple.

I was so busy watching the little mark on the tree trunk—I didn't want to lose sight of it, not until that last bucket was finally hanging there—that it took me a second to realize what was happening. I didn't notice that we had a problem until I heard the sound.

The awful, terrible, terrifying sound.

It was the sound of the shafts groaning in protest.

42

In that split second, I realized what was happening. Dinah was so busy heading for the tree that she had forgotten the rule about sharp turns. The horse was leaning so far into the right-hand shaft that it was on the verge of breaking!

I realized all that, but I knew I didn't have time to explain it. Dinah hadn't noticed a thing, and I had no idea if Betsy was paying attention, either.

It was all up to me.

Luckily, I knew what to do. I grabbed the left rein and tugged. From driving before, I knew that that should be all it would take.

It was. The horse responded instantly, shifting back toward the left. Then he stopped in his tracks.

"Huh?" Dinah said. I think that's what she said, anyway. I was too busy being grateful at escaping our close call that I was sort of distracted. I quickly explained why I had done what I'd done.

"Oh, wow!" Dinah exclaimed. "Your quick and brilliant thinking saved us all!"

"Oh, I don't know," I said modestly. Actually, I knew she was right—I had saved us from a lot of trouble. The sleigh could have broken or tipped over, the horse could have been badly hurt. . . . But that was all behind us now. I didn't want to rub it in.

"Yes, you did," Dinah insisted. "I really almost blew it— just to tap one maple tree. It wasn't worth it. Definitely."

I was really starting to blush by now. Deep down, I'm really a shy and humble person. Well, sort of. "Who says we can't tap it now?" I asked. I grabbed the equipment from the back of the sleigh and got to work. In a few minutes we were heading back to the Sugar Hut—a little older, and a little wiser.

FROM: LAtwood
TO: Steviethegreat
SUBJECT: Friendly reminder . . .
MESSAGE:

Hi! How's the report going? Are you still working on the part about your trip to Vermont? Because I just remembered something that happened while you were away and I wanted to remind you in case you forgot about it. It's Phil's unmounted Pony Club meeting. Remember? You had promised him you'd go over to Cross County for it, and then you couldn't reach him before you left for Vermont because he was on that class trip. So you made Carole and me promise to call him for you when he got back. . . . Well, you probably remember. I don't know if that's the kind of thing you want to include in your report, but it does become sort of important later because of what the meeting turned out to be about.

Anyway, I hope the writing is going well. We missed you at Pine Hollow today, though of course we understood why you couldn't make it. (At least I understood. But you know Carole. She thinks school is just a place to go between trail rides! Ha ha!) Anyway, Max let me groom our favorite new Pine Hollow resident today, and it was absolutely wonderful. What a sweetie! Let me know when you get to that part of your story. I'll definitely want to help you all I can!

Not to totally change the subject, but you missed another exciting episode of *The Rich and the Weird* at the stable this afternoon. Veronica stopped by, which of course shocked us, since we didn't have lessons or anything. Anyway, I heard her ordering Red to saddle up Garnet for her. So I figured she just felt like going for a ride. That's kind of unusual, but no big deal, right? I didn't think much about it. Then she disappeared toward the tack room, and I figured she was going to hover over Red and give him a hard time while he did her work for her. No surprises there, either. Except a few minutes later I happened to glance out the window of Diablo's stall, and I saw Veronica rushing down the driveway. Yes, rushing. As in *on foot*. And her family's limo was nowhere in sight. Don't ask me where she was going, but Red was pretty peeved when he came out a minute later with Garnet all saddled and ready. Pretty bizarre, huh? Even for Veronica!

Anyway, I don't want to distract you from your paper. I'll see you tomorrow at lessons, and I'll be dying to hear all about it. Don't forget what I told you about keeping things formal and straightforward. Teachers love that. And don't forget—substance!

Welcome to My Life . . .

Okay, Miss Fenton, we're going to have a little change in format here. You see, my trip to Vermont soon got so exciting that it was like being swept up in the events of some epic film. You know, like *Ben Hur* or *Star Wars*. So I think the best way to get that across is to write it as if it were a film script. I even called my close personal friend, teen movie star Skye Ransom, to help me with the details. I spent over an hour on the phone asking questions about how real Hollywood movie scripts are written. It was a very educational conversation, and I think you'll find that I learned a lot from it.

Without further ado, Stevie Lake Productions presents . . .

DANGER IN VERMONT!

An Action-Packed Blockbuster Movie Script by S. Lake

FADE IN
INTERIOR Dinah's bedroom, early morning
CLOSE-UP on STEVIE, an exceptionally attractive middle-school girl, sleeping peacefully in the spare bed. A stack of schoolbooks sits on the floor nearby, and a history textbook lies open on the pillow next to her, revealing a picture of Paul Revere.

STEVIE
(mumbles in her sleep)
1775 . . . 1775 . . . 1775 . . .
One if by land, two if by . . . (snores) . . .

The bedroom door opens, and DINAH enters. She is fully dressed and smiling.

NARRATOR (voice-over)
Early the next morning . . .

DINAH
(loudly)
Time to get up!

STEVIE
(yawning)
What's the hurry? Is it time to go collect
the sap?

Stevie sits up and rubs her eyes.
DRAMATIC MUSIC

NARRATOR (voice-over)
But it wasn't time to collect sap yet. It was
too cold outside. Instead, it was time for Stevie to go with Dinah to her riding class.

STEVIE
(bounding out of bed, completely wide
awake and refreshed at the thought of
riding)
Cool! Let's go!

Stevie pauses just long enough to carefully place her history book back on the pile with the other schoolbooks.

STEVIE
(lovingly)
I'll get back to *you* later, Mr. Revere. After
all, you must be the most interesting patriot
and silversmith in all of American history!

FADE TO
INTERIOR The Slatterys' front hall. Stevie, Dinah, and
MRS. SLATTERY are there.

DINAH
Bye, Mom. We're off to riding class.

Mrs. Slattery waves one finger warningly as Stevie and Dinah prepare to leave the house.

MRS. SLATTERY
(worried)
Make sure you follow Mr. Daviet's instructions. Remember, no cantering and no leav-

48

ing the ring without an experienced rider. And keep your hard hat on, and always take your vitamins, and wait at least an hour before swimming, and . . .

DINAH
(wearily)
Yes, Mom.

The two girls EXIT.

CUT TO
EXTERIOR The Slatterys' neighborhood. Dinah and Stevie are walking through the snow toward Sugarbush Stables.

DINAH

My parents think riding is too dangerous. They knew someone who had a freak accident on a horse and got brain damaged or something. They're sure the same thing will happen to me. That's why they spend hours before each class warning me to be careful. It's totally boring, but I have to let them do it or they won't let me ride at all.

STEVIE

Then you should definitely let them do it. Besides, it's important to always listen to your parents and other adults, like teachers

49

and headmistresses, for example. They're older and wiser than we are.

> DINAH
> Yes, that's true.

CUT TO
INTERIOR Sugarbush Stables. There are no other people in sight, and no sounds aside from those made by horses in their stalls.

> DINAH
> (worried)
> Uh-oh. There's nobody here. I have the funny feeling something's up.

> NARRATOR (voice-over)
> Dinah was right. Something *was* up. But our heroines didn't discover the truth until they encountered Jodi Hale.

CUT TO
INTERIOR A different section of the stable. CLOSE-UP on Dinah and Stevie, looking happy. There is the sound of a DOOR, and JODI walks out of one of the stalls. Jodi is a few years older than the other girls. She is dressed in stable clothes, but her hair is carefully styled and she wears makeup. She is scowling. Dinah and Stevie look surprised at her entrance.

JODI
(nastily; to Dinah)
Your riding class is canceled.

Dinah blushes. Stevie looks surprised at the older girl's meanness.

STEVIE
(very politely)
How come class is canceled, Jodi?

JODI
Because most people are busy with the sugaring. Also, Mr. Daviet has to spend the whole day at the Sugar Hut, so he can't teach.

DINAH
But Goldie's here.

PULL BACK to reveal a horse in the stall behind Dinah. CLOSE-UP on GOLDIE, a perfectly gorgeous and wonderful golden palomino gelding. His eyes shine with friendly curiosity. His beautiful pale mane floats gently in a slight breeze. He stares lovingly at Dinah.

DINAH
(hopefully)
Can we at least go for a trail ride, Jodi?

51

JODI
(rudely)
Forget it. You know the rules. I'd have to go
with you. You've got to have an experienced
rider along on a trail ride. And I've got Mark
Carey coming over here in half an hour for a
lesson in tacking up. So scram, dummies.

DINAH
(meaningfully)
Uh-huh. I just bet that's why Mark's coming
over here.

Stevie suddenly smiles. She has an idea.

STEVIE
(innocently)
Tacking up? Great, I could use some pointers
on that. Maybe Dinah and I should just join
in on that lesson. I forget, which do you put
on first, the saddle or the bridle?

Jodi gives Stevie a dirty look.

JODI
I just had a thought. Stevie is an extremely
experienced rider. I've heard she's one of the
best riders in the whole state of Virginia, or
possibly the whole entire East Coast. So why
don't you two go out alone?

DINAH
(eagerly)
Can we go on the Rocky Road Trail?

JODI
Whatever. But don't tell Mr. Daviet.

DRAMATIC PAUSE as Jodi looks around to make sure no one is listening.

JODI
The Rocky Road Trail has been closed all winter. Mr. Daviet doesn't want anybody on it until he has a chance to check it out later in the week. So be careful and keep your mouths shut and everything will be fine.

DINAH
(trustingly)
Okay, Jodi. Whatever you say.

Stevie nods, looking a tiny bit worried.
CUT TO a few minutes later. Stevie and Dinah are riding through breathtaking Vermont scenery. They are in the mountains, following a clearly marked riding trail.

STEVIE
(happily)
The scenery here is stupendous, Dinah. All

this snow reminds me of some of the many things I've learned in science class this year. For instance, did you know that the freezing point of water is thirty-two degrees Fahrenheit? That's the same as zero degrees Celsius.

DINAH
(admiringly)
Wow, Stevie. You sure do know a lot about science.

STEVIE
(modestly)
Oh, it's nothing. I just always try to do my best.

Suddenly there is a THUMP. Stevie's horse, EVERGREEN, jumps in surprise but calms down again quickly.

STEVIE
What was that?

DINAH
(not worried)
Just a clump of melting snow falling from a branch.

Stevie reacts, understands what Dinah is saying, and nods.

DINAH

You'll hear a lot of that at this time of year.
The horses won't even notice it next time.

At that moment there is another THUMP. The horses
don't flinch.
PULL OUT to show more of the scenery the girls are riding
through. We see the entrance to several trails, including a
very steep, mountainous one.

DINAH
(points to steepest trail)
There's the Rocky Road Trail. Let's go on it.
Is that okay with you?

STEVIE
(surprised that she is asking)
Of course. I love steep trails. And Jodi
seemed to think it was safe enough.

The two girls turn their horses toward the steep trail.
FADE OUT
DRAMATIC MUSIC

NARRATOR (voice-over)
(ominously)
Little did those two innocent girls realize the
horror and danger that awaited them on the
Rocky Road Trail . . .

FADE IN on Stevie and Dinah riding at a higher point of the Rocky Road Trail. They are leaving an area thick with evergreen trees, entering a flat, open plateau covered with snow.

DINAH

Thanks for filling me in on all the news from Willow Creek, Stevie. Oh, look, there's a clearing. Why don't we trot for a while? Maybe we can even canter!

STEVIE
(doubtfully)

On the frozen ground? Isn't that dangerous? The horses could slip, and we both know the rules. Safety first.

DINAH
(ashamed)

You're right as always, Stevie. Sometimes I can hardly believe how smart and responsible you are, especially since you're so cool and popular, too. No wonder everybody likes you so much. Okay, then, we won't canter. Let's just try a trot.

Dinah urges Goldie forward without waiting for Stevie's reply.

NARRATOR (voice-over)

Stevie was worried about trotting on the

frozen ground. But she was too stunned by the beautiful mountain scenery to say so for a moment . . .

PAN OVER beautiful mountain scenery

> NARRATOR (voice-over)
> . . . a critical moment that would change both their lives forever . . .

DRAMATIC MUSIC gets louder, then fades away as Goldie trots with difficulty through the deep snow on the trail. Stevie, still looking worried, urges Evergreen after them at a very slow, cautious trot.

> STEVIE
> (calling to Dinah, who is ahead)
> Wouldn't you rather just walk? That would be the responsible thing to do. And we're both very responsible people.

> DINAH
> (admiringly)
> All right, Stevie. You know best, after all.

There is a loud BOOM. It's another clump of snow hitting the ground. It is followed by a loud CRACK.
Evergreen flinches.

STEVIE
What's that?

DINAH
It's the sound of ice melting. As the weather
warms, the water in the icicles expands—remember that lesson in science class? You
studied extremely hard for that quiz, as I recall, although your teacher unfairly marked
you down for some minor errors on stuff that
wasn't even in the chapter we were supposed
to read—and the ice can crack as it melts.
It's a weird sound, isn't it?

Stevie nods, and the two girls ride on.

DINAH
(pointing, holding both reins in one hand)
Look, there's an interesting rock formation
up the mountain, just ahead. We climb on it
during the summer, and—

An extremely loud BOOM interrupts her from somewhere
nearby.
Goldie takes off, terrified by the sound. Dinah is taken by
surprise and does her best to keep her balance and hold on.

DINAH
AAAAAAAAAHHHHHHH!!!!!!!

STEVIE
(reacts instantly)
Hyaaa!

She signals to Evergreen, who leaps forward after the runaway.

DINAH
(terrified)
Stevie!

STEVIE
I'm coming, Dinah! Hold on!

Suddenly the woods are filled with the booming sounds of cracking ice. There is also another sound: the sound of wood breaking and rocks skittering and cracking against one another.

STEVIE
(gasps)
Avalanche!

PAN FORWARD to reveal rocks rolling down the hill, straight toward the trail ahead of Dinah.

STEVIE
(pale and scared)
And Dinah's riding straight into it!

PAN FORWARD to show Stevie's point of view.

SLOW MOTION Goldie is rearing about thirty yards down the trail. Small rocks tumble down the mountainside through the snow, kicking up puffs of snow and mud. In the middle of it is Dinah, clutching the horse's mane for dear life. Goldie rears again, standing majestically on both his hind legs, whinnying and screaming in horror, his legs trembling with fear. As soon as he lands on all fours again . . .

END SLOW MOTION Goldie bolts. Dinah flies from the saddle and lands hard on the snowy ground. She is obviously too stunned by the fall to move.

STEVIE
(gasps)
Oh, no! She's landed right in the path of the oncoming rocks!

QUICK FADE TO BLACK

NARRATOR (voice-over)
(dramatically)
Meanwhile, back at Pine Hollow . . .

FADE UP TO
EXTERIOR Pine Hollow Stables. A sunny early-spring day.
CUT TO Stable interior. CAROLE and LISA are standing in the hallway. Lisa, a pretty girl with shoulder-length

brown hair, is holding the receiver of the public pay phone attached to the wall. She is dressed in spotless preppy clothes and polished high boots, and her expression is very serious. Carole, leaning against the wall beside her, is a cute girl wearing an I ♥ HORSES T-shirt. She has a currycomb stuck in her thick, curly dark hair. She is busy cleaning a complicated pelham bit or a cavesson or some other piece of tack throughout most of the scene.

LISA
(as she dials carefully)
It's time to keep our solemn promise to Stevie and call Phil to tell him she can't make it to his Pony Club meeting.

CAROLE
(a bit distracted)
Huh? Oh, sure, whatever. Listen, do you think I need to add a little bit of corn oil to Starlight's diet, since I've started jumping him a lot more lately? I do. I think I'll go talk to Max about it right now.

She starts to leave. Lisa grabs her by the arm.

LISA
(scolds)
Pay attention, Carole. We have a job to do here. Don't get flaky.

CAROLE
(abashed)
Oops. Sorry. What's our job again?

LISA
(sighs, then explains patiently)
We have to call Phil for Stevie. Although I can't help feeling awkward about it. After all, Phil is Stevie's beau, her paramour, her inamorato, her sweetheart, her suitor. I can't help questioning the ethical conundrum of us, her female best friends, calling him on the phone—which, in case you were wondering, was invented by Alexander Graham Bell in 1876—when she isn't here. It's just a silly little thing, but I can't help worrying obsessively over it.
(sighs again)
Still, a promise is a promise. And we promised her we'd call him.

CAROLE
Oh yeah! I forgot all about that. I guess I was distracted by thinking how Starlight's mane looks so shiny and beautiful in the morning light. Do you think I should do his mane in high braids before our next lesson? He would look really good like that. Mrs. Reg has some spare thread in her office. I think I'll go look . . .

Carole starts to hurry off again. Lisa drags her back, rolling her eyes.

CUT TO

INTERIOR The home of PHIL MARSTEN. Phil, a very good-looking boy with deep, intelligent green eyes and a killer smile, is sitting on the couch doing his homework.

The phone RINGS. Phil picks it up.

> PHIL
> Hello? Oh, hi, Lisa. How are you today?

CUT TO

INTERIOR Pine Hollow, as before. Lisa is speaking on the phone while Carole continues to clean the piece of tack she is holding.

> LISA
> Good morning, Phil. I'm very well, thank you. And yourself?

She pauses for his answer before continuing.

> LISA
> (politely)
> Oh, marvelous. I'm so glad to hear that you're well as well. But listen, Phil. I'm afraid I have some terrible news about Stevie. Well, perhaps I shouldn't say "terrible." You see, technically speaking, the actual definition of the word "terrible" could be

63

construed to be the same as the word "terrifying," which this news indubitably isn't. And, of course, if you want to accept an alternate definition of "terrible," which is "repulsive or objectionable," that would also not supply an accurate description of this—

> CAROLE
> (interrupting)
> Give me that.

She grabs the phone from Lisa's hand.

> LISA
> Hey! I haven't had a chance to tell him the news yet.

> CAROLE
> (ignoring Lisa)
> Hey, Phil, I just remembered something I wanted to ask you. It's very important, so listen carefully. Okay, you know Starlight, right? Do you think he's better at stadium jumping or hunter seat equitation?

CUT TO
INTERIOR Phil's house.
CLOSE-UP on Phil's face. He looks confused.

PHIL

Uh, well, I don't know. What do you think, Carole?

CUT TO
CLOSE-UP on Carole.

CAROLE

I'm glad you asked! I think he shows so much natural talent that he could be great at any kind of jumping. Why, just the other day I was working with him in the indoor ring, and Max had left up a small course—let's see, I think there was a post-and-rail, a double oxer, a chicken coop . . .

CUT TO the clock on the wall in the Pine Hollow office. The minute hand sweeps forward about fifteen minutes.
CUT TO
CLOSE-UP on Carole.

CAROLE

(still on the phone; speaking very quickly)
. . . and so then I took him through the course one more time, and do you know, his hooves didn't so much as touch a single rail on any of the jumps! Starlight is perfect. Did I ever tell you about the time he . . .

65

CUT TO the clock again. The minute hand sweeps forward forty-five more minutes.

CUT TO

INTERIOR The stable hallway. Lisa is looking at her watch, her expression disgruntled. Carole doesn't notice. She is still talking on the phone.

> CAROLE
> (leaning against the wall, still talking fast)
> . . . and then another disease I just learned about is lymphangitis. That's problems with the lymphatic tubes, which drain fluid away from the tissues of a horse's hind legs. Their legs can become terribly swollen and may even start to ooze fluid if left untreated. Fortunately it's treatable, as well as being easy to prevent by cutting back on the horse's feed on days he won't be getting much exercise. Then there's lungworm, which is—

> LISA
> (interrupting)
> Carole! Carole! We have to tell him about Stevie, remember?

Carole looks annoyed for a second at being interrupted. Then a light dawns in her eyes.

> CAROLE
> (to Lisa)

66

Oh, yeah! I guess I forgot about that.
(into phone)
Listen here, Phil. Stevie can't come to your Pony Club meeting. She's away. Now, where was I? Oh yeah. Lungworm . . .

CUT TO
CLOSE-UP on Phil, looking shocked and heartbroken.

PHIL
(interrupting Carole)
What? What do you mean, Stevie can't come to the meeting?

CUT TO

CAROLE
(shrugs)
Huh? Oh, she's in Vermont or someplace. Maybe it's New Hampshire. Or New Mexico. What difference does it make? Anyway, I know there's a stable there, so at least she'll get to ride while she's away.

PHIL (offscreen; through phone)
But that's terrible. I really wanted her to come to my meeting. It won't be the same without her. Things are never the same without her sparkling personality and bril-

liant wit, of course, but this time they'll be even less the same.

CAROLE
(shrugs again)
Hey, what can I say? Tough break. So anyway, how's your horse, Teddy? Have you taught him any more dressage moves or anything? By the way, did you know that the word "dressage" comes from a French word that means "training"? Also, it has been around for ages. In the fourth century B.C. . . .

PHIL (offscreen; through phone)
Wait! Carole, I have to ask you something. Something important.

CAROLE
What? Does it have something to do with Starlight?

CUT TO

PHIL
No, not really. I just wondered if you and Lisa would like to come to my meeting instead. You know, in Stevie's place. That way you can tell her about it when she gets back.

CUT TO

                    CAROLE
                   (confused)
              Uh—wha—ah . . . Okay.

Carole hangs up the phone and turns toward Lisa.

                    CAROLE
          Phil just invited us to the meeting.

                     LISA
                 (looks worried)
          Us? But Stevie is his girlfriend.

                    CAROLE
          Oh yeah. I guess I forgot about that.

                     LISA
Oh dear. This is truly a moral quandary. I certainly hope Stevie doesn't think we're trying
to steal her boyfriend. Oh dear. Oh dear.

FADE OUT on Lisa's worried face.

Hi, guys! You wouldn't recognize me these days. I'm getting so much work done on my report that I'm thinking of taking up writing school reports as a career someday! (Just kidding.) But seriously, it's getting pretty scary. I mean, I've practically moved into the den with the computer (actually, I had to—whenever I leave, even for two minutes to go to the bathroom or to get a snack, my brothers try to sneak in and take over). And I think by this point just about every reference book in the house is stacked on the desk or floor next to me. I really want to make sure to include lots of specific facts and information to prove how much research and thought I'm putting into this. I've managed to work in quite a few extra facts (and some really cool long words) so far.

Anyway, I'm right in the middle of it, but I just found something I had to tell you about. It happened while I was in my room. I was searching through that top shelf in my closet—you know, the one my mother calls the abyss? Anyway, I was looking for this e-mail from Dinah I printed out yesterday. It had a whole bunch of useful info in it about sugaring off and stuff, so of course I didn't want to leave it lying around where my rotten, scheming brothers could find it and take it hostage. (Don't even get me started on their latest pathetic attempts to pry me away from the computer so they can play their stupid game!) But I guess I hid it a little too well, because while I was digging around on the shelf, I uncovered some papers I had totally forgotten about. One was a math quiz I was hiding from Mom and Dad, and then there was some paperwork from Max and a couple of magazines and some dirty socks and other stuff. . . . But anyway, the important thing is that I found a letter I wrote to you guys when I was in Vermont.

What letter, you ask? Well, don't worry. You're not losing your memories. I never quite got around to sending it, and I probably forgot to tell you I ever wrote it. See, I was going to send it to you both in care of Pine Hollow so you'd be sure to get it at the same time. But I couldn't remember the exact address, or whether the zip code was the same as at my house. Well, anyway, you get the idea. It's kind of a shame, too, because the letter is really long and, if I say so myself, pretty exciting.

The point is, the letter will be a perfect addition to my report! This is where the multimedia part really starts to come in, see? I'm going to attach it to the report in the appropriate spot and it will help tell the story. (Of course, I did have to cross out a few things I didn't want Miss Fenton to read. But she'll probably just think they're misspelled words or something.)

You guys already know about all the stuff I talk about in the letter. But I'll be sure to finally give it to you once Miss Fenton hands my report back!

By the way, Lisa, thanks again for loaning me your dictionary. It's a lot easier to use than the huge one in my living room. I'll be sure to return it as soon as my report is finished, or when I find mine, whichever comes first. But you would be totally proud if you could see how much I'm using it. I must have learned twenty new words today alone. Miss Fenton is going to be *surpassingly* impressed!

Talk to you guys later!

Carole Hanson and Lisa Atwood
c/o Pine Hollow Stables

Willow Creek, VA

Hi, guys!

You'll never guess what happened today! I almost got caught in an avalanche!

Don't worry, I'm okay. But it was really scary.

What happened was, Dinah and I went for a trail ride on this mountainous trail called the Rocky Road Trail. There's still lots of snow around up here, but the weather is getting warmer, so it's starting to melt. And when big clumps of snow melt and fall from trees and stuff, they make a lot of noise. So does melting ice, though I'm not exactly sure why.

So while we were riding, there's this huge BOOM! from some ice melting. And Dinah's horse, Goldie (you guys would love him, by the way. He's a palomino, so of course he reminds me a little of

72

Delilah. He's almost as sweet as she is, too) freaks out and races off. Then he stops and starts rearing, and to make a long story short, ends up dumping Dinah on the ground, right in the path of this huge avalanche of rocks and snow. I guess the melting started it, or maybe the noise. I've heard they can start that way. ~~In fact, I think my science teacher may have spent some time droning on about that a few weeks ago. Of course, I had better things to do than listen, like catch up on my sleep, for instance. Ha ha.~~

I was totally petrified, as you can imagine. But I knew I had to do something to help Dinah. I could already tell she was at least stunned by the fall, maybe hurt. And all these rocks and stuff were rolling and bouncing toward her down the steep hillside.

I had already started chasing Goldie after he spooked. I was worried about Dinah getting control of him again. (Between you two, me, and the wall, Dinah isn't quite as good a rider as she could be. But she tries hard, and she's getting better.) But then when I saw the avalanche, I had to stop. I couldn't endanger myself and Evergreen (he's the horse I was riding). That wouldn't do any of us any good. So I felt totally helpless as Dinah sort of crawled behind this big boulder to shield herself from the avalanche. (Actually, I guess it was more of a rockslide than an avalanche, but at the time I wasn't worrying too much about what to call it. I was too busy hoping we'd all get out of it in one piece!)

Carole, before you ask, don't worry about Goldie. He had already run well out of range of the rocks, so he was safe.

Dinah was another story. The big rock she was hiding behind was maybe three feet across, so it was shielding her from the worst of the shower of little stones and clumps of snow that were flying down the hillside, though I could see that a few of them were bouncing and hitting her arms and legs—hard. At least Dinah was wearing a riding helmet and her head was pretty well protected behind the rock, and she had her arms wrapped around it, too. (Her head, not the rock.)

Still, as I watched and waited, hardly daring to breathe (and hardly able to keep Evergreen from turning and bolting away from all the noise), I couldn't help thinking some really scary thoughts. For one thing, it had taken us a really long time to ride this far. What if something really bad happened to Dinah? What was I going to do? It was getting warmer, but it was still awfully cold up there. You get the picture.

But a new, even scarier thought popped into my mind after a few seconds. At first the rockslide had been made up mostly of pebble-sized stones. But I noticed more and more larger rocks mixed in with the shower, and that made me wonder. Maybe the slide had been caused at the top by something big….

It didn't take long before I found out that that was true. Peering up the mountainside as far as I could see, I spotted THE ROCK. Actually, it was more like a boulder. It was at least as large as the rock that Dinah was hiding behind, and it was lumbering down the hill among the smaller rocks and pebbles, slowly but steadily.

And it was heading straight for Dinah!

I screamed at her to move, knowing that if that rock hit her (or even the rock in front of her), she was doomed.

Luckily, Dinah listened. She moved as she had never moved before. She shot out from behind that protective rock, dashing for safety. I just kept yelling for her to run faster. I had one eye on her and the other on that big rock, which was getting closer… closer…

Dinah was yelling for help and sort of stumbling and crawling. I wasn't sure if the deep snow was keeping her from running nor-

74

mally or if she was already hurt, and I didn't bother to think much about it. I shouted, "Here! This way!" or something like that, so she would know which way to go. It was the only help I could give her, and that was a really horrible feeling.

But then I realized there was something else I could do. No, actually it was something else I <u>had</u> to do. Dinah wasn't moving fast enough, and that boulder was practically on top of us by now, bouncing back and forth crazily but coming closer and closer.

I gave Evergreen a sharp kick—I didn't want to waste any time arguing with him. Luckily, I didn't have to. He sprang forward bravely, breaking into a canter even in that deep, mushy snow, and headed right where I was aiming him, despite the still-falling rocks.

"Give me your hand!" I yelled to Dinah, hoping against hope that she would understand what I was doing.

She stuck her hand in the air. I shifted both reins to my left hand and leaned over to the right. Closer and closer. It was going to be tricky. I was directing Evergreen with my legs, and he was doing everything I asked. Dinah's face looked frozen, not from the cold, but from horror and fear and pain. But she kept her hand up, reaching toward me.

I leaned out of the saddle, straining toward her as we thundered past. For a second I thought I was going to miss. But I strained down a little more, and at the last possible second I felt Dinah's hand grasping mine. I gripped it as hard as I could and yanked upward. I thought my arm was going to rip out of its socket, but I kept pulling. Dinah was pushing herself at the same time, and as soon as she was high enough she grabbed at the saddle with her other hand and held on tight. She somehow managed to haul herself up onto the horse's rear as we cantered on as fast as Evergreen could go.

That was when I dared to look uphill again.

The boulder was almost on us. It struck a tree, bounced right, and crossed the trail just a yard or two behind us. It smashed into the rock Dinah had just been hiding behind, shattering it and sending chunks of it flying. One chunk barely missed Evergreen's rump. Then the big boulder continued on down the hill into the flat meadow below us, where it finally lost momentum and stopped, leaving everything around us silent again, except for the sound of Evergreen's snorts.

It was over. We were safe. I could hardly believe it.

"Is it really over?" Dinah asked.

I nodded and told her we were safe, then asked if she was okay. She said she was, basically, but she got hurt when Goldie threw her.

As if on cue, Goldie poked his head out from the trees ahead of us, looking kind of sheepish. So we knew he was okay.

Dinah was another story. When she tried standing, one of her ankles gave out. She was covered with scratches, and we could tell she was going to have a lot of bruises very soon.

I thought the first thing we should do was get her to a doctor, and I said so. But Dinah said, "No way." She was afraid we would get in trouble, and that we would get Jodi in trouble.

Oh, wait, you don't even know who Jodi is, do you? Well, she's Betsy's older sister—Betsy is the third member of our sugaring-off team. She's nice, I'll tell you more about her in my next letter. (My hand is getting tired already, and I really want to tell you the rest of this story.) Jodi works at Sugarbush Stables, and she's not exactly nice. She's not exactly not nice, either, but I can't say I'm crazy about her. Anyway, I definitely don't like her as much as Dinah does—she practically worships the ground Jodi rides across. So she was totally against the whole doctor thing because she knew everyone would find out we'd gone riding alone, when actually Jodi should have come with us (or not let us go at all). And they would probably figure out that she had only let us go so she could be alone with her boyfriend, and, well, you get the idea.

So Dinah promised me that she'd be okay. After all, if we had avoided being killed by the rockslide, we could certainly take care of a few cuts and bruises.

I wasn't sure what to do. I know everybody thinks I'm kind of daring and adventurous and everything, but I'm not completely irresponsible, no matter what people like my parents and Miss Fenton might think. So I was worried about Dinah and her injuries. Still, she could move and talk. And she's my friend, and I'm definitely not a squealer. If she didn't want me to tell, I wouldn't tell.

But there was more to it than that. I recently found out that Dinah's parents are really paranoid about her riding. They're sure she's going to be horribly injured every time she sets foot in a stable, and I know they'd love nothing more than for her to stop riding altogether. And I have the funniest feeling that if they find out about this, they'll decide to ban her from riding.

So I promised not to tell, and we started homeward—very, very slowly. Dinah couldn't ride because she was super sore in the spot where she'd landed, which happens to be the exact same spot that sits in a saddle. So I led Goldie and Dinah walked, slowly and carefully. She didn't mount until we were within sight of the stable again, and then she kind of rode standing up in the stirrups. We hoped that would fool anyone who saw us.

It didn't fool Jodi. She started to freak out until we promised her we weren't going to breathe a word to anyone. (Well, I guess I'm telling you guys. But you know what I mean.) She was totally relieved, although I was kind of annoyed that she didn't even seem that worried about how Dinah was feeling. I let that go, though, since she did offer to take care of the horses for us. She also told us Betsy was waiting for us at the Sugar Hut so we could get started collecting sap. (Which is really interesting. I'll tell you all about it in my next letter.)

It didn't take a genius to see that Dinah was in no state for collecting sap. She could hardly walk without wincing. So she suggested I go ahead to the Sugar Hut without her while she went home to soak in a long, hot bath, hoping that would make her feel better. I was afraid that her mother would get suspicious, but Dinah loves to take baths, so she thought it would be okay.

Collecting sap with Betsy was loads of fun, although I kept worrying about Dinah the whole time. Also, it was kind of awkward having to lie to Betsy about where Dinah was. I like Betsy, and I don't like lying to people I like (which is why I usually only lie to Veronica, my brothers, and Miss Fenton. Ha ha!). But I didn't really have much choice.

But I pulled it off somehow, and before long I was back here at the Slatterys' house. Dinah wasn't feeling too hot, and she couldn't bear the thought of going back to the Sugar Hut later for the next step. Besides that, she looked like a total mess. With all her bumps and bruises, not to mention a limp and this huge, red scrape down one side of her face, there was no way people wouldn't notice there was something wrong. But Mr. Daviet had told me that all the team members had to show up that evening to get credit.

That's when I came up with my brilliant idea—to give Dinah a makeover!

She was kind of skeptical at first. But what choice did she have? We got to work.

Mr. Slattery was the first one to see the new Dinah, and he was pretty surprised. I guess he didn't think much of my makeover. But I thought it was awesome. I had dressed her in baggy clothes to cover most of the scratches and bruises on her arms and legs and to keep them from hurting any more. That also covered her leg injury, as long as she tried to keep from limping while anyone was watching.

Then there was her hair. Makeup just wasn't going to be enough to hide that big scrape on her face. So I came up with another way. I piled most of Dinah's hair up on top of her head. Then, on the right side, I arranged it so that a hand-sized curl swept down across her right eye, past her jaw, and back up again. It was fastened behind her ear with a large bow. It took me about half a can of hairspray and a lot of mousse to get it to stay that way (and of course, Dinah had to adjust to seeing out of only one eye), but the end result did what it was supposed to do. It hid that scrape completely.

Mr. and Mrs. Slattery kept giving me funny looks as I explained that this look was all the rage in Virginia. But I guess they believed me, because they didn't say another word about it all through dinner.

At the Sugar Hut, I had a lot of fun watching Mr. Daviet boil the sap to create the syrup. It was kind of a complicated process, though it seemed simple, and I'll tell you about it some other time. The important part is, at the end we used part of what he made to make something called sugar on snow. You make it by dribbling some hot syrup over fresh snow, which almost magically creates these twisty, stringy bits of chewy maple-flavored stuff that's just about as delicious as anything I've ever tasted.

We had a few close calls during the evening. For instance, when everyone went inside the Sugar Hut, which was really warm from all that boiling, I realized that Dinah couldn't take off any of her warm, baggy layers without someone noticing her injuries. So I convinced everyone to head back out for a moonlight Frisbee game. That did the trick. And everybody seemed to believe that Dinah just had a stomachache earlier (when she was supposed to be collecting the sap with us). One other weird thing happened, though, and I'm kind of worried about it. I think Jodi said something nasty to Dinah. I saw Jodi hurrying away from a spot in the woods near the hut, looking angry, and when I went to investigate, I found Dinah there crying her eyes out. I was afraid her injuries were hurting her worse, but she claimed that wasn't it. But she wouldn't tell me what was wrong.

By the way, I'm writing this in Dinah's room. Mr. and Mrs. Slattery wanted us to stay downstairs after we got back from the Sugar Hut. But I could tell that Dinah really needed to get to bed right away. So I told Dinah's mom I needed to spend an hour or two reading <u>To Kill a Mockingbird</u>, and I wanted Dinah to explain some fraction problems to me since she studied the same thing last semester. ~~Ha! As if I could even think about homework on an action-packed trip like this!~~ Anyway, Dinah fell asleep ages ago, and it's getting late, so I guess now I'll sign off and hit the sack, too. It's been a long day. I miss you guys—I hope you remembered to explain things to Phil for me. I'm sure you did. ~~I miss him, too. I was hoping we'd get a little quality time together after his Pony Club meeting, if you know what I mean. But oh well. My love life will just have to wait.~~

I'll write again soon and let you know what happens with Dinah. And I'll see you when I get back!

Love,
Stevie

Welcome to My Life . . .

When morning came, I was still really worried about Dinah. Especially about that mysterious encounter with Jodi in the woods the night before.

"What really happened last night?" I asked her.

"Oh, I just got hit on the head with a falling icicle," Dinah claimed.

I knew she was lying, which made me kind of angry. But I could tell that she was hurting, and she wasn't in the mood to talk. So I could understand—sort of. Sometimes there are times when I don't feel like talking to anyone, even my best friends. They understand almost everything— that's why we're best friends—but I guess nobody can understand every single thing about someone else. That's why people just need to work things out on their own sometimes. I figured that was what was going on with Dinah right then, so I left her alone.

Actually, I ended up leaving her alone almost all day. I went collecting with Betsy again while Dinah stayed home. It wasn't easy passing off Dinah's behavior to her mother and Betsy, but I managed. Of course, I don't believe in lying. Lying is wrong, and I would never lie in most situations, like at school. But this was an emergency. Anyway, after collecting, Betsy invited me to go skiing with her. I was excited about that, since I had never tried skiing before. But I wished Dinah could have come, too.

Later that day I stood at the top of the mountain on my skis, and THEN I FELL DOWN ON MY BUTT IN THE SNOW, AND WHEN I TRIED TO GET UP I FELL ON

MY FACE. THEN I FELL ON MY BUTT AGAIN. BE-CAUSE I'M A CLUMSY, DUMB GIRL WHO IS TO-TALLY INFERIOR TO ALL BOYS, ESPECIALLY MY BROTHERS. THEY ARE THE BIGGEST GENIUSES IN THE ENTIRE UNIVERSE, AND THE COOLEST, TOO. THEY ARE SO FAR SUPERIOR TO ME IN EVERY WAY THAT I COWER IN THEIR PRESENCE, LIKE A WORM IN THE PRESENCE OF A SUPER-ADVANCED ALIEN RACE OF GENIUSES.

SO ANYWAY, THEN I TRIPPED AND FELL DOWN THE MOUNTAIN, AND MY SKIS FELL OFF, AND I WENT FLYING DOWNHILL SO FAST THAT I BECAME A GIANT SNOWBALL. I ROLLED AND ROLLED, AND WHEN I HIT THE BOTTOM I BUMPED MY HEAD SO HARD MY BRAIN FELL OUT INTO THE SNOW. LUCKILY IT'S SO TINY THAT I COULD SCOOP IT UP WITH ONE FINGER AND SHOVE IT BACK INTO MY HEAD BY STICKING MY FINGER UP MY NOSE.

AND THEN I STARTED THINKING ABOUT MY SUPERHUMAN BROTHERS AND HOW MUCH I AD-MIRE THEM. HOW COULD I EVER HOPE TO COM-PETE WITH THREE INCREDIBLY GOOD-LOOKING, INTELLIGENT, AND

FROM: Steviethegreat

TO: PhilmStar

SUBJECT: GRRRRR!!!!!!!!!!!!!!

MESSAGE:

Okay, Phil, my idiot brothers have gone too far! It's not enough that they have to make my life a living nightmare. Now they've stooped to sabotaging my schoolwork, too! I just got back from talking to Dinah (yeah, yeah, I know it's long distance, but I figured my parents wouldn't mind since it's for school. And we only talked for forty-five minutes) and found them gathered around the computer, giggling like the big dorks they are. Naturally, I thought they were playing Awesome Jawsome. But no. They had hijacked my report and were typing in stupid stuff that passes for humor in their pea brains. Anyway, I chased them around the house a few times just to teach them a lesson, and now I'm back, getting ready to fix what they did.

By the way, I had another great idea to add more "substance" (that's one of Lisa's words, in case you couldn't guess) to my report. Remember how I told you on the phone last night (or was it Tuesday night? I'm spending so much time working on this report that I can't even keep track of time anymore! *Aaah!*) about how I want to come up with more unusual things to fill in my report? Well, I found this letter I wrote to Carole and Lisa while I was in Vermont, and that's working out so well that I've been trying to come up with more stuff like that. So I was thinking about how Adam Levine's mother is a doctor, and that gave me a great idea. I'm going to ask her to write up a medical diagnosis for what happened to Dinah during my visit. I'll ask her to throw in as many serious-sounding medical terms as she can. I figure that will add a lot of realism and stuff and make Miss Fenton realize that I'm serious about this. Details, details, details . . .

Speaking of realism, I'm starting to feel the tiniest bit guilty about something. I'm afraid I might be exaggerating some stuff, just a little, in my report. For instance, I might have made Jodi Hale sound a little bit meaner than she actually was in a few spots. I know she kind of deserves it, since she really did turn out to be a jerk. But I didn't really know how much of a jerk she was yet at that point in the story. You know what I mean?

Oh well, maybe I'm getting worried about nothing. The important thing is to make the story clear and believable so that Miss Fenton understands exactly what happened. Right?

And it's definitely important to make sure she understands. Because I was talking to some kids after school today, and one of them (a ninth-grader) had just failed his big biology test . . . and Miss Fenton assigned him to eight weeks of summer school! Just like that!!! She didn't even give him a chance to explain. So now I definitely know that I'm lucky even to be doing this report (not that it feels like it when I'm hunched over the computer instead of riding or something else that's fun) and that I'd better make darn sure it's the best report Miss Fenton has ever read in her entire life. Because I could never survive two whole months of summer school—let alone a whole summer without riding! Gulp!

Anyway, I'm getting closer to the part of my report about the fox hunt. So be prepared—I'll definitely want your input! Maybe we can talk about it Friday night (oops, I mean tomorrow night—see what I mean about losing track of time?) when we all get together. By the way, my dad promised to drive me, Carole, and Lisa over to that pizza place in your town. Then we should be able to walk to the movie theater, right? Did you remember to ask A.J. if he can come? I hope he can—I haven't seen him in ages! (Well, okay—since the fox hunt.) I'm just glad my parents finally agreed to let me go out. They're so impressed with how hard I've been working on this report—not to mention the A-minus I got on my makeup history quiz—that they decided I'm not grounded anymore! :-)

Welcome to My Life . . .

I stood at the top of the mountain on my skis, looking down the steep, steep slope. Betsy had taught me the basics when we arrived. And I had learned (mostly by trial and error) that the first rule of skiing is Slide, don't lift. So I thought I was ready.

I wasn't. It must have taken us an hour to make it down the hill the first time. But I learned as I went, thanks to Betsy's patient teaching, and before long I was schussing like a pro. Well, almost.

That was when Betsy told me she had something to show me.

"Let me show you this little side path," she said. "You're good enough now, and it is part of the the beginners' trail."

I followed obediently. At first I couldn't even see any trail. All I saw was a row of fir trees with their snow-covered branches hanging all the way to the ground. Betsy went straight up to one of the branches, lifted it up, and went under. I followed.

As soon as I went under that branch, I felt as though I'd stepped into a magical kingdom. Suddenly there was total silence. The snowy tree branches around and above us created a large, silent hideaway, sort of like a natural cathedral. I was afraid to move—I didn't want to shatter the dream and make this wonderful vision disappear.

Next Betsy showed me a rock, which she said she and Dinah called the palace throne. We sat there, viewing our silent, snowy kingdom, and talked.

But before I describe what we talked about, I wish to share something deeply personal. The specialness of the snow cathedral was something that I truly wish to express, and I think I can do that best through the medium of poetry.

Cathedral in the Snow
An Original Poem by Ms. Stephanie Lake, Esq.
(inspired by W. Wordsworth)

I wandered lonely through the snow,
And loved the view of vales and hills,

When all at once my eyes did show
Something that down my spine sent chills;
A magical kingdom on the ski slope,
I'm going to describe it well, I hope.

The walls were made of snowy branches
The air just reeked of evergreen;
More special than trips to dude ranches,
Was this whole resplendent scene.
And at one end, a tree trunk shone;
I gasped and sat—it was a throne!

How special was this snow cathedral?
The English language has no words.
Just as some shapes are polyhedral,
So some feelings make us soar like birds.
Forgive me if I make no sense;
But all that beauty made me dense.

I hope this poem gives you some idea about what I was feeling that day. I don't mind saying, all the wise words of my English teachers through the years at Fenton Hall helped make me the poet I am today. I hope it also gives some indication of how full of poetry and literature I was on that trip, and how I was sort of doing my English homework in spirit, even if I hadn't actually picked up *To Kill a Mockingbird* at that point. Isn't Life itself one big classroom?

Anyway, Betsy and I sat in the snow cathedral talking about things—mostly skiing at first. She told me that everybody in her family—actually, just about everybody in Vermont—skis.

"What about horseback riding?" I asked her. "Are you all riders, too?"

"I guess so," she replied. "Jodi and I have been riding for a long time."

"She's really good, isn't she?" I commented, remembering what Dinah had said.

Betsy shrugged. "Sort of," she said. "Personally, I think she's more in love with the glamour of riding than she is with horses. She knows her stuff, but it's like she almost doesn't care."

That made me think. Could Betsy really be describing the same person Dinah admired so much? It was hard to believe that two people—two close friends, even—could see someone in such totally different ways. I wondered if Betsy was just being hard on Jodi because they are sisters. I mean, occasionally I can be a teeny, tiny bit unfair to my brothers, just because they're my brothers. (And incidentally, they can be the same way to me. Only worse, because they're much less mature than I am.)

Betsy didn't seem to want to talk about that, though, so I let it drop. Instead, we talked about how her parents were taking riding lessons. Her father even wants to learn how to jump!

"Mom mostly likes to go on trail rides, though," she said. "Fortunately there are zillions of trails through the woods around here, so she doesn't get bored."

"Oh, I know there are," I said.

Then I froze. I couldn't believe what I had just said.

"You do?" Betsy turned to me, looking curious. "How?"

"Uh—um—well, yeah—ah . . . ," I said, or something to that effect.

I realized I had almost given away Dinah's secret. I had almost told Betsy that Dinah and I had gone riding on Rocky Road Trail!

Luckily, I'm a fast thinker. (You've pointed that out yourself, remember, Miss Fenton?) "Uh, Dinah and I were talking about them last night. She told me there were zillions."

Betsy didn't suspect a thing. We went on to chat about other things, but I couldn't help feeling a bit guilty. I liked Betsy. I didn't like lying to her. Even for a good cause.

Anyway, our day on the slopes eventually came to an end, and I returned to Dinah's house. As soon as I entered the kitchen, Mrs. Slattery pounced on me.

"Stevie, you've got to convince that girl to eat," she said, looking worried. "I'm really starting to think this stomachache of hers may be something serious. She's been holed up in her room all day."

I bit my lip. It seemed that our little stomachache tale was going over a bit too well. "Don't worry, Mrs. Slattery," I said quickly. "I'm sure all she needed was this one more day of rest. I'll go check on her right now."

I took the stairs three at a time and hurried down the hall to Dinah's room.

She was happy to see me. I guess she was pretty bored sitting around her room all day by herself when the rest of us were out having fun. I don't blame her.

I filled her in on my fun day with Betsy. Then we got down to business. I told her what her mother had said. "So how *are* you, really?" I asked.

"More or less okay," she said. "Fortunately, I've managed to keep my mother from noticing my face, but everything really hurts."

"Let's take a look," I said.

I checked over all her injuries, from that horrible scrape on her face to the mess of bumps and bruises on her legs. I kind of felt like Judy Barker, the vet who takes care of the horses at Pine Hollow, checking over one of her patients.

I decided to go with that feeling. After all, I'm pretty good at tending to horses myself, even if I'm not a vet. And how different could human injuries really be from equine ones?

I decided that most of Dinah's injuries would certainly heal on their own. But there was one thing that bothered me a little. It was a distinctly horseshoe-shaped bruise just above one knee. It was purplish and swollen and looked really disgusting and painful.

"I think I remember Goldie using that knee as a starting point for his hundred-meter dash," Dinah joked weakly as I poked at her knee. "It's hard to put weight on it."

I pondered the problem for a moment. Of course, I already knew that the best thing would be to let a doctor take a look at it right away. But there was no way Dinah would go for that. Dr. Stevie would have to do the trick.

Luckily, I had just the thing. "You need a leg wrap," I decided.

Dinah laughed. "You think I'm some kind of horse?"

"Not really," I said. "But if you saw that kind of swelling on a horse, you'd wrap it, right?" I was kind of proud of myself for thinking of that. I hurried to the bathroom to retrieve an elastic bandage, and before long Dinah's sore leg was wrapped up just as neatly as Max could ever ask.

"Makes me feel like having oats for supper," Dinah said with a giggle that told me she was feeling a little better already. She even whinnied.

I chuckled along with her, enjoying the sound of her laughter. I hadn't heard it since before the accident, and it sounded really great.

"Now it's time to walk you around the paddock a few times," I said. "If you don't keep moving at least a little, you're going to stiffen up."

Explanatory note:
Miss Fenton, what follows is an official medical diagnosis from a member in good standing of the local medical community. I explained what happened to Dinah to Dr. Levine and asked her to diagnose her symptoms so that you could understand exactly how serious her condition really was. I trust you will find it informative and helpful.

Stevie

Medical Diagnosis of
Miss Dinah Slattery

Disclaimer: What follows is not to be construed as a true diagnosis, since I have never met the patient in question nor observed her symptoms (which Stevie tells me are long since cleared up anyway). In addition, I write this with no access to my medical references, since I am currently standing in a stable aisle after my son's Pony Club meeting. Besides which, being a cardiologist, I wouldn't normally handle this sort of patient anyway. But Stevie Lake can convince anybody to do just about anything, and for some reason this seems quite important to her, so against my better judgment, here goes . . .

The patient, Dinah Slattery, was injured in a fall from a bolting horse, followed by exposure to a snow-related rock slide. Her injuries include the following:

• Sizable epidermal abrasion on the right cheekbone

• Numerous purpura (bruises) caused by falling rocks and/or by falling from a horse to the ground

• Several lacerations to the arms, legs, and torso of unknown size and severity

• Possible minor stress injury to the patella

92

and/or lower femur caused by a violent blow from a blunt object (most likely a horse's hoof)

DIAGNOSIS: The patient should see (or, rather, should have seen) a physician immediately for general first aid and a close examination of her injured knee as described above, as well as to ascertain that there were no internal injuries or head trauma.

FROM:	Steviethegreat
TO:	DSlattVT
SUBJECT:	The great irony of life
MESSAGE:	

You'll never believe who I ran into last night. Never. I must have the worst luck in the entire universe!!!!

Here's what happened. I took a teeny, tiny break from my writing, just long enough to go out for pizza and a movie with Phil, Carole, Lisa, Phil's friend A.J., and a couple of other kids from Cross County. I've been working so hard on my report all week that I figured I deserved a break—*needed* one, before my brain exploded from all that writing and remembering and research. Obviously my parents agreed, since they let me go. As I was leaving, Mom even said something about being proud that I was being so RESPONSIBLE about the project. (She really said that. I only wish I'd had a tape recorder with me! I could have included it in my report. Oh well, maybe I can get her to repeat it later.)

So anyway, I was feeling pretty good about things as we left the movie and headed to this pizza place near Phil's house. Hungry. Happy. Proud.

Then we walked into the restaurant, and my heart totally stopped. I swear it did. I mean, I know people say that all the time. But I am one hundred percent sure that I was probably legally dead for a second there.

Because sitting at a table right near the door, chomping down on a slice of mushroom pizza, was . . . (drumroll, please)

MISS FENTON!!!!!!

Can you believe that? I couldn't. Naturally, she spotted me right away.

"Good evening, Stephanie," she said in that dry, deliberate voice of hers. "I'm surprised to see you so far afield."

I suppose I must have stammered something in response. I seem to recall trying to introduce my friends and forgetting Carole's name. And I think I called Phil "Philip Marlowe" instead of Phil Marsten.

Because I was sure I knew exactly what she was thinking: *There's that irresponsible Stephanie Lake, goofing off when she's supposed to be working hard to save her grades. Too bad. I guess I'll have to flunk her out of school after all. HA HA HA HA HA HA HA HA HA!*

Okay, she probably wouldn't have laughed about it, even to herself. But the rest is probably pretty close, don't you think? I mean, do you remember what she said to us that time we got sent to her office for stealing all the frogs from the high-school biology lab and releasing them into the school toilets because we thought they'd go down into the sewers and breed into a mutant race of superfrogs that would destroy the school? You started crying and saying we were sorry, while I tried to convince her that, as third-graders, we deserved a second chance. She just stared at us and said, "I'm sorry, girls. A second chance is not something to be deserved; it is something to be earned." Then she made us help the janitor clean the high-school bathrooms every day for a month. :-(

And that was when we were little kids! So I'm afraid I may have blown it. If my report had to be good before, now it has to be beyond great. It has to be stupendous. Extraordinary. Unsurpassed. Inimitable. Unparalleled. Transcendent. (See? That thesaurus I borrowed from Lisa is coming in handy!)

So if all that is true, what am I doing spending valuable report time writing to you??? Oops. Gotta go . . .

Welcome to My Life . . .

Dinah and I managed to keep anyone from suspecting anything for the next few days. We redid her makeover each morning and blamed her imaginary stomachache for the fact that she still spent an awful lot of time hiding out in her room. But every day it got harder to keep it up. Mrs. Slat-

95

tery started talking more and more about things like doctors, milk of magnesia, and Kaopectate. We knew it wasn't going to be easy to trick her much longer.

But that was nothing compared to how hard it was getting to keep the truth from Betsy. I thought we should just go ahead and tell her—I was sure she could be trusted—but Dinah disagreed.

"We can't take any chances," she said, limping along with me through the snow toward the Sugar Hut one morning. We were going to meet Betsy to do some more collecting.

I just shrugged. I figured it was her decision to make. That didn't mean I had to agree with it. But it did mean I had to honor it.

"Okay," I said. "But it's not going to be easy to fool her once we start collecting. It's going to be an awful lot of work. Are you sure you're up for it?"

"I was thinking about that," Dinah said. "I have an idea. We have to convince Betsy to let me do all the driving today."

I immediately saw what she meant. "That's a great idea!" I cried. "If you're driving, that means you won't have to do any walking and collecting because you'll have to stay with the sleigh."

"Right," Dinah said. "And Betsy will never have to know the truth."

Betsy didn't seem thrilled about the idea of Dinah driving, but she agreed. And our plan worked for a while. But before long I could tell that in Dinah's current condition, even driving was a pretty big strain. Soon she was wincing every time she had to pull on the reins to get the horse to stop.

Finally Betsy noticed, too. "Is something wrong?" she asked.

"No," Dinah assured her quickly. "I'm just not as good at this as you are."

"Then let me do it," Betsy said. It wasn't the first time she had said it. It was clear she was itching to take her turn at the reins, though Dinah and I kept putting her off.

"No, I'm fine," Dinah said now. "I've just got to learn to do this right."

"That's for sure," Betsy replied.

I winced at the tone in her voice. She didn't sound very happy with Dinah, and in a way I couldn't really blame her. I knew I had to change the subject.

"There are some more of our buckets!" I sang out as cheerfully as possible.

Betsy and I set to work. We emptied the buckets into the vat on the back of the big, flat sleigh. Then we removed the spiles from the tree trunks. Sugaring time was coming to an end, and we had been instructed to remove our equipment that day.

"That's another four spiles down," Betsy commented as she tossed the equipment onto the sleigh.

I nodded and quickly counted the spiles already there. "Why, yes," I said, thinking of the fraction homework waiting for me back in Dinah's bedroom, as I frequently had over the past few extremely busy days. "And by my calculations, that means we have collected exactly four-fifths of the total number of spiles we set out."

"Boy, you sure are good at math, Stevie," Betsy said admiringly.

Dinah heard us from the driver's seat and nodded. "Stevie is always talking about how much she's learned in Ms. Snyder's math class this year. It's just too bad her test grades don't always reflect her true comprehension and love of fractions and everything else about math. I think that really says something about our constrictive educational system."

I sighed. "I could stand around here and talk about math all day. But we'd better keep moving if we want to collect the last one-fifth of our spiles."

The others nodded. Betsy and I swung up onto our seats on the sleigh, and Dinah got the horse started again.

A moment later the sleigh went over a bump in the road, jolting us all around in our seats.

"Ouch!" Dinah cried before she could stop herself.

"What's the matter?" Betsy asked.

"Nothing." Dinah and I both said it at the same time. I gulped, realizing that Betsy might find it rather strange that I was answering for Dinah.

Luckily, Dinah changed the subject before Betsy could comment. "How are your parents coming with their riding lessons, Betsy?"

Betsy smiled. "Oh, they're doing great," she said. "In fact, they're going on a trail ride this morning."

"They are?" Dinah said, looking surprised. "I thought Mr.

Daviet said nobody could go out on any of the trails until sugaring off was over."

"He did." Betsy shrugged and laughed. "But you know how convincing my father can be. He told Mr. Daviet he wouldn't have time to go for another few weeks if they couldn't go today. And guess what? Mr. Daviet said he'd take them on a trail that's been closed because of the snow this winter. He wants to see if it's ready to be opened to other riders."

All of a sudden I had a bad feeling in the pit of my stomach. I could tell Dinah was thinking the same thing I was. She sort of stiffened on the seat next to me.

"What trail?" we both asked in a single voice.

"Rocky Road," Betsy replied. "Isn't that neat? I'm sure they're going to love it. It's such an exciting trail ride—or so I've heard."

Sure it's exciting, I thought. *At least if you consider tumbling rocks, landslides, and avalanches exciting.*

I was really feeling sick by now, and it had nothing to do with the bouncing sleigh ride. All sorts of horrible images were flashing through my mind. Falling rocks. Terrified horses. Horribly injured riders.

I knew we had to do something. That trail wasn't safe, not even for an expert like Mr. Daviet. It certainly wasn't safe for inexperienced riders like the Hales.

I guess Dinah was thinking the same thing. "They can't go!" she blurted out.

Betsy looked surprised at her outburst. "Of course they can," she said. "Like I said, Dad told Mr. Daviet—"

Dinah's face was white. "I don't mean they can't go riding; they can't go on Rocky Road."

"Why not?" Betsy asked.

"It isn't safe!" Dinah said urgently.

Betsy looked a little annoyed. "I think Mr. Daviet's a better judge of that than you are," she said. "After all, if *he* thinks my parents—"

"That's not what I mean," Dinah said. "The trail isn't safe. I mean, it can't be safe at this time of year. All that snow melting is probably dislodging some of the boulders and rocks, and it could—" Dinah stopped talking because Betsy was staring at her.

"You were on it," Betsy said. "That's how you know."

Dinah didn't answer. She just nodded.

"That's what happened, and you're hurt, aren't you?" Betsy asked.

I gulped, glancing at Dinah to see what she would do. I guess we should have known that Betsy would guess the truth.

Dinah stared at the reins in her hand for a moment. "It was a big boulder," she said finally. "It missed me by inches. Stevie saved me. The same thing could happen to your parents—only Stevie won't be there to save them. We can't let them go on that trail."

Betsy turned pale. "We've got to warn them," she said, grabbing the reins from Dinah. "Hold on tight, or we won't get there in time! They're going out at eleven."

I glanced at my watch. It was ten minutes to eleven. That didn't leave us much time.

100

Betsy slapped the horse's rump vigorously with the reins, and the lumbering old workhorse sprang to life.

I held on tight as we raced over the snowy roads. We didn't talk much. We were all concentrating grimly on the horse, the sleigh, the road. I suspected that the horse's brisk trot was faster than he had gone in many years. Would it be enough?

It seemed to take forever. But finally the Sugar Hut came into view. I checked my watch again. Five past eleven. Were we too late?

As we pulled up at the door, Betsy flung down the reins and we all leaped out of the sleigh. Betsy was in the lead as we dashed inside. "There's an intercom that connects the Sugar Hut with the stable," she explained breathlessly as we ran.

Seconds later she was waiting for someone to pick up at the other end. I held my breath. My mind was swirling with all sorts of different thoughts. I was still scared for Mr. Daviet and the Hales. But I also couldn't help feeling a strange sense of relief. At last our secret was out. And I, for one, was glad. Usually I like secrets. But this hadn't been the fun kind of secret. Not at all.

"Mr. Daviet?" Betsy said, interrupting my thoughts. "You're still there?" Her voice was filled with relief.

I let out the breath I'd been holding. We were in time!

It didn't take long for Betsy and Dinah to explain. Finally Dinah hung up the intercom. She sat down on a wooden bench, leaned back against the rough-hewn log wall, and started to cry. All I could do was sit down and put my arm around her, being careful not to touch any of her injuries. I

101

didn't say anything, figuring she needed to let it all out. I guess Betsy thought the same thing, because she just sat silently on Dinah's other side, patting her on the knee until Dinah's parents arrived a few minutes later to take their daughter to the doctor.

They dropped me off at their home on the way. I went inside, feeling unsettled and worried. I was worried about Dinah's injuries, of course, but now that she was going to a real doctor, I was sure she would be fine. I was a lot more worried about other things. After all, we'd had some pretty good reasons to keep that secret. In some ways it really was a relief to have it out in the open, but that didn't mean there wouldn't be consequences. For one thing, Jodi was in big trouble with Mr. Daviet now. But more importantly, we had given Dinah's parents something real to worry about. They might tell her she couldn't ride anymore. That was about the worst thing I could imagine.

I spent the next hour or two trying to figure out how to convince the Slatterys not to make Dinah stop riding. At the same time, I was thinking about how all this had happened. I felt kind of guilty about it, because I knew it was partly my fault. If I hadn't been there, Dinah wouldn't have been on that trail.

Still, I knew at least one person was more to blame than I was: Jodi. I was realizing that I didn't like Jodi at all. She had sent us out on that trail, knowing full well that we could get into trouble, just so she could be alone with her boyfriend. That wasn't cool. Some people may consider me kind of a rule-breaker sometimes, but there was no way I would ever even think about putting someone else in danger like that. That was just wrong.

I was still thinking about that when the Slatterys finally got home. I hurried to meet them. First I checked to make sure Dinah was going to be okay.

"I'm fine," she told me. "In fact, the doctor admired the leg wrap. I thought you'd want to know that." She smiled.

Next I turned to Dinah's parents. "Mr. and Mrs. Slattery, there's something I need to say. This wasn't Dinah's fault, really. It was mostly mine. It wouldn't have happened if I hadn't been here."

"Thanks, Stevie," Mr. Slattery said. "Dinah told us everything. We have an idea where the fault lies. We understand what the two of you were doing and why."

"So you're not going to punish Dinah?" I asked hopefully.

"No, we don't mean that," Mr. Slattery said.

My heart sank like a stone. So this was it. I was sure they were going to tell Dinah she could never ride again.

Mr. Slattery went on. "Dinah won't be allowed to ride for a month," he said. "I mean a month *after* her cuts and bruises heal."

I could hardly believe my ears. A month? In one way, that seemed like a lifetime. I couldn't imagine not being able to ride for a month.

But it wasn't a lifetime. Not even close. Dinah would be riding again before summer!

I tried not to look as happy and relieved as I felt. I didn't want Dinah's parents to get the idea that their punishment was too light or anything.

Dinah and I went upstairs so that she could change. As soon as we were safely inside her room, she turned to me and grinned.

"Isn't it great?" she said. "It was all I could do to keep from cheering. I was sure they'd tell me I couldn't ride ever again." She shrugged and sighed happily. "My parents are okay."

I had to agree with that.

After Dinah had changed, we lay back on the twin beds in her room. Something was still bothering me a little. I couldn't help wondering if what had happened had changed Dinah's opinion of Jodi. It bothered me that my friend admired someone like that, although I sort of understood why she did. It was because Jodi was older, and sort of glamorous, and a good rider. Still, I didn't like the thought that even after all that had happened, Dinah might still like her.

I'm not very good at keeping quiet when I'm wondering about something. So after a few minutes, I spoke up. "I've been thinking about Jodi," I said hesitantly. "I've been thinking she was wrong."

"You bet she was," Dinah said. Her voice was angry, which surprised me. I had been expecting her to jump to Jodi's defense.

I sat up on the bed. "She shouldn't have let us go out on the trail, and she shouldn't have asked us not to tell."

"That, too," Dinah said.

"What else?" I asked.

"What she said to me that night . . . ," Dinah began, blinking a few times.

104

I thought back to that night outside the Sugar Hut. Everybody had been laughing, playing Frisbee, having fun—everyone except Dinah.

"Is that what made you upset?" I asked.

Dinah nodded, blinking again. I guessed that she was trying not to cry, which meant that whatever had happened must have really hurt her. I waited for her to go on.

"Jodi found me outside," Dinah said. "She'd figured the reason we'd gone outside was because I didn't want to take off my overclothes and show my cuts. I guess she was afraid I'd change my mind, so she came over to convince me that that wouldn't be a good idea."

"What did she say that upset you so much?" I asked.

"She told me that if I told anybody, she'd see to it that I'd never ride Goldie again. She also said I didn't deserve to ride him anyway because if I couldn't stay on a horse like Goldie, I was never going to be a good rider. I had this awful picture of spending the rest of my life riding in circles in a little ring. I was on a pony and Jodi Hale had the lead rope. It was awful!"

Even with everything else I knew about Jodi, I could hardly believe she'd been so mean. I also couldn't believe Dinah hadn't told me, though I guessed she had felt too ashamed to share it with anyone, even me.

"Let me tell you something," I said. "I may not be the best rider in the world, but I'm pretty good. Just about nobody could have stayed on Goldie at that moment. If a horse is totally determined to lose his rider, he's going to lose his rider, and I never saw a horse more determined

105

than Goldie was right then. I couldn't have stayed on him. Even Carole would have gone flying. The miracle was that you stayed on through that tremendous rear. You were fabulous!"

Dinah sniffled, looking astonished. "I was?"

"You were. And you are." I gave her a very careful hug.

Suddenly Dinah remembered something important. "Tonight is the annual Sugaring Off Square Dance!" she exclaimed.

We only had a few hours to get ready. But we were pretty sure we were up to the challenge. The only tricky part would be dismantling Dinah's now unnecessary "fashionable" hairdo!

FROM: HorseGal
TO: Steviethegreat
SUBJECT: Hi!
MESSAGE:

I would have called, but I don't want to interrupt your writing. How's it going? By the way, I meant to tell you this at Horse Wise today: If you want, I can write you a complete description about Topside's condition and training during the time you were in Vermont. If you're going to feature him more in the rest of your report, it could be really helpful to include that information so that Miss Fenton will understand what kind of horse he is and everything. I could probably have it finished by Tuesday's lessons if you want. Just let me know how many pages you need!

Speaking of Horse Wise, wasn't it nice not to have to put up with Veronica for a change? I wonder why she skipped? Max didn't even seem to notice. He's probably as glad she wasn't there as the rest of us were!

Talk to you later!

FROM:	Steviethegreat
TO:	HorseGal
SUBJECT:	Thanks
MESSAGE:	

It's really nice of you to offer to write about Topside. But even though I know your description of his condition would be really interesting and everything, I'm not sure Miss Fenton would appreciate it, since she's not really a horse person. So I don't want to waste your time, especially when I'm going to need your help more when we get to the part of the story that has to do with the racetrack, since you were more involved with all that than I was. Okay?

Speaking of which, I'd better run—I checked out a book on horse racing from the school library yesterday, and it seems to have disappeared. I think it might be under my bed, or maybe in the basement where I was looking for the photo album with the pictures Mr. Slattery took of me and Dinah in Vermont. Anyway, I'd better start looking for it. I just hope my brothers didn't have anything to do with its disappearance, or I'm going to break their stupid Jawbone disc over their pointy heads!

Anyway, I can't believe I haven't even started talking about Prancer and Pepper yet, let alone the fox hunt. And I only have eight days left to finish this report! AAAAAAH!

YO, STEVIE!

DON'T THINK WE HAVEN'T NOTICED HOW YOU'VE BEEN HOGGING THE COMPUTER ALL WEEK. IF YOU KNOW WHAT'S GOOD FOR YOU, YOU'LL FINISH YOUR STUPID REPORT ALREADY AND LET SOMEBODY ELSE HAVE A TURN. IF YOU DON'T, THE REVENGE OF THE AWESOME JAWSOME WILL BE SWIFT AND POWERFUL!

YOUR AWESOME BROTHER,
ALEX

Welcome to My Life . . .

Well, Miss Fenton, by now I'm sure you can see how exciting and action-packed my trip to Vermont was. In fact, reliving it through this very fascinating assignment has been so exciting that I almost forgot I hadn't told you yet what was happening back home with Carole and Lisa and that Pony Club meeting. So here goes . . .

DECISION IN VIRGINIA!
(the slightly less action-packed blockbuster sequel to DANGER IN VERMONT!)

Another Nail-Biting Cinematic Production by Stephanie Lake

FADE IN
INTERIOR Carole's father's car. COLONEL HANSON, a handsome, distinguished Marine colonel, is driving. His daughter, CAROLE, sits in the front seat, reading a book called *The Amazing Wide World of Horses*. LISA sits in the back, staring out the window with an anguished expression.

LISA
Oh dear.

She wrings her hands and sighs.
Carole looks up from her reading.

CAROLE
Did I hear you say "ear"? That's funny. You see, I was just reading a passage in my book about how horses can move each ear independently to listen for sounds.

109

Lisa rolls her eyes.

LISA
That's not what I said. I was worrying about what we're doing. Do you really think we should be going to Phil's Pony Club meeting? I mean, he is Stevie's boyfriend. Won't she be mad at us? You know—angry, irate, sullen, indignant, rageful, cross, wrathful, furious, acrimonious, resentful . . .

CAROLE
Oh. I see what you mean. She might hate us when she gets back!

CLOSE-UP on Colonel Hanson. He laughs loudly. PAN TO Carole and Lisa, looking perplexed at his sudden outburst.

CAROLE
What's so funny, Dad?

COL. HANSON
You two are! I don't think you have to worry about Stevie getting mad. She knows you guys are her best friends. That means she trusts you, and she trusts Phil. And in case you haven't noticed, she's not exactly the most uptight person in the world. So why in the wild blue yonder would she get mad?

Why, if Stevie were here right now, she would probably tell you that you're being totally ridiculous. She would probably say you're getting all freaked out for no good reason. She might even say that you're going out of your way to find something to worry about because you're so bored without her magnificent presence to keep you entertained.

                    CAROLE
                    (nodding)
Yes, you're absolutely right. I guess we just went a little crazy because we miss Stevie so much. Right, Lisa?

                     LISA
                   (smiling)
Of course. Why didn't we see it before?

                    CAROLE
Hurry up, Dad. Now I can't wait to get to Phil's Pony Club meeting! I hope it has something to do with horses. . . .

CUT TO WIDE-ANGLE SHOT of the Hansons' car pulling into the driveway of Cross County Stables and stopping in front of the door.
PAN IN on Carole and Lisa climbing out of the car as Colonel Hanson watches them. Colonel Hanson salutes.

COL. HANSON
At ease, privates!

FADE OUT
FADE IN
EXTERIOR Sugarbush Stables, night. The outside of the
building is festooned with hanging lanterns, which sway in
a gentle breeze, causing gorgeous twinkles on the crisp
snow below.
CUT TO
INTERIOR Sugarbush Stables, transformed. The barn area
has been turned into a party space, with a huge table
stacked with refreshments, and maple-leaf garlands hanging
from the rafters. At one end of the room, a real live
SQUARE DANCE BAND is playing a lively tune. More
than a hundred people are in the room, laughing and talking and dancing and generally having a great time.

NARRATOR (voice-over)
That night, at Sugarbush Stables . . .

PAN IN on STEVIE and DINAH. They are near the refreshments table, sipping punch and talking. Stevie is leaning on the back of the chair in which Dinah is sitting. They
both look positively fantastic. Stevie is wearing a long,
swishy skirt, and her hair looks incredible. Dinah is wearing
jeans, but her hair looks nice, too. She has neat, profes-
sional-looking bandages over her injuries.

DINAH

I'm so glad Betsy forgave us for lying to her.

STEVIE

Me too. We should have known she would guess something was wrong and start to worry. And she did. She even guessed Jodi was part of it.

DINAH

She really did appreciate our stepping forward to save her parents, though. I'm glad we did it.

STEVIE
(nodding sincerely)
Me too. I guess this is why my teachers always tell me to tell the truth. I should have remembered that in the first place. After all, teachers are the wisest people in the world. Except maybe for headmistresses, whom I like to think of as superteachers.

SQUARE DANCE CALLER (offscreen)
Everybody grab a partner!

DINAH

Why don't you go ahead and dance, Stevie?

113

I'm still way too sore to do-si-do, but that
doesn't mean you shouldn't have fun.

STEVIE
(blushing)
Thanks. But I don't have anybody to dance
with.

Suddenly at least a dozen very cute teenage guys rush over.

CUTE GUY #1
Did I hear you say you need a dance partner, Stevie?

CUTE GUY #2
(pushing Cute Guy #1 aside)
No way! I got here first!

CUTE GUY #3
You're both wrong! I want to dance with
Stevie.

Stevie waves her hands and smiles.

STEVIE
Guys, guys! You'll all get your chance. I feel
like I could dance all night!

CUTE GUYS (in unison)
Hooray!

Stevie grabs Cute Guy #1 by the arm, and they make their way to the dance floor.

MUSIC VIDEO SEQUENCE

Stevie square-dances with guy after guy. She is a natural on the dance floor. Even the caller looks impressed by her style, grace, and technique.

After music video ends, CUT TO

CLOSE-UP on Stevie, who has just finished square dancing with Cute Guy #47. The band starts another song.

> MAN'S VOICE (offscreen)
> May I have this dance?

PAN OUT to reveal that the man is MR. DAVIET, the owner of Sugarbush Stables. He is smiling at Stevie and holding out his arm.

Stevie takes it, blushing.

> STEVIE
> You really want to dance with me?

> MR. DAVIET
> Certainly. I wanted to ask you about your miraculous recovery. You know, from that injured leg you had when you first arrived.

> STEVIE
> (looking embarrassed as she remembers the fib she and Dinah and Betsy told)

Fresh air. It's the best medicine there is. Plus
exercise. Shall we dance?

They begin to dance. Once again, Stevie is a paragon of
grace.

MR. DAVIET
Don't worry. I was going to offer you the
sleigh anyway. Since you've never used
snowshoes before, you would have been at a
terrible disadvantage.

STEVIE
(smiling)
That's very true.
[See, Miss Fenton? He really said that. I swear!]

FADE OUT on Stevie and Mr. Daviet do-si-do-ing.
FADE IN on WIDE-ANGLE SHOT of the party a few minutes later. Everybody is still having fun; the band is still
playing; etc.
PAN IN to CLOSE-UP of Stevie and Dinah, who are hanging out near the refreshments table again. This time Stevie
is also sitting, exhausted from all that dancing.

STEVIE
(happily)
This is wonderful!

She waves an arm to indicate the party.

116

DINAH
(smiling mysteriously)
Ah, and the best part is yet to come.

STEVIE
(confused)
What do you mean? Did you bring my math
book along so that I could do those fraction
problems? It's a dream come true!

DINAH
No, no. Something even better than that.

STEVIE
(eagerly)
Better than fractions? What could—

JODI
(harshly; interrupts Stevie)
Dinah!

Dinah gulps and turns. PAN OUT to reveal JODI HALE
standing in front of the girls, hands on hips, looking angry.
She is dressed in dirty jeans, and her hair looks like a rat's
nest. Or at least not like she's at a party. Standing beside her
is DORKY BOYFRIEND, a rather unattractive teenage boy
in equally messy old clothes.

JODI
(glaring at Dinah)
Proud of yourself?

DINAH
(clearly uncomfortable)
It was to help your parents. They could have
gotten badly hurt—just like I was.

JODI
They're better riders than you could ever be.
Anyway, rocks fall on that trail sometimes,
but not all the time. What's the big deal?

Stevie's jaw drops open in astonishment. She bites her lip to
keep from yelling at Jodi. This is Dinah's fight. Dinah stands
up, ignoring her injuries. She looks angry. Her fists are
clenched. She looks very noble. Jodi shrinks back a bit before her magnificence.

DINAH
Jodi, I used to think that all I wanted in the
world was to be like you. I admired you more
than anybody else I knew.

The sounds of the party fade away, and soft but dramatic
MUSIC begins to play instead—something like "The Battle
Hymn of the Republic" or the theme from *Rocky*.

DINAH
I tried to be like you, but I've found in the last
few days that I just can't do it. I also don't

want to do it. There are differences between us. For one thing, I know the difference between right and wrong. I also know the difference between safe and sorry. For a while I forgot those things, but now I remember, and I'm not going to forget them again.

Dramatic MUSIC STOPS, replaced once again by the sounds of the party. Jodi steps forward, scowling defiantly, her hands on her hips.

> JODI
> There are other differences between us. The biggest one is that you'll never be a good rider if you can't stay on a skittish horse. I'll always be better than you are.

She spins around and looks at her dorky boyfriend.

> JODI
> Come on, Mark. Let's get out of here.

They EXIT. Stevie puts out a hand to comfort her friend.

> MR. DAVIET (offscreen)
> If it's any comfort to you, Dinah, you should know that Jodi won't be riding at Sugarbush Stables anymore.

Dinah and Stevie gasp and turn.

PAN OUT to reveal Mr. Daviet standing nearby. He has heard the entire exchange.

> MR. DAVIET
> You did something you shouldn't have done, but Jodi did something inexcusable. She put my riders at risk. Even worse, she asked you to cover for her. She won't ride any of my horses again. Ever. You, however, will have many opportunities to continue riding here. And I'm glad. You're a wonderful student. I wish I had more like you. For one thing, you keep your head in an emergency. Now, the trick is to avoid emergencies in the future!

Dinah stammers, not knowing what to say. Just then the band starts a new, loud song. MR. SLATTERY approaches and bows before Stevie.

> MR. SLATTERY
> I heard you're the best dancer the state of Vermont has ever seen. Will you dance with me, Stevie?

FADE OUT as Stevie accepts.
FADE IN on the bandstand, a few minutes later. Mr. Daviet is standing at the microphone.

MR. DAVIET

Your attention, please. We have a few cere-
monial items to take care of, and then we can
return to dancing. First of all, as many of you
know, Mrs. Daviet has been at the Sugar Hut
finishing the evaporation process on the final
batch of sap. She's also been making our first
batch of sugar. It's our tradition here to have
our first sugar sampled by our newest worker.
I have the sugar here, so will our newest
worker please come to the bandstand?

PAN TO Stevie, who is watching the action from one end of
the room, next to Dinah. She glances around, obviously wondering who will come forward. Everyone turns to look at her.

STEVIE
Me?

CUT TO Mr. Daviet onstage, smiling.

MR. DAVIET

Of course. Besides, you've got to have something sweet to give you energy so that you can
keep dancing all night. Come on up here!

CUT BACK TO Stevie, making her way toward the bandstand. As she goes, everyone she passes smiles or congratu-
lates her or pats her on the back. She is beaming with

happiness. Soon she reaches the bandstand, where Mr. Daviet is waiting for her. Just then MRS. DAVIET enters, carrying a platter filled with little chunks of maple sugar.

MR. DAVIET
(gesturing to platter)
Go ahead, Stevie.

Stevie takes a piece and drops it quickly. She blows on her fingers.

STEVIE
Ouch! It's hot!

She picks up the sugar again and blows on it. Then she tastes it.

STEVIE
Delicious!

The crowd applauds. Mrs. Daviet and several ASSISTANTS begin passing out morsels of maple sugar to everybody in the place.
PAN BACK TO Mr. Daviet, still onstage. He pulls a piece of paper from his pocket.

MR. DAVIET
There's one more thing. All the sap was gathered by my junior riders, and in order to get

them to do a lot of work for free, I make it into a contest.

The crowd laughs.

> MR. DAVIET
> (grinning)
> Anyway, we've finished tallying up the amount of sap that was brought in by each team of three students. The team that brought in the most sap is guaranteed to have first pick of horses for classes all summer. This year one team was clearly superior: the team of Dinah Slattery, Betsy Hale, and our newcomer and star square dancer, Stevie Lake!

The crowd erupts into loud cheers.
PAN TO Stevie, looking thrilled as she hugs Mr. and Mrs. Daviet and anybody else who happens to be standing nearby.
PAN TO Betsy, out in the crowd, jumping up and down excitedly.
PAN TO Dinah, sitting in her chair near the refreshments table. CLOSE-UP on her face. She looks stunned. Slowly her mouth forms a single word.

> DINAH
> (whispering)
> Goldie!

QUICK FADE TO BLACK

So as you can see, Miss Fenton, my trip to Vermont was very eventful. Not only did I get to see my friend Dinah (and make some new friends, like Betsy, Evergreen, and the Daviets), but I also learned some valuable lessons about loyalty, honesty, risk-taking, and of course, square dancing. In addition to all that, I learned practically everything there is to know about the extremely fascinating and scientifically important process of sugaring off. Unfortunately, all that learning didn't leave me much time for doing homework. Actually, it didn't leave me any.

So naturally, my unfinished assignments were very much on my mind when I arrived at Pine Hollow the day after my return. I found Carole and Lisa in the paddock, working Starlight on a longe line. As soon as they saw me, they tied up Starlight and we had an impromptu Saddle Club meeting—our first in more than a week, which has to be some kind of record.

"We're so glad you're back!" Lisa exclaimed. "We have the most wonderful news!"

"It's a big secret, but you're going to love it," Carole assured me.

I groaned. I'd had enough of secrets for a while, and I said so. But as soon as they told me what the secret was, I felt a whole lot better about it. Of course, before they told me, they had to go into this whole long speech about Phil inviting them to his Pony Club meeting and their not being sure whether they should go, blah blah blah. Before long I felt like just shaking the secret out of them. But they finally got to the point.

Carole grinned. "Does the word 'tallyho' mean anything to you?"

I could hardly believe my ears. "A hunt?" I exclaimed. "There's going to be a fox hunt?"

"And we get to be in it!" Lisa said.

"It's going to be at Cross County in a few weeks," Carole explained. "It's an annual hunt for all the young riders, and this time they're allowed to invite friends."

"And that means us?" It was just too incredible for words. We were all going to get to ride in a real fox hunt! It would be so exciting—hounds, horns, the thrill of the chase. . . .

It was such thrilling news that all thoughts of Paul Revere, fractions, and *To Kill a Mockingbird* flew straight out of my head. And so we come to the next part of my story. . . .

FROM: DSlattVT
TO: Steviethegreat
SUBJECT: Your assignment
MESSAGE:

Okay, it's like midnight and I'm so sleepy I'm about to drop. At least it's Saturday so I don't have to get up for school tomorrow. I can't wait for summer!

Anyway, the reason I'm writing is that I've been thinking about your report all day. I was also thinking about Miss

Fenton, and how she's always getting worked up about telling the truth and being careful and all that kind of stuff. So the point is, I started getting worried that when you tell her what happened up here in Vermont, she might get the wrong idea about you, and then you'd be in more trouble than ever. So I got inspired, and I wrote a short essay about you, explaining all the good stuff you did up here just in case she misses the point. Here goes:

Stevie Is:
The Perfect Friend

Why is Stevie such a good friend, you ask? Allow me to list just a few of her many fine qualities, in alphabetical order for clarity and organization, since this is a school project.

Stevie is BRAVE. She raced in to save me from a horrible rockslide, even though it meant risking her own safety.

Stevie is CAREFUL. She didn't want to canter in the snow because it was too dangerous.

Stevie is HELPFUL. She pitched in with all the hard work of sugaring off.

Stevie is HONEST. She didn't want us to keep my accident a secret because she always likes to tell the truth, the whole truth, and nothing but the truth.

Stevie is LOYAL. She kept my secret even though she didn't feel right about it.

Stevie is RESOURCEFUL. She figured out a way to keep my secret for days and days, even though it seemed impossible. And even though, like I said before, she's so honest that she didn't want to do it.

Stevie is RESPONSIBLE. Being responsible may be one of the most important things someone can be. And Stevie is. Responsible, I mean. She took responsibility for her part in my accident. And she was responsible enough to try to talk me into going to the doctor right after it happened. She also tried to be responsible about doing her homework while she was here. But I talked her out of it and kept her so busy that she didn't have time. So it was really all my fault that she didn't get it done.

Stevie is WONDERFUL. She has every quality that a friend—or an above-average student—should have. Don't you agree, Miss Fenton?

There you have it. What do you think? I hope you decide to use it. I think it will really help Miss Fenton understand you better.

I was also thinking about the multimedia thing. Remember how you said on the phone that you were going to try to find more different kinds of stuff to include? Well, I remembered that I saved an article that came out in our local newspaper after you left. I always meant to send you a copy, because it actually mentions you, but I forgot until now. I scanned it into my computer and I'm attaching the file to this e-mail, so you can put the article in your report just as it appeared in the paper. I thought that would add a nice multimedia touch. (See? I may have moved, but great minds still think alike, right?)

By the way, it was really great talking to you on the phone the other day. We have to do that more often! :-)

ANNUAL SUGARING OFF AT SUGARBUSH A SWEET SUCCESS

SUGARBUSH, VT—

It doesn't get much sweeter than this!

Local equestrian Daniel Daviet has once again proved that sugaring-off season can be a time of fun for young and old alike. Daviet, who owns and operates Sugarbush Stables, has made a tradition of his own during maple sugar season. He sponsors a sap-collecting contest for his young riders, with the prize being special riding-class honors.

"The kids seem to have fun," Daviet remarked during the annual post-collection bash at the stables. "And it's a nice way to keep a Vermont tradition alive."

This reporter could not agree more.

This year two members of the winning team are local seventh-graders Elizabeth Hale and Dinah Slattery. Both girls enjoy riding at Sugarbush Stables very much and hope to enter the sugaring contest again next year. We wish them luck.

Steven Lake, a ten-year-old boy visiting from Virginia, made up the third member of the winning team. Ms. Slattery told this reporter, "We never could have done it without Steve. He was a real inspiration."

Thanks for coming, Steve. May your visit to the Green Mountain State leave you with many sweet boyhood memories!

Welcome to My Life . . .

Well, Miss Fenton, as you can see from the unsolicited essay from Dinah, my trip to Vermont probably made me a better person. Of course, she may have exaggerated a tiny bit about a few things, like the part about me being brave. I only did what I had to do. But let me assure you that the part about my homework is the absolute truth. I'm sure I would have gotten it all finished by the time I got back if there hadn't been so many distractions up in Vermont.

In any case, despite my excitement about the upcoming fox hunt, I was determined to keep up with my homework once I returned to Willow Creek at the end of spring break. First, though, I had a very important responsibility to attend to. Namely, the next meeting of my Pony Club, which is called Horse Wise. In case you're not familiar with it, the U.S. Pony Club was started in 1953 for the purpose of teaching young people more about horse care and good riding. Some people are a bit confused by the name, *Pony* Club, because they think we must all ride tiny Shetland ponies or something. But most of us in Horse Wise ride full-size horses, just like we do at our regular riding lessons. I myself normally ride a Thoroughbred gelding named Topside. He's a wonderful horse and very well trained, since he used to belong to Dorothy DeSoto, the famous championship rider.

My friends both have their favorite mounts, too. For Carole, it's obvious—she always rides her own horse, a bay gelding with a lopsided white star on his forehead, named

129

Starlight. Lisa's favorite is always Pepper, a wonderful, sweet-tempered old dapple-gray gelding who has been at Pine Hollow for years and years.

However, at the Horse Wise meeting in question, we weren't going to be doing any riding. That's because it was an unmounted meeting. We have those every other week, because Max believes there's more to being a good horseperson than just good riding. So in our unmounted meetings we learn about stuff like stable management and grooming and all sorts of other things. We also sometimes have guest speakers. On that fateful day, our speaker was Judy Barker, the vet who takes care of the horses at Pine Hollow as well as those at many other stables in the area.

My friends and I were sitting on the floor in the indoor ring, paying close attention as Judy spoke (though I was, perhaps, slightly distracted by the thought of my upcoming math test).

"The most important health care a horse gets," Judy told us, "is from its rider."

That made sense to me. But I wasn't surprised. Judy really knows her stuff.

Judy went on. "Now I would like each of you to fetch the horse you usually ride and your grooming bucket so we can get some hands-on practice. We'll meet up again in the side paddock in a few minutes."

I hopped up and followed my friends out of the indoor ring. "This should be interesting," Carole said.

"Definitely," I agreed. "I love learning new things, whether it's at the stable or, say, in history class."

"We know," Lisa said. "You're a very fine student, Stevie. It's one of the qualities I admire most about you."

I hurried to Topside's stall. He was munching on some hay when I got there, and he seemed happy to see me. I slung his grooming bucket over one arm, then snapped a lead line to his halter and led him out to the paddock, arriving at the same time as most of the other Pony Clubbers.

We got right down to work. Judy told us to start grooming as usual, saying that grooming was an excellent time to check out our horses' physical conditions and check them for soundness.

Meg Durham was the first to find something out of the ordinary. She was grooming Patch, a calm pinto she often rides. "What's this?" she called, pointing to his left foreleg.

Judy went to take a look. I happened to be working near Patch, so I leaned over to see. Patch had a small, raised lump, about half an inch across, just above the fetlock.

The vet saw it, too. She nodded, not looking too worried. "Anybody know what this is?" she asked the group.

Lisa had come forward from her place beside me to peer at the bump. "Patch is allergic to flies," she said. "I bet it's a fly bite."

"I bet you're right," Judy agreed. "It should go away on its own. The best thing to do for Patch is spray him for flies."

Meg went inside to get the fly spray, and the rest of us got back to work. I was enjoying myself. At first I was distracted with anticipation at the thought of reading *To Kill a Mockingbird* when I got home, but soon the warm spring sun and the familiar task of grooming took over. Topside was having an even better time than I was. Like most horses, he adores being groomed. He kept letting out these little grunts and sighs of contentment as I worked.

Of course, I was also following Judy's advice and checking over the horse's body while I groomed him. I was just thinking that Topside had to be the healthiest horse in the state of Virginia when I noticed Lisa frowning.

"What's wrong?" I asked. "Is Pepper okay?"

Lisa shrugged. "He just doesn't seem very interested in the grooming. It's like he's not alert or something."

I could understand why she was worried, but I doubted it was any big deal. Pepper had always been healthy. "He probably just doesn't feel in top condition because he's not fully groomed yet. Wait to see how he feels when his coat's shiny, okay?"

Lisa smiled gratefully and got back to work. But when Judy stopped by a few minutes later, I heard Lisa repeat her concerns.

I watched over Topside's back as Judy checked Pepper over quickly. When she finished, she gave Lisa a reassuring smile. "He's just getting old." I stopped my brushing and watched as Judy pried Pepper's mouth open and showed Lisa his big, yellowish teeth. "Look at the wear on these teeth and the angle of the jaw," Judy said. "Max probably knows for sure, but I'd guess Pepper is somewhere in his mid-twenties. In horse years, that makes him nearly ninety. I'm sure Max is going to retire him soon."

My jaw dropped. I could tell that Lisa was just as surprised.

Pepper was *ninety?* No wonder he sometimes had trouble keeping up with Topside and Starlight on our trail rides lately. It was pretty amazing that a horse his age could even manage a trail ride anymore! I guess that just goes to show what good care Max takes of all his horses. (And, of course, what good care Lisa always takes of Pepper when she rides him.)

I went back to concentrating on Topside, and I didn't pay much attention to the other kids' comments and questions. That is, not until I heard Carole's voice.

"Judy," she called. "Something's wrong with Starlight."

I glanced over at Carole, surprised. A worried frown creased her forehead, and she was running her hand down Starlight's right foreleg.

Judy hurried over. "What is it?"

"Look," Carole said. "When I run my hand down his leg, it feels warm and swollen at the knee."

"Just the right knee?" Judy asked.

Carole blushed a little. I guess that meant she'd forgotten to check the other leg, which just goes to show how worried she was. Normally she remembers to do everything right when it comes to horses (even though she still sometimes forgets her own telephone number, ha ha!).

She quickly checked Starlight's left leg. "It's just the right one that's swollen," she reported.

Judy felt Starlight's legs for herself. "Has he been limping or favoring his right leg lately?"

Carole shook her head. Then she unclipped his lead rope and led him around so Judy could see for herself.

"That's good news," Judy said. "Whatever it is, it barely shows in his walk yet. That means we've caught it early, before much damage has been done."

By this time, the entire group was watching Starlight. Judy spent a few more minutes examining his knee, then stood and faced us.

"It could be a couple of things," she said. "But they all come down to the same prescription for now. Does anybody know what that is?"

It didn't take long for various Horse Wise members to come up with the various steps of the prescription—complete rest, bandages, and hosing the sore joint.

I glanced over at Carole. She looked upset, and I couldn't blame her. Starlight's problem didn't seem to be too serious, but it still meant that she wouldn't be able to ride him until he was better.

"How long will Starlight need to rest?" she asked Judy.

Judy shrugged. "Hard to say. It could be as little as two weeks. We'll see."

I felt terrible for Carole. For her, two weeks without riding was almost as bad as two years. Lisa and I did our best to comfort her, but we knew it wouldn't be easy for her. She did her best to put on a brave front as she secured Starlight to the paddock fence and headed inside to get some bandages.

"Poor Carole," Lisa said to me. "This is going to be really tough on her."

"I know," I agreed, picking up a comb to work on Topside's mane. "But if anyone can help Starlight recover

134

quickly, it's Carole. She'll probably take better care of him than anyone has ever taken care of any horse in the history of the world."

Lisa giggled, but she still looked kind of sad. I felt sad, too, for Carole's sake. We all know there's more to horse care than riding, but still, riding really is an awfully big part of it!

A few minutes later I saw Max coming out of the stable building and heading toward us. Carole was right behind him.

"Here she comes," I whispered, nudging Lisa, who was bent over one of Pepper's hooves. "Let's see if we can cheer her up, okay?"

But we never got a chance to try. Max had an announcement to make. "Don't stop working," he told us. "Just work and listen at the same time, because I've got some news. I've just been speaking with a former student of mine. It seems that she's been spending some time working with a student of hers who's going to be appearing at a horse show in western Virginia. She suggested that she come over here the day after the show and have a reunion of sorts—"

I gasped, suddenly certain that I had guessed exactly who Max was talking about. "Dorothy DeSoto!" I blurted out, so excited that I almost dropped my comb. "She wants to see Topside!"

"—with the horse she rode in the show ring for so many years," Max went on.

I hardly heard him. My mind was filled with the thrilling news. Dorothy DeSoto! Coming *here*! Soon! It was almost too good to be true. "Oh, it's going to be so great to see her!" I exclaimed.

Suddenly I noticed that Max was glaring at me, looking slightly disgruntled. "Do I get to finish, or do you know the rest of the good news?"

"There's more?" I asked, wondering what it could possibly be. When Max nodded, the answer popped into my mind. "Oh, then it has to be that she wants to actually ride Topside."

"Who's doing the announcing? You or me?" Max grumbled. But I was pretty sure I saw a twinkle in his eye that meant he was sort of amused. At least I hoped so.

I decided to play it safe just in case. "Sorry, Max," I said contritely. "Please go on. I'll be as quiet as a mouse."

Max went on to give us the rest of the news. He explained that Dorothy would be coming to Pine Hollow on Sunday, two weeks and one day from that very day. She would be reunited with Topside and perform a dressage demonstration for anybody who wanted to watch it.

I was absolutely thrilled. Dressage is one of my favorite forms of riding, and Dorothy was the best of the best when she was competing. She can't ride competitively anymore because of an injury, but she trains horses and she's still the best. A dressage demonstration featuring Dorothy DeSoto was huge news!

I could tell that Lisa was excited, too, and even Carole had perked up quite a bit. She came over to where I was standing.

"It's going to be great, isn't it?" I said to her.

She nodded and smiled, then bent to pick a brush out of Topside's grooming bucket. "Let me give you a hand," she suggested. "After all, we want to make sure Topside is in perfect shape for his big day, right?"

I grinned at her, happy that she didn't seem too bummed out about Starlight's knee. "Definitely," I agreed, getting back to work with renewed gusto.

FROM: Steviethegreat
TO: HorseGal
SUBJECT: Legs
MESSAGE:

Hi, Carole! I have a very important question for you. I just got to the part of my report where I'm talking about Starlight's leg problem. Lisa keeps telling me to make sure my report has substance, and we all know she's the expert when it comes to school! What exactly did Judy think was wrong again? Can you e-mail me back as soon as you get this? I want to make sure I get all the details right. Because I know how Miss Fenton feels about details. . . .

Welcome to My Life . . .

Well, Miss Fenton, this is your lucky day. I've just received an e-mail from renowned local equine expert Carole Hanson regarding the leg injury I discussed in the previous section of my report. I feel I must tell you that Carole attacked this topic with her usual exhaustive enthusiasm, so I found it necessary to edit her essay a bit in the interest of length. I don't want you to still be reading when school starts again in the fall! Ha ha! But seriously, I only cut about eight or nine pages. Okay, maybe it was more like twelve. But what's still here basically sums up the whole thing, without all the long explanations and lists of fairly disgusting horse diseases and the history of the horse in America and stuff like that. I know you like a lot of detail, Miss Fenton, but trust me—in this case, less is more.

Anyway, here it is. I hope you find it very informative.

Knees, Vets, and Heartbreak
A Personal Essay by Carole Hanson

"No foot, no horse."

It's an old horseperson's saying, but still a true one. You see, a horse's feet and legs are perhaps the most important parts of its body. In the distant past, wild horses relied on their legs to save them from dangerous predators by carrying them away as quickly as possible. However, a horse's legs are very slender and fragile compared to the rest of its body. Some people don't realize that a horse has no muscles at all below its knees and hocks, just bone and tendons. Some people also don't know that a horse carries its entire weight on one leg during a gallop. . . .

Different breeds have legs of differing thickness and strength. For instance, a Thoroughbred has very long, slender legs because it is bred for speed. A heavy workhorse, on the other hand, has larger joints and thicker legs. . . .

One of the most important things to look for in a horse is good conformation, including good legs. There are a number of defects you should watch for in both the forelegs and the hind legs. . . .

My horse's name is Starlight. . . .

I love to go riding with my friends in The Saddle Club. That's a club that Stevie Lake, Lisa Atwood, and I started when we realized we were all horse-crazy. . . .

Anyway, one day earlier this spring the three of us were at our weekly Pony Club meeting. That's when I discovered the swelling on Starlight's knee. Luckily, Judy Barker, our stable vet, was at the meeting. After I discovered the swelling, which I did while running my hand down Starlight's leg . . .

I knew that there were a number of possible diagnoses for the swelling in his knee—anything from a localized trauma or infection or a ligament or tendon strain to infectious diseases such as equine viral arteritis, pleuritis, influenza, or even severe diarrhea. However, Judy suspected a mild carpitis, which would clear up in a matter of weeks without medication or other procedures. As usual with horses, though, there are no guarantees. . . .

So there we were, the three members of The Saddle Club, sitting in TD's eating sundaes and talking about Starlight. I couldn't believe I couldn't ride him for at least two weeks. I didn't know what I was going to do with my time—other than taking care of him, of course. My friends tried to reassure me, but I was still depressed. I knew I could ride a Pine Hollow horse, but then Max would have to charge me. And I didn't even want to think about asking my father for extra money for that.

Eventually we changed the subject to Dorothy DeSoto's upcoming visit. She was going to give a special dressage demonstration, and we were all excited about that. Dressage is a very interesting sport, with a long and fascinating history beginning in the fourth century B.C. . . .

Stevie is probably the most serious about dressage out of the three of us. . . .

Then our talk turned to Pepper. Lisa decided to make Pepper the topic of an essay she had to write for school. The topic was Life, and I didn't blame her for wanting to write about Pepper. What's life without beloved horses? I myself love everything about them. . . .

. . . and Pepper is the perfect example of all that. But now, I couldn't help wondering if he was getting too old to be ridden. Lisa told us that Max wanted her to start riding Comanche because Pepper was coming close to retirement. We were all still thinking about that (and eating our ice cream) when Judy Barker came into the restaurant.

She greeted us cheerfully, but I guess we were a little less happy to see her than usual. I was upset because of not being able to ride for two weeks. Lisa was upset because soon she wouldn't be able to ride Pepper at all. I guess Stevie wasn't upset about anything in particular, except that as a loyal friend she was upset on behalf of Lisa and me.

Judy was sympathetic. She started to talk about how horses get sick sometimes, which I already knew. I mean, it sometimes seems as though there are thousands of things that can go wrong. . . .

But of course most of those things will probably never happen to Starlight. It was just his leg that I was worried about.

That's when Judy gave me her great news. She wanted me to be her assistant!

It was a perfect plan. She needed someone to help her on her rounds. I needed something to do with my time now that I couldn't ride. Besides that, she would pay me for my time by taking care of Starlight for free. That was a big relief, since vet bills can be expensive and I knew my dad was already spending a whole lot on Starlight's boarding and the rest of my riding expenses.

I knew there was a lot I had to learn about a veterinarian's job, and I was eager to learn. . . .

. . . and that is why proper horse care—with special attention to the legs and feet—is vital for every good rider to learn.

141

Welcome to My Life . . .

There you have it. Carole's essay pretty much sums up what happened next. We went to TD's (you know, that ice cream parlor over at the shopping center near Pine Hollow) to talk over what had happened at the meeting. Carole was moping about Starlight, Lisa was moping about Pepper, and I was just trying to act sympathetic (which I was, of course) even while I felt like cheering because of the news about Dorothy DeSoto.

Judy Barker's invitation for Carole to work as her assistant cheered us all up, at least a little. But I think it was something she said that reminded Lisa about that Life essay she had to write for school.

Come to think of it, during this whole time that I'm writing about, both of my best friends were kind of preoccupied with these really serious issues of life and death and health and sickness and stuff like that. I was distracted by other things, which I'll get to in a minute. Lisa was taking the news about Pepper's upcoming retirement pretty hard. In addition to worrying about Starlight, her new job with Judy gave Carole a lot to think about. She had to see a lot of sick horses, and while most of them got better thanks to Judy's excellent care, a few of them didn't. That must have been pretty hard for Carole to handle, considering how she feels about all horses.

Anyway, I had some serious stuff on my mind at that time, too. For instance, my history paper on Paul Revere was almost due, and I had that big science test coming up.

But I'm sure you'll understand that my first priority had to be to help my friends. It was my sworn duty as a member of The Saddle Club. Plus, there was that dressage demonstration to look forward to. I may not be serious about many things, but as Carole mentioned, I'm very serious about dressage. It's a very exacting and demanding sport, requiring lots of discipline and responsibility, sort of like taking a science test or something. And naturally, I wanted Topside to be in top condition when Dorothy arrived.

So we were all pretty busy for a while. Carole got to visit lots of interesting places with Judy. One of the most interesting was a place called Maskee Farms, which is a racing stable owned by a man named Mr. McLeod. That was where Carole first met Prancer, a beautiful young Thoroughbred with the sweetest disposition in the world. Carole discovered that Prancer loved kids, even though she was nervous around most adults.

Then there was Lisa. She always spends a ton of time worrying over her homework, but this essay was different. Lisa was agonizing over it, even after she turned it in. I don't know why. Teachers always love everything she does, and her English teacher gave her an A on the Life essay and even read it out loud to the class. But Lisa was still all worked up about it. She seemed to think the essay hadn't deserved an A. I didn't quite understand that, since in my case my grades usually seem to be *lower* than I think they should be, not higher. But Lisa certainly seemed worried about something.

I suspected it probably had something to do with Pepper.

Lisa had hardly ridden another horse since she first set foot in a stirrup, and I figured she was having a hard time adjusting to the idea that she would soon have to switch to a different horse.

I decided to step in and help her out. Sometimes Lisa just sits around and thinks and worries too much for her own good. I'm no Sigmund Freud (1856–1939), but I think she probably gets that particular bad habit from her mother. I decided that as a good friend, it was time for me to step in and take some action. So one day I arranged things with Max so that Lisa could take her first trial ride on Comanche.

"You're going to love him," I assured her as I led the way toward Comanche's stall. I meant it, too. Comanche is a terrific horse—he's a deep chestnut gelding with lots of spirit and personality, with a quick, bouncy trot and a wonderful canter. He's really fun to ride. I would swear he has a better sense of humor than some people I know. (I don't mean you, Miss Fenton.)

"I'm not so sure about this," Lisa said uneasily when I told her the plan.

I did my best to be patient with her. Lisa isn't always as excited about trying new things as she could be, and I could tell she was kind of nervous. Personally, I thought it was pretty cool that she was getting the chance to get to know a whole new horse. Then again, I've ridden lots of different horses since I started riding, and like I said, Lisa hadn't had nearly as much experience.

"Come on, chin up," I said. "Let this young boy show you his stuff, okay?"

"Okay," Lisa agreed, though she still didn't seem very enthusiastic.

I had tacked up Comanche before Lisa arrived, so he was ready to go when we reached his stall. His eyes were sparkling with anticipation, and his ears perked forward alertly as we opened the door to lead him out. He looked so lively and ready for fun that I was almost sorry that I wasn't the one who was getting to ride him. I let Lisa get acquainted by leading him to the outdoor ring while I hurried to get Topside, who was also ready and waiting. Then I headed for the outdoor ring, stopping only long enough to touch the lucky horseshoe that every rider at Pine Hollow touches before each ride.

We both mounted and walked around the ring a few times to warm up. Lisa looked kind of nervous, though so far she and Comanche seemed to be getting along fine. He was responding to her aids perfectly and not giving her a bit of trouble.

"Ready to let him show you his stuff?" I called when I thought the horses were limber enough. Lisa didn't respond, but I continued anyway. Sometimes she just needs a little nudging. "Okay, let's trot."

I signaled to Topside, who swung into his easy trot immediately. Then I glanced over my shoulder to see how Lisa was doing.

She was posting evenly as Comanche trotted along briskly. I noticed she had a rather disgruntled expression on her face. "What's wrong?" I asked her, guiding Topside until he was trotting right beside Comanche.

"It's his trot," Lisa said, sounding a little breathless from

145

the fast pace. "It's so choppy. I feel like a sack of potatoes bouncing around up here."

I shrugged. "You look okay," I told her.

"Only because I'm posting," Lisa replied. "I could never sit Comanche's trot like I do with Pepper. It's not smooth enough." She sighed loudly. "I'm even having trouble riding it while I'm posting."

"Balance," I told her supportively. "That's the most important thing. Anyway, the best is yet to come."

I signaled for Topside to move into a canter. He obeyed instantly. Comanche started cantering, too.

Lisa's expression changed almost immediately. I thought I knew why. Comanche has the smoothest, most wonderful canter—it's almost like riding a rocking horse, though of course it's much faster, which makes it that much more fun.

"Oh, this is wonderful!" Lisa cried to me.

"I knew you'd love him!" I called back, happy that Lisa had at last realized how wonderful Comanche was—thanks, in part, to me.

FROM: LAtwood

TO: Steviethegreat

SUBJECT: Your report

MESSAGE:

Hi, Stevie! Happy Monday. I know your report is due in exactly one week, and as I was thinking about that today I had a great idea. I went to the school library during my study

146

hall and did a little research on horse racing. It's no big deal, just a few notes—I typed them onto one of the school computers and then put the file on a disk. I was going to give it to you at Pine Hollow today, but since you didn't show up I figured I could just attach the file to this e-mail. It's a little long, so it may take a while to download. But I'm sure you'll find lots of stuff you can use in your report. Feel free to just include the whole thing if you want.

As I was researching the topic, I realized how much we learned about racing in just the short time we spent at the track. For instance, before we went I never knew that when the horses all come out on the track before the race it's called the post parade, or that those people who lead the post parade are called outriders. I was also surprised at how much smaller the saddles are than the ones we use, and how much higher the stirrups are. I found a whole bunch of more specific information on racing tack, which is included in the file, along with some interesting info on the history of racing and training methods and some more technical stuff.

Anyway, happy writing! I'll see you tomorrow at lessons. (You're coming, right? I mean, not even I would miss a riding lesson because of a school paper!)

Welcome to My Life . . .

During the whole time I'm writing about, Carole was spending a lot of time with Judy on her rounds. One day they went back to Maskee Farms for another check on Mr. McLeod's racers, and they found out that Prancer would be

147

racing in just over a week. And the best part was that Mr. McLeod and Judy invited Carole to go to the racetrack to watch her! Lisa and I were really happy for her when she told us at our next Saddle Club meeting, though of course we couldn't help being a tiny bit jealous, too. I had seen plenty of horse races on TV, and they always looked so exciting.

In fact, Lisa and I were still thinking about that when we got to Pine Hollow the next day. At least I still was. I couldn't believe Carole was really going to have the chance to see all those gorgeous Thoroughbred racehorses at the track and be a part of all that fun. I mean, all horses are born to run. But Thoroughbred racehorses are bred and trained for it, too. It was sure to be a memorable experience, especially for a horse-crazy girl like Carole.

Lisa and I went to Starlight's stall. We had agreed to take over his care that day so Carole and Judy could get an earlier start. As we were hosing down his leg, I was still thinking about Carole's big news.

"Isn't Carole lucky to be going to the racetrack?" I commented, giving Starlight a pat.

"She sure is," Lisa agreed. "Have you ever been to a racetrack?"

"No, but my parents go sometimes," I said. "As a matter of fact, they were talking about going again soon."

"How soon?" Lisa asked quickly.

I glanced at her. Suddenly I realized what she was thinking, and I couldn't believe I hadn't thought of it myself. "What a great idea!" I cried. "I'll start nagging them about it right away!"

"Do you think it'll work?" Lisa asked.

I was pretty sure it would. My parents had always enjoyed their trips to the track in the past, and once they heard about Carole being there I figured I could talk them into taking us. In fact, I could only think of one potential problem. "But will your parents let you go?" I asked. Lisa's parents can be—well, let's just say they're conservative. They tend to get nervous whenever Lisa's out of their sight for more than two seconds.

But Lisa didn't look worried at all. "You know my parents, Stevie. They think your parents are wonderful. If your parents say it's okay, they'll let me go."

We continued with Starlight's treatment, massaging his swollen leg after we finished hosing it. Then we took him back to his stall and started to replace the wrap on his knee. A few minutes later, Max stopped by. "How's it coming, girls?" he asked, leaning on the half door of the stall.

"Just fine," I told him. "We think the swelling is going down. Maybe. A little bit."

Max chuckled. "Glad you're so certain. But as long as it's not getting worse, it's a good sign. When you're waiting for a horse to heal, patience is a good quality."

"At least *he's* healing," Lisa put in. Her voice sounded kind of angry, and I guess Max noticed, too, because he shot her a surprised look.

I suspected that Lisa's harsh words had something to do with her feelings about Pepper. Max must have been thinking the same thing, because he asked Lisa how her first ride on Comanche had gone.

149

Lisa shrugged. "Okay, I guess."

"You know," Max said, "I just stopped by and checked on Pepper. He seemed a little restless. Would you have time to take him out on a trail ride—say half an hour—if somebody could go with you?"

"Like me? On Topside?" I asked.

"Like you, on Topside," Max confirmed.

I did my best to keep a straight face as I nodded. "I bet we could squeeze it in."

We quickly finished up in Starlight's stall, then rushed to get our horses ready. We tacked up Pepper and Topside in record time and were soon mounted and riding off across the rolling fields behind Pine Hollow.

I glanced over at Lisa as we rode along at a sedate walk. She looked happier than she had in days. "I really love this horse," she said, her eyes shining. "He's just so gentle."

I glanced at Pepper. At that second, he nodded his big gray head up and down, as if agreeing with Lisa's words. I couldn't help smiling at that.

It was a gorgeous day, perfect for riding. After a while, I could tell that Topside was getting a bit bored with walking. At least I was pretty sure he was. And I was *very* sure that I was. Max had told us not to overwork Pepper, but I didn't think a short trot would do him any harm. "Want to trot?" I suggested.

"Of course," Lisa agreed quickly. Soon both horses were trotting, with Pepper seeming to enjoy the exercise every bit as much as Topside did.

We slowed down again when we got to the woods. "That was wonderful," Lisa said.

I smiled, glad that she sounded so happy. "I think Pepper enjoyed it as much as you did."

"More," Lisa said. "And, you know, it turns out that Pepper has been enjoying this kind of thing with lots of people for a long time. Remember that essay I wrote?"

How could I forget? It was all she had talked about for days. But I just nodded. "Didn't you get an A?"

"Yes, I got an A, but that wasn't the thing I wanted to tell you about. Ms. Ingleby read it out loud in class. She did it because she liked Pepper. And it turned out that practically every kid in my class had ridden Pepper at one time or another. A lot of them were pretty upset that Pepper is getting old. One girl was even crying."

I wasn't surprised that a lot of people felt so strongly about Pepper. He was a pretty special horse. I still loved him myself, even though I hadn't ridden him in ages.

Lisa wasn't finished. "Even Ms. Ingleby had ridden Pepper when she was a little girl. That's why she read my essay. It was kind of neat. It's like this one horse ties a whole lot of people together. Isn't that odd? I mean, how many riders have sat in this saddle, on this horse, and enjoyed it as much as I'm enjoying it now?"

I tried to imagine the answer. "Hundreds, I guess," I said. "It makes it seem all the more as if Pepper has earned his retirement, doesn't it?"

Lisa smiled. "Too bad we can't give him a black-tie dinner and a gold watch to take to Florida," she joked. "But I think he'd be happier with some warm mash anyway."

I almost didn't hear what she said next. I had just had one of those ideas—the kind that I knew was destined to be one of those stupendously wonderful, earth-shatteringly fantastic ideas that everyone would remember practically forever. It was so perfect I could hardly keep myself from shouting with joy that I had thought of it.

But I didn't tell Lisa about it. I knew it would be even better if it was a surprise, to her at least. I would need a little help from a few other people. Max, for one . . .

I was still thinking about it when I got home that day, trying to figure out how all the details would work. I was humming as I entered the kitchen to scrounge up a snack.

Then I saw my mother sitting at the kitchen table reading a magazine, and I remembered our racetrack plan. I gave Mom a big, loving smile.

"Hi!" I said brightly. "How's my favorite mother in the whole wide world?"

She lowered the magazine and gazed at me through slightly narrowed eyes. "Suspicious," she replied. "What do you need? Money? Or is today report card day?"

I laughed. Mom has a terrific sense of humor sometimes. "Very funny," I said. "Actually, I was thinking about how you and Dad were just saying that we should do more things as a family."

Mom raised one eyebrow. "Yes?"

I shrugged. "Well, I think it's a great idea. We should do something together this weekend. Say Saturday afternoon.

Of course, the boys wouldn't have to come," I added quickly, shuddering at the thought of Chad, Alex, and Michael at the racetrack. They always make fun of everything having to do with horses, mostly because they know it bugs me. That's how immature they are. "Actually, maybe Lisa could come instead. She's been kind of depressed lately because Pepper's retiring. She could use some excitement. So she should definitely come with us."

Mom was looking slightly confused by now. "Where are we going?"

I smiled. "Why, to the racetrack of course," I said.

"Hmmm," she said.

I felt a twinge of nervousness. It's hard to tell what Mom is thinking when she says "hmmm" like that. Maybe it was time for the direct approach. "So can we go?" I asked. "Please? Carole is going to be there because Judy's the vet for some of the horses that are running on Saturday and they asked Carole to come along because one of the horses really likes her, not that that's such a surprise, since every horse ever foaled just adores Carole from the second they meet her, but still, it's kind of a big deal, so of course Lisa and I don't want to miss it, and we were talking today about how it would be really cool to surprise Carole by showing up and so I remembered how much fun you and Dad had when you went to the track last summer and you were saying a couple of weeks ago that you should do it again now that racing season is here, and—"

"Stop!" Mom cried, holding up both hands in a position of surrender. "Please, enough already! You've convinced me."

"Really?" I could hardly believe it had been that easy.

She nodded. "On one condition. Well, actually two. First, if your father agrees."

"And second?"

She let out a mock groan. "If you promise to stop explaining!"

I grinned and pretended to zip my lips shut with my finger. Then I unzipped them just long enough to say, "Thanks, Mom!" before skipping out of the room and heading upstairs.

I was thrilled. I couldn't wait to go to a real racetrack and see Prancer. Carole had been talking about her so much that Lisa and I felt as though we knew her already. And now we were going to get to watch her run!

But I couldn't spend too much time thinking about it. I had other things to do. It was time to start working on my other plan—the plan that would make a whole lot of people happy. And somehow, just at that moment, bringing more joy and pleasure to the world seemed more important than anything else—even studying for my math quiz.

FROM: FentonHall

TO: Steviethegreat

SUBJECT: Your assignment

MESSAGE:

Hello, Stephanie,

This is Miss Fenton writing from the school computer. I

write to remind you that your extra-credit assignment is due exactly one week from today. I trust you are already hard at work and that this message is completely unnecessary. However, I know that your life is full of many distractions, so I thought it prudent to send you this friendly reminder. I expect to see your completed report on my desk bright and early next Monday morning.

Happy writing!

Welcome to My Life . . .

While I was making my plans and Lisa was continuing to worry about Pepper, Carole was learning all kinds of stuff while working with Judy. Most of it isn't really relevant to this assignment, though of course it's all very interesting and I would be glad to discuss it if you're interested, Miss Fenton.

Carole and Judy went back to Maskee Farms for one final health check on the horses that would be racing that weekend, including Prancer. When they got there Mr. McLeod told Judy that he was afraid Prancer might be favoring one of her hind legs. I wasn't there, of course, but Carole told me all about what happened next (several dozen times, actually), so I'm pretty sure it went something like this:

First Judy looks over Prancer in her stall and doesn't find anything wrong. So she steps back. "Let's get her moving," she says. "Somebody lead her out."

Mr. McLeod points at Carole. "You," he barks. "Lead her out." He tosses a lead rope at her.

Carole catches it and goes to Prancer's stall. The beautiful filly is overjoyed to see her. Her deep brown eyes light up, her gentle face nudges Carole's hair, her dainty ears prick forward eagerly. Carole clips the rope on her and leads her out. She leads her past Judy and Mr. McLeod, first at a walk and then at a trot. The two adults peer intently at the horse's legs, watching for any sign of hesitation or discomfort.

"She looks good to me," Judy says at last.

"Hmmm," Mr. McLeod says. "Better safe than sorry. Let's try her at a faster gait. But there's no one here to ride her. At least no one small, like a jockey . . ." Suddenly his gaze falls on Carole. "You!" he barks. "Can you ride?"

Carole's jaw drops. "M-Me?"

"Of course she can," Judy says. "Carole's a terrific rider. Let's saddle 'er up!"

Carole moves as if in a daze. Mr. McLeod tells her where the tack is, and she rushes to get the filly ready. She is going to ride a real racehorse! It's unbelievable!

(Actually, it *was* unbelievable. Carole had to tell me and Lisa at least three times before we figured out that she wasn't pulling our legs.)

Finally the filly is all set. The lightweight racing saddle is much smaller than the ones Carole is used to, and the stirrups a bit higher. Still, a saddle's a saddle.

And moments later, Carole finds herself high up on the back of a real, live racehorse! It's like a dream come true.

Prancer's motions are smooth, almost seamless. Every movement she makes is sleek and graceful. Carole walks her, then trots her, while Judy and Mr. McLeod watch.

156

Carole feels kind of self-conscious, but she soon realizes they aren't watching her. They're watching Prancer, trying to see if her leg is bothering her in any way.

"Let's take her around the practice track," Mr. McLeod suggests. He points the way to his farm's practice track—which looks like a real racetrack, just a little bit smaller—and Carole rides Prancer there, still enjoying the filly's fluid gaits.

Then the dream gets even better. Prancer steps onto the track. Following Mr. McLeod's directions, Carole takes her to a trot, then a canter. . . .

And then, with just the slightest pressure from Carole's legs, the filly breaks into a gallop!

Carole adjusts her position, leaning forward to maintain her balance at the new, much faster gait. She can feel the incredible power and speed of the horse beneath her as the filly's long strides eagerly gobble up the track. Wind whistles past her ears, whipping back her hair even under her hard hat. Prancer is practically flying! And Carole is the pilot!

All too soon, Carole realizes it's time to stop. She pulls up the filly, who is dancing with eagerness to keep running but obeys Carole's commands.

It is one of the most special days of Carole's life. She knows she will never forget it—or Prancer.

Miss Fenton, being the astute and erudite woman that you are, you can probably already guess that Carole had totally fallen in love with Prancer. But what you may not realize is that she was also falling in love with her job helping Judy. I'm not saying she's definitely decided to be a vet or anything—it's still on the list, but so are lots of other careers (like being a jockey, now that she's seen what that can be like)—but she loves to learn about anything having to do with horses, so hanging out with someone who knows as much as Judy was her idea of big fun. Even though she had to witness a lot of sad and upsetting things, like sick and injured and poorly treated and dying horses, as well as wonderful things, like newborn foals and miraculous recoveries.

Anyway, my point is that I thought it would be useful to this part of the story if we had a word from Judy Barker, the vet Carole has been working with. I asked her to write a brief statement explaining how important Carole is to all her patients, especially Prancer. Her statement follows.

Statement from Judy Barker

My name is Judy Barker. I am an equine veterinarian from Willow Creek, Virginia. Stevie Lake has asked me to write a few words about Carole Hanson. I'm not much of a writer, but I'll do my best, since Stevie seems to think it's important.

I asked Carole to assist me on my rounds because she's one of the best young horsewomen I've ever met. She takes horse care and horse health very seriously. I had already been considering asking her to join me on my rounds when her own horse, a bay gelding named Starlight, developed a slight swelling in his foreleg. Knowing that Carole would need something to take her mind off her worries, I made the offer, and she accepted.

Since that time, Carole has been an invaluable part of my practice. She accompanies me on my rounds as frequently as her sched-

ule allows. Her understanding of and enthusiasm for horses has helped carry us through good times and bad.

Carole was especially helpful with one patient recently, a Thoroughbred filly named Prancer. Carole had a good rapport with this horse, which came in handy when the filly needed comforting and soothing after a terrible accident when she was suffering a great deal of pain and fear. Carole's steadfast courage and helpfulness throughout a very tense and tragic situation were of great comfort to me and also, I strongly suspect, to Prancer.

To sum up, Carole has been a wonderful assistant. Through her young and enthusiastic eyes, I see my patients in a whole new way.

Welcome to My Life . . .

See, Miss Fenton? Wasn't that a touching note? Judy really appreciates Carole's help, and no wonder. Carole is good for the horses she works with. Just like those same horses are good for her. They help her learn, and they took her mind off Starlight's leg problem enough so that she wouldn't worry too much.

People are good for horses. Horses are good for people.

Isn't that a life lesson more valuable than anything that we could learn from mere homework? I leave it to you to decide.

HEY, DORKY SISTER!

SINCE WHEN DO YOU LIKE HOMEWORK SO MUCH, ANYWAY? WE KNOW THE TRUTH. YOU'RE JUST TRYING TO KEEP US FROM PLAY-

159

ING AWESOME JAWSOME BECAUSE YOU'RE A BIG LOSER. WELL, WE'RE ON TO YOU. SO WATCH OUT—THE JAWBONE WILL GET YOU WHEN YOU LEAST EXPECT IT!!!

HA HA HA HA HA HA HA!

LOVE,
MICHAEL

FROM: HorseGal

TO: Steviethegreat

SUBJECT: How's it going?

MESSAGE:

I just had another idea for an essay I could write for your report. That last one (about Starlight's leg) turned out pretty well, if I do say so myself. I'm glad you're using it. But sometime, if you don't mind, I'd like to see exactly what you cut out. I know you said it was just a few words here and there, but I want to make sure everything is still clear. There are a few places where it could be easy to get confused, like the part where I explain the positioning of the navicular bone in the foot versus the flexor tendon and pedal bone, or the section about the differences between introductory-level and training-level tests in dressage. And since Miss Fenton isn't really a horse person, well, you can't be too careful, right?

But anyway, my new idea is that I could write something

160

giving my impressions of the whole racetrack scene. I spent a lot of time thinking about it afterward, as you know. And I still think it's really interesting (and kind of weird) that the whole racing industry centers around the connection between horses and making money. I mean, we ride and love and care for and appreciate horses every day, but we never expect them to repay us by earning money for us the way Mr. McLeod and other people in the racing industry do. It still seems like such a strange way to think about such wonderful animals, to me at least.

Of course, that doesn't mean that the racetrack isn't an exciting place. I mean, we all had fun that day, didn't we? At least until the accident. It's a whole world devoted to horses, and that can't be all bad. In fact, it was pretty exciting.

So anyway, I could talk more about that stuff in my essay, along with the interesting information I learned about racing (I just found a book at the library about the history of racing, so I could include some of that info, too) and my experiences behind the scenes with Judy and Prancer and all the rest of it. I could probably turn that into ten pages or so pretty easily, and I'm sure your headmistress would be really impressed, especially if I made sure to include a lot of cool racing terms like "furlong" and "photo finish." What do you think?

161

So get this. Now Carole wants to do some ten-page dissertation on horse racing for my project. If Miss Fenton only knew how many millions of words I was saving her from reading, she'd probably just give me an A for the rest of my school career! Well, maybe not. But you know how Carole can get when she's enthusiastic about a subject. And of course, when it comes to horses, she's enthusiastic about EVERY subject. Anyway, I managed to talk her out of her latest contribution by telling her that I was afraid all the research she'd done might end up making me look bad—you know, as if I was making my friends do my assignment for me. Come to think of it, that might work equally well the next time Lisa starts blabbing on about footnotes. . . .

Anyway, despite how it sounds, I really do appreciate all their help and support. Yours, too, of course. That stuff you wrote about me being honest and responsible was brilliant. I *was* pretty worried that some of the facts of the story up to that point might have made me sound, well, you know—not quite as honest and responsible as someone like Miss Fenton might think I should be. You know? So thanks again.

Now all I have to do is convince her that spending the day at the track instead of working on my English paper was

162

the right thing to do. Naturally, I know it was. But teachers and other adults can be so unreasonable sometimes. Thank goodness Mom and Dad didn't suspect I hadn't even gotten past chapter one of *To Kill a Mockingbird* by the day we went to the track (let alone started the paper, which was due the next Tuesday), or they never would have agreed to it. Instead of cheering on all those beautiful Thoroughbreds, I would have spent the day locked in my room with my nose buried in my book.

Speaking of which, you'll never guess who I saw at the school library today with her nose buried in a whole huge stack of books.

Veronica!

Yes, you read right. Veronica diAngelo was making like a study buddy after school. Don't ask me why. But I saw it with my own eyes when I stopped in to return a book. I assumed it must be just one more symptom of her weirdness disease. But then I noticed that she didn't even seem to be reading. She had a book open in front of her, but she was just sort of staring into space. She didn't even see me watching her.

I was about to go over and say something to her—I mean, I was pretty curious about this. She hasn't made a snotty remark or insulted me in well over a week now. But just then Betsy Cavanaugh came into the library and saw me looking at Veronica.

"Poor thing," she whispered, with this really sympathetic look on her face. "She's just killing herself on that assignment."

"What assignment?" I asked quickly. Veronica is in a lot of my classes, and I started to panic that while I was concentrating on my extra-credit report, one of my teachers had slipped in some huge project when I wasn't paying attention.

Betsy looked uncertain. "Well, I guess it's not really a secret," she said, glancing around to make sure no one else could hear. "Miss Fenton is making Veronica write an extra-credit report. You know, because her grades have slipped these past few weeks."

I tell you, my jaw practically dropped on the floor at that one. I couldn't believe it. So Veronica has the same assignment I do! Isn't that bizarre? Who would have guessed that Little Miss Perfect could ever have problems with her grades just like the rest of us? I'd always assumed that she just paid all the teachers to give her As and Bs, or maybe paid her servants to do her homework for her. I wouldn't put it past her.

That's not all. After Betsy wandered away, I got ready to leave. But just then I saw Veronica suddenly glance at her watch. Then she gasped, jumped up with a worried expression on her face, and rushed straight out of the library, brushing right past me without even noticing I was there. Naturally, she didn't bother to put away any of the books she'd been using, either.

I can't even begin to imagine what's up with her. It's totally mysterious. Maybe after I finish my report I'll have time to figure it out!

But it will definitely have to wait until after I finish. Because right after I left the library, I ran into Miss Fenton. And from what she said, I know now—if I didn't before—that this report had better be good. It went something like this:

MISS FENTON: Hello, Stephanie.

STEVIE: Hi, Miss Fenton. I was just on my way home to work on my report.

MISS FENTON (looking down her nose like she always does): Good. Because I'm really looking forward to reading it. And I expect all your hard work to show.

STEVIE: Oh, it will! And I am. Working. Hard, that is. Um, gotta go.

MISS FENTON (calling after me): Monday morning, Stephanie! Bright and early! *Ha ha ha ha ha ha ha ha ha!*

Okay, I made up that wicked laugh at the end. But the rest is true. She was giving me this really intense look when she said it, like she suspected I was really goofing off all day instead of working on the report. Which is so totally not true this time. I've just got to make sure there's no way she can possibly think that I didn't put my best effort into this.

So I'd better get to it, huh? I'm going to try to call Dorothy DeSoto now to ask her some questions about that dressage demonstration she did. I want to include a lot of information about it in the report. Do you happen to know the time difference between here and London? Never mind. I'll just go ahead and call—if she's sleeping, she won't pick up the phone, right? And I can just leave a message.

Wish me luck—I'll need it!

165

MEMO

TO: All Horse Wise Members
FROM: Max
RE: Fox hunt

As some of you may have heard by now (thank you, S.L.), the Cross County Pony Club has invited all members of Horse Wise to participate in their upcoming fox hunt. We will be holding a mock hunt of our own prior to the real hunt to give us all some practice in the field. We'll discuss that further next week.

You'll find permission slips attached to this memo along with the schedule for the meetings etc. leading up to the hunt. Please have your parents sign the slips and drop them off at the office by Friday so I'll know who will be participating.

Foxhunting is a sport with many traditions and a long history. In order to participate in the upcoming hunt, you must learn to appreciate same. You will be expected to familiarize yourself with the following list of terms by our next meeting.

Master of the hounds—The person who is in charge of everything about the hunt except tracking the fox.

Huntsman—The person in charge of tracking the fox.

Whippers-in—Riders assigned to assist the huntsman and help keep the hounds on the track.

The field—Everybody on the hunt who *isn't* the master of the hounds, the huntsman, one of the whippers-in, or a hound.

Drag meet or *drag hunt*—A hunt in which the "fox" is actually a bag of scent that has been dragged across the countryside to lay an artificial trail for the hounds to follow.

Capping fee—A sum of money paid by visitors to a hunt official. (Don't worry, you can save your allowances. Our hunts will be free to Pony Club members.)

Couple (of hounds)—The proper foxhunting term for a pair of foxhounds. The hounds are always referred to as such—"a couple of hounds" rather than "a pair of dogs."

Giving tongue—What the hounds do when they are on the trail of a fox.

Full cry—Similar to above; indicates they're following a trail.

Riding to hounds—Another way of saying going on a hunt.

Holloa—The call a whipper-in makes when he spots the fox breaking cover.

Breaking cover—Running out into the open.

Larking—Jumping unnecessarily during a hunt; a sure sign of an ignorant hunter.

Thank you for your attention. If you have any questions about this list you may feel free to ask me or Mr. Baker, the director of Cross County.

Tallyho!

Welcome to My Life . . .

The above memo is what's known as foreshadowing. (See? Despite what Ms. Milligan may claim, I do pay attention in English class!) You see, Max handed the memo out to us at our Horse Wise meeting on the morning of Prancer's race. Because in case you've forgotten in all the excitement of more recent events in this report, we were all still looking forward to that fox hunt that Phil's Pony Club was sponsoring.

Judy picked Carole up at the stable right after the meeting. Carole still had no idea that Lisa and I were coming to the track, too.

"Bye, Carole," I called after her innocently as she left. "Have a really fun day!"

Lisa giggled. "Say hi to Prancer for us, okay?"

"Bye!" Carole called back, hardly stopping long enough to wave as she followed Judy to her truck. Seconds later, they were gone.

Lisa and I went back inside to finish taking care of our horses. We chatted a little bit about the memo Max had just given us and how exciting it was that we were going to be in a real fox hunt soon. But mostly we talked about our upcoming day at the races.

I was feeling a little bit sleepy. I had been up very late the night before, finishing every last word of *To Kill a Mockingbird*. It had been such a fascinating book that I didn't really mind, but I couldn't help being kind of tired. I figured the excitement of the racetrack would help perk me up, though.

"Come on," I said. "Let's hurry and finish up here. We don't want to be late!"

We finished our stable chores in record time and ran all the way back to my house. My parents were ready to go. Fortunately, my three brothers—who, as you know, Miss Fenton, are not among the most intelligent or discerning students at Fenton Hall—had declined to join us and were nowhere in sight. So the four of us climbed in the car and took off.

Lisa and I talked about Prancer the whole way there. Even though we'd never laid eyes on her, we were totally sure she was going to win her race. After all, she had The Saddle Club cheering her on! I guess my parents weren't that interested in hearing about her, though, because they kept trying to distract us with boring questions about stuff like the weather and our homework. (Not that homework itself is boring, of course. But you know what I mean.)

We finally arrived at the track. My dad paid our way in, and then we all huddled just inside the gate.

"Okay, girls," Dad said. "We have reserved seats in the clubhouse, but we don't have to stay there the whole time. Feel free to wander, but stay together. And check in with us at least every hour, okay?"

"Sure, Dad," I agreed. I grabbed Lisa by the arm as she started some long-winded thank-yous for the ride there, and dragged her off as my parents headed for the entrance to the clubhouse (which was really just a part of the grandstand, which is the building where the audience sits to watch the races).

"This is so exciting, isn't it?" Lisa said, staring wide-eyed at the bustling scene surrounding us.

It really was amazing. In case you've never been to the racetrack yourself, Miss Fenton, I'll do my best to describe it. First of all, you have to picture the track itself—a huge oval, a mile around, of smooth brown dirt. The finish line is a wire hung over the track in front of the grandstand. The starting gate (you've probably seen those on TV, at least) is attached to a tractor thing that pulls it to the right spot or whatever distance the race is supposed to be. There are people out there, including some people on horseback—outriders, they're called. But on the whole, the scene out on the track itself is fairly peaceful—in between races, at least.

It's just the opposite inside the grandstand. There are people everywhere—sitting in the stands, buying food at the snack bar, standing in line to place bets at the betting windows, wandering around staring at their race programs. And everybody seems to have an opinion on who's going to win. For instance, as we were walking over to buy ourselves a program, Lisa and I overheard two men talking about Mr. McLeod's horses, including Prancer.

We spent a few minutes exploring the rest of the track. Then we bought a large popcorn to share and headed upstairs to our seats. We didn't want to miss the start of the first race.

"I wonder what Carole is doing right now," Lisa remarked as we got comfortable.

I shrugged and peered down toward the track, not wanting to miss my first glimpse of the post parade, which is what it's called when all the horses walk in front of the stands before heading to the starting gate. "Who knows?" I said. "Probably having tons of fun behind the scenes."

"Probably," Lisa agreed, reaching for another handful of popcorn.

Just then the horses appeared, so we were pretty quiet for a while. My parents returned with their betting tickets, which I expected to be interesting-looking but were really just boring little slips of white paper with some numbers on them.

"Who did you bet on, Mr. Lake?" Lisa asked politely.

My dad grinned and winked at us. "I overheard a tip," he said. "The number four horse. It's practically a sure thing."

My mother rolled her eyes and laughed. "That's what you kept saying the last time we were here," she told him. She leaned over to help herself to a few pieces of our popcorn. "It's a good thing I made you stop betting after you lost twenty dollars, or we wouldn't have been able to buy gas for the ride home."

My dad laughed good-naturedly at my mom's teasing. I grinned at Lisa, glad that everyone seemed to be having such a good time. I know I was! That's the kind of life experience you just can't get from a textbook.

Then I turned my attention back to the post parade. Each sleek racehorse pranced by with a jockey on its back. Each racehorse also had another horse walking beside it. I had seen the same thing on TV.

Lisa noticed, too. "Why are those other horses there?" she wondered aloud. "Is it just to keep the racehorses calm?"

I shrugged. "Probably. Remember, these are Thoroughbreds we're talking about. I mean, Topside is so calm and even-tempered most of the time that it's easy to forget that a lot of Thoroughbreds are pretty jumpy. It probably helps to have a calmer horse lead them."

My dad heard us and leaned over. "I can't believe *I'm* actually about to tell *you two* something about horses," he joked. "But I think those horses are known as lead ponies."

I grinned at him. "Hey, maybe you're not totally useless after all, Dad!"

(Don't worry, Miss Fenton, I was only kidding. I actually have a great and profound respect for my father and all adults.)

After the post parade, all the horses warmed up by cantering or galloping for a few minutes. Then they all headed around the track to the starting gate. Some track workers loaded them in one by one, and then, with a clang of a bell and a whoop from the crowd, they were off!

It was an exciting race. Three different horses kept battling for the lead, but in the end a spunky little bay mare leaped forward just in time to win.

"That was great!" I cried, a little breathless from the excitement of it all. Thinking back, I realized I had been shouting and cheering the whole time, even though I wasn't exactly sure which horse I'd been cheering for. The only bad part was that I'd been so excited that I had ended up spilling most of the popcorn all over the floor.

"It sure was!" my dad agreed. Glancing over, I saw that he was grinning broadly. "I just won some money!"

I checked the tote board that showed the numbers of the winning horses. Sure enough, the little bay was number four!

"Cool!" I said. "Does that mean the next round of popcorn is on you?"

My dad grinned as he got up to go cash in his ticket. "I'll even throw in some sodas."

And now, Miss Fenton, if you will indulge me—I found myself so inspired by the athletic poetry of those noble racehorses that I have composed a brief ode in their honor. I think it will help make clear what an unmissable and life-changing experience this was, regardless of what other experiences I might have been neglecting at the same time (like those word problems I never quite got around to doing). Here it is:

A DAY AT THE RACES
A completely original poem by S. Lake

There once was a nice girl named Lake
Who decided she wanted to take
A trip to the track.
She might never come back!
'Cause the horses there just took the cake!

First came a cool post parade
Of the track a big circle they made
Each with an outrider
Riding beside 'er
Then they headed to the starting gate.
With a ring of the bell they were off!
At their speed no one ever could scoff

173

The browns and the bays,
The chestnuts and grays,
Left me too breathless even to cough!

I learned so so so much that day
All the learning just blew me away
Who will win, who will show?
Does it matter, or no?
That's important, now wouldn't you say?

Anyway, I think that poem sums up some of what I was feeling about the grandeur and majesty of racing—which is known as the sport of kings, by the way.

So the next couple of races came and went. There was almost half an hour in between each one, so Lisa and I had plenty of time to wander around and see the sights.

"Hey, I wonder where Carole is? I can't believe we haven't even seen her," I said once we got back to our seats.

Lisa nodded. "I'm starting to think we may not see her at all," she said. "Judy's probably keeping her busy back in the—"

Suddenly she let out a loud gasp. I turned to see what she was staring at. It was Carole! She was down by the rail near the gap leading back to the stable area. One of Mr. McLeod's horses, Hold Fast, had just walked past, and Carole was waving at the jockey.

My dad had looked up. He spotted her at the same time I did. "Look, there's Carole."

"We've got to get her attention," I declared. Without waiting for Lisa to answer, I took a deep breath and shouted as loudly as I could: *"Caaarooole!"*

Lisa joined in, and Carole heard us almost immediately. After looking around for a second, she spotted us waving wildly at her from our seats. She grinned, looking surprised, and waved back.

"Wait there!" I shrieked at the top of my lungs, hoping she could hear me. Then I turned to Lisa. "Come on. Let's go say hi."

We raced downstairs and found our way to where Carole was.

"There's so much to tell you guys," she said breathlessly. "You just wouldn't believe everything that goes on here and everything I'm learning. This whole place, this whole thing—horse racing, I mean—is another world. It's hard to believe it's all done with the same animals we love so much at Pine Hollow."

"Purebred Thoroughbreds aren't exactly what we're riding at Pine Hollow," Lisa put in. "Except for Topside, I mean."

"But they're all horses, aren't they?" I commented.

"You'd hardly think so around here," Carole said. "It's more like they're some kind of precious commodity."

"I don't know about you, but that's just the way *I* feel about them," I said.

"Me too," Carole agreed. "Definitely. But it's more than that. It's money. It's business. It's something we never think about."

175

"I think about money all the time," I said.

"That's because you always spend everything you've got," Lisa said. (She was just kidding. I'm as responsible about money as I am about everything else.) "To you, two dollars is a precious commodity. I think what Carole's saying is that these animals are worth hundreds of thousands of dollars, and they're treated as if they're royalty."

"That's it exactly," Carole said. "We're used to horses that may be worth a couple of thousand dollars, which isn't exactly pocket change, but these horses are worth zillions, and the whole purpose is for them to earn even more zillions. That's a big difference."

"You can say that again," I agreed. I had finally caught on to what she was trying to say—that racing was a business, not just a sport, so the horses themselves were valued for things other than the things we valued horses for, like a nice personality or a smooth trot. They were valued for their speed, and that was worth a lot.

Before we could talk about that anymore, we heard someone calling Carole's name. It turned out to be Mr. McLeod.

"I'm glad I found you," he told her. "I need your help. Can you get to the stables quickly?"

"Sure," Carole said. And with a quick wave, she was gone.

"I wonder what that was about?" Lisa said.

I shrugged. "Who knows? I'm sure she'll tell us later. What do you want to do now? Prancer's in the sixth race, so we have plenty of time before it starts."

"I know," Lisa said. "I heard some people talking about

going to watch the horses being saddled in the paddock. Wouldn't it be cool to watch Prancer getting tacked up? Maybe Carole will be there, too, if she's helping Judy and Mr. McLeod."

"Brilliant idea!" I exclaimed. "Let's go!"

We asked someone for directions, and soon (after stopping at the snack bar just long enough to gobble down a couple of hot dogs—all that cheering is hungry work!) we found ourselves at the fence just outside the saddling area, which as Lisa had said was called the paddock. And it really was mostly like a big paddock with a few open-sided stalls marked with numbers, where the horses stood while their trainers got them ready to race. A couple of horses were there when we arrived, but we didn't see any that matched Carole's description of Prancer.

We leaned on the fence and watched for a while. Then, suddenly, Lisa started elbowing me in the ribs. Hard.

"Ouch!" I protested. "What's your problem?"

Lisa didn't even hear me. She was staring at a path leading to the far side of the paddock. I had already guessed that it led to the stable area, since all the horses seemed to be coming from that way. Now I looked and saw a small buckskin horse walking through the paddock gate, followed by a tall, elegant bay filly. And the buckskin was being ridden by a very familiar-looking, curly-haired girl!

"Carole!" I cried. "What's she doing?"

"Call me crazy," Lisa replied, "but I think she's riding Prancer's lead pony!"

I was about to start calling out her name again, but Lisa

stopped me, explaining that Carole probably had a job to do and we shouldn't disturb her. So I kept quiet, though it wasn't easy—especially as we watched Carole dismount from the buckskin pony and start assisting Mr. McLeod and some other people in tacking up Prancer.

Then the adults stood back, and Carole led the beautiful filly out of the saddling stall and started walking her around the ring. When she passed in front of us, I couldn't resist. "Carole!" I cried. "Over here!"

Carole glanced over, saw me, and grinned. She waved to us.

"Is this for real?" Lisa called out. "Are you riding the lead pony?"

Carole nodded and started leading Prancer in a tight circle so she could talk to us. "Mr. McLeod wanted me to do it because he thinks I have this magical ability to calm this filly down. Isn't it weird? She isn't nervous or upset at all!"

Just then, almost as if she had understood every word Carole was saying, Prancer turned to snuffle at Lisa and me. It reminded me of when Topside is feeling feisty and looking for treats. I grinned and gave the friendly horse a pat, and so did Lisa.

"She's beautiful!" Lisa exclaimed.

"And loving!" I added, rubbing the filly's soft muzzle. "I'm sure she's going to win. I'll tell my dad to bet a bundle on her." I didn't bother to tell her that to my dad a "bundle" would be about two dollars and fifty cents.

"Let your dad do his own betting," Carole advised. "But

for now, go back to your seats. I'm going to be in the post parade, and I want to see somebody cheering for Prancer."

"I'll cheer for Prancer," I promised. "But mostly I'm going to cheer for you."

Lisa and I gave Prancer a few final pats. Then Carole turned her to continue circling the paddock.

"You heard what she said," Lisa said as we watched her go. "Let's get back to our seats so we don't miss a millisecond of that post parade."

A few minutes later, Lisa and I were safely in our seats as the first horse stepped onto the track. We had filled my parents in on the news, and they watched almost as eagerly as we did for Carole to appear.

Prancer was the second horse in line. "There she is!" Lisa shrieked, pointing and jumping up and down in her seat. "There's Carole!"

"I see her!" I replied, not taking my eyes off our friend for a second. Carole was sitting up straight in the saddle, a thrilled smile on her face. She was watching Prancer carefully as the filly stepped along beside the lead pony on her long, elegant legs. It looked to me as if Prancer was determined to stay as close to Carole as possible. She kept swinging her head over the pony's neck, almost as if looking to Carole for reassurance. The jockey, a tiny man in bright blue-and-white silks (that's what the jockey's uniform is called, in case you were wondering, Miss Fenton) sat quietly on Prancer's back, letting Carole do the leading.

"She looks good out there," my dad commented. I guessed he was talking about Carole rather than the horse. "Very professional."

The four of us hardly said another word throughout the whole post parade. But we did cheer—loudly—as Prancer passed in front of our part of the stands. I wanted to make sure Carole heard us. She must have, because she looked up, spotted us, and waved.

Before long the post parade broke up and the horses started warming up for the race. Carole steered her pony to one side as the jockey galloped Prancer partway around the track. I had a hard time deciding between watching Carole and watching Prancer. So I did my best to do both.

Then Carole rode off to one side with the other lead riders, and I concentrated all my attention on Prancer. After her warm-up run, she turned and headed for the starting gate with the rest of the horses. Soon they were all loaded into the gate.

"And they're off!" the public-address system blared. The announcer continued, giving the positions of the runners as they pounded down the track toward the first turn. But I wasn't paying attention. I was only interested in one horse, and I could see her jockey's blue-and-white silks near the front of the pack. Seconds later, Prancer burst out in front of everyone else.

Lisa was gripping my arm so tightly that her fingernails were digging into my skin. But I hardly noticed. "She's winning!" I gasped.

"I know! I know!" Lisa cried. We both knew that they

still had to travel a long way before crossing the finish line. But Prancer was racing ahead, opening up space in front of the other horses, looking wild and free and happy, her nostrils flared wide and her legs flashing almost too fast to see.

And then it happened.

It was so sudden that if Lisa or I had blinked just then, we might have missed it. Prancer stumbled. Her right foreleg bent under her body, the angle all wrong, terribly wrong. The jockey's arms flew up at the sudden change in direction. But I wasn't watching him. I was watching the horse, my heart in my throat.

Prancer lurched forward, then back. Somehow, she was also still moving forward as her three healthy legs tried to continue, to keep running the race.

Then a loud gasp went up from the entire audience as, after one final flailing attempt to keep going, Prancer pitched forward and fell onto the track, flinging her jockey off to one side.

My heart was pounding and blood was racing through my temples. I gripped the rail at the front of our box so tightly that my knuckles turned white. I couldn't believe this was happening. But it got worse.

"The other horses!" Lisa choked out.

I grabbed her hand and squeezed it tight, feeling helpless as we watched the rest of the field catch up to the fallen Prancer. Her jockey was rolling across the track, trying desperately to get out of the path of those deadly, flashing hooves. But Prancer couldn't roll away. She lay there helplessly as the other horses surrounded her.

I closed my eyes, afraid to look. When I opened them again a second later, the field of horses was well past. "Did they hit her?" I asked, afraid to hear the answer.

"I don't think so," my mother said grimly. "The other jockeys managed to steer around her. And her jockey got out of the way in time."

I nodded. But it was only a small comfort.

For the first time, I noticed that an ambulance was already on the track, rolling toward the jockey. Several people had emerged onto the track and were running toward him and Prancer. I recognized Judy among them.

Just then, I also spotted Carole. She was still on her lead pony, riding toward Prancer at a full gallop, urging her little horse to go still faster. Even from this distance, I could see that her face was covered with tears.

That made me realize that I was crying, too. So was Lisa.

The next few minutes passed very slowly. Some horse or other must have won that race, but we didn't see it. We watched as Carole arrived at Prancer's side before anyone else. She slid off her pony, leaving it ground-tied, and went to check on the jockey. I guess he was okay—he was already sitting up—because she almost immediately went to Prancer's side. She flung herself down on the track beside the horse and reached for the filly's leg.

It looked to Lisa and me as if Prancer calmed down as soon as she saw Carole. Before that, Prancer had been thrashing around and shaking her head, as if she wanted to get back up and keep running. But when she spotted Carole, she almost completely stopped struggling.

Carole felt Prancer's leg, just as we had seen her feel many another horse's leg, including Starlight's just a week or two before. But what she might find had perhaps never been so important.

"Do you think it's broken?" I whispered, my voice breaking a little on the words.

My mother put a comforting hand on my knee. "There's no way of telling," she murmured. "We just have to wait and see."

I gulped. My mother may not know a whole lot about horses aside from what I tell her, but she had seen enough races to know what might happen next. If Prancer's leg was broken, there was a good chance the vet would want to put her out of her misery right there and then.

We watched as Judy arrived at Carole's side, along with another man we assumed was the track vet and a couple of other people, including Mr. McLeod and the jockey, who seemed to be fine. They all gathered around Prancer and Carole, hiding them from view for a few minutes.

Finally the little crowd of people moved aside and we could see Carole once again.

"What's happening now?" Lisa wondered.

I just shook my head. And crossed my fingers. Soon we would know. . . .

I saw Carole at the filly's head. She stood up, then leaned down again over Prancer. I could see her lips moving and guessed that she was talking gently to the horse. Then she took the filly's reins in one hand.

"They're going to see if she can stand," my dad said.

I nodded, dropping Lisa's hand so I could cross my fingers on that hand, too. Lisa saw what I was doing and did the same. "Come on, Prancer," she whispered.

Prancer knew what Carole was asking her to do. She rolled partway over, her legs flailing around for a hold on the ground.

Carole managed to direct the horse's movements, encouraging her to put her weight on her left foreleg instead of the injured right. I held my breath. I think everyone else in the stands was doing the same thing, because there was hardly a sound for the next several seconds as Prancer struggled to stand—to save her own life.

She shifted her weight and brought her hind legs under her. Her hindquarters lifted a little bit. She braced her left foreleg against the track surface. Slowly, awkwardly, the horse lurched upward—and a moment later she was standing on her three good legs!

"She did it!" I gasped. Then I let out a loud whoop. "She did it!" I cried at the top of my lungs. I was vaguely aware that Lisa was shouting beside me. Even my parents were cheering, along with everybody else who'd been watching.

My gaze shifted from Prancer to Carole. At almost the same moment, Carole looked up, her eyes searching the stands. Lisa and I waved our arms to help her see us. Carole waved back, tears still streaming down her cheeks but a big smile lighting up her face.

Then she turned back to Prancer. Giving the filly several comforting pats and a big hug, she began to lead her, slowly, painfully, but steadily, back toward the stable.

"What do we do now?" Lisa asked worriedly after they had disappeared. The track workers had already set about preparing for the next race, but we were no longer interested in any of that. All our thoughts were with Prancer and Carole.

"Simple," I said. "We go help."

My father frowned. "Now, I'm not sure that's a good idea, girls," he said. "The public isn't allowed back in the stable area, and—"

"Dad!" I protested, wiping away most of my tears and frowning at him. "We're not the public. We're Carole's best friends, and we have to go. Carole needs us."

"Prancer needs us," Lisa added.

My father hesitated and glanced at my mother. "Well," he said reluctantly. He let out a sigh. "Maybe you're right. But I don't want you concocting some crazy scheme and sneaking back there without permission."

I widened my eyes, trying to look as innocent as possible. *"Moi?"* I asked in my best French accent.

Sensible Lisa came to the rescue. "I don't think we'll need any crazy schemes," she pointed out. "We can just explain exactly why we need to go back there and exactly how much Carole probably needs our support right now."

"Hmmm. The truth?" I pretended to think about it for a second. "It's so crazy, it just might work." (Of course, I was just kidding. The truth almost always works, as I well know, since I almost always tell it.) "Let's go."

Without giving my parents any time to change their minds, we hurried off to the stable area.

I let Lisa do most of the talking when we ran into the

185

guards. She has the kind of face and voice that just demands trust from everyone, including adults. Before long the guards were practically in tears, and they were waving us through and pointing us in the direction of the barn where Mr. McLeod's horses were staying.

We were so worried about Prancer that we hardly had time to look around, so I really don't have a very strong impression of what the stable area was like. The important thing was that we found the right barn almost immediately. We hurried inside, looking for Carole.

We found Judy instead. She was standing in the aisle, talking to Mr. McLeod while various other people scurried around busily. Prancer was standing in the stall just behind Judy, her head hanging lower than usual. "There she is," I whispered to Lisa. I wanted to rush over to see what was going on, but at the same time I was afraid we would only be in the way. I wasn't sure what to do now that we were in the stable.

Judy saved me from that decision. "Girls!" she said, spotting us and waving us over. "I'm so glad you're here. I think Carole's taking this pretty hard." As she talked, Lisa and I patted Prancer, who seemed glad to see us even though she was clearly still in pain.

Lisa nodded. "Where is she?"

"I'm not sure," Judy replied. "She disappeared a few minutes after we brought Prancer in." She glanced at her watch. "The X ray should be ready now. I've got to go take a look at it."

Part of me really, really wanted to know what that X ray said, since I knew it could mean the difference between life and death for Prancer. But I knew we would find that out sooner or later. Right then, Carole needed us.

"Let's check all the empty stalls," I told Lisa briskly.

She nodded, and we hurried down the aisle, peering over each half door. We didn't have to speak to know that we were both thinking the same thing: Carole must have hidden herself away somewhere to try to deal with her worry and grief. That was the only reason she would have left Prancer's side right then.

We checked every stall in the barn, but Carole was nowhere to be found. "What's that?" Lisa asked when we reached the end of the row.

I looked where she was pointing and saw a large, square shed just beyond the stable area. The big double doors were shut tight.

"Looks like some kind of storage building," I said. "Let's go."

We hurried forward and pulled one of the doors open. It was easy to tell that the building was some kind of feed storage area. The warm, familiar smells of hay and grain drifted toward us, and after a few seconds I could make out the shapes of bales and barrels.

I also spotted another familiar shape. "Carole?" I said.

Carole looked up at us, her face streaked with tears. Without a word, Lisa and I rushed inside and wrapped her in the biggest, warmest three-way hug we knew how to give.

After a moment Carole pulled back and looked at us. I could see the worry and fear in her eyes. "Prancer?" she said.

"Judy's reading the X ray now," Lisa said.

"I can't stand it," Carole said.

"We know." I reached forward to hug her again, wishing there was something more I could do to help her. But I was totally helpless. Suddenly, though, I realized that there was someone who could help Carole at that moment. "I think Prancer needs you now," I told her.

Lisa nodded. "We saw her and she seemed glad to see us," she said. "Except she kept looking over my shoulder."

"I think she was looking for you," I told Carole.

Carole smiled a little. "She's an amazing horse. A truly amazing horse."

"All the more reason to be there for her now," I pointed out, offering Carole my hand to help her up.

Carole took it. She also took the tissue that Lisa had pulled out of somewhere or other and was offering to her. After Carole had blown her nose and wiped her eyes, we headed out of the shed and returned to the stable building.

There were more people than before, clustered around Prancer's stall as we approached. Judy was still there, of course, along with the track vet and Mr. McLeod and some of the other people we'd seen earlier. They were peering at a large X ray, which Judy was holding up to the light. Several official-looking people with clipboards were also on the scene, making notes and speaking into tape recorders and cell phones.

Carole ignored them all. She walked past them, past Judy and the X ray, straight to Prancer's stall. Lisa and I followed.

Prancer was still standing awkwardly on her three good legs, with her injured right foreleg lifted off the floor. But she gave a little hop forward when she saw Carole approaching and sort of whiffled her lips in what could only have been a greeting.

Carole reached into her pocket and pulled out a sugar lump, which she fed to the filly. Prancer's big teeth crunched down on the treat as Carole let herself into the stall and gave her a big hug. Prancer nuzzled her affectionately as Lisa and I stepped forward to pat her.

I was making a real effort not to turn and race over to the adults and demand to know what was going on. It was so hard to wait—but I knew we had to. We had to trust Judy. She wouldn't keep us in suspense any longer than necessary. And I didn't want to disturb her while she was figuring out how to save Prancer.

Still, I knew I had to do something to keep myself busy or I would go crazy. So I did the only thing that seemed natural. I grabbed a grooming brush that was sitting on a trunk nearby and started brushing some of the dried sweat and dirt from the filly's bay coat.

Prancer seemed to appreciate it. She nodded her head up and down, just like Topside does when I groom him. Lisa joined in, picking at the tangles in the filly's dark mane with her fingers, while Carole continued to hug Prancer and murmur loving words of encouragement.

A moment later, I heard the track vet's voice above the low murmur of adults nearby. "Too bad," he said.

From my position near Prancer's withers, I saw Carole stiffen. She kept hugging and murmuring, but I could tell she was listening as hard as I was. So was Lisa, her fingers shaking a little as she worked at a particularly stubborn knot.

"Not really," Mr. McLeod was saying. "The insurance money would be nice, and I know I'll never recover my investment, but look at that horse. Would anybody want to destroy her?"

At his words, all the adults suddenly turned to look at Prancer—and at us, standing there hugging and grooming her as if we were just returning from a trail ride rather than waiting for the most important decision of her life.

Judy looked surprised for a second. Then she burst out laughing. Carole released her hug. Feeling a little embarrassed, I shifted the brush to my other hand and stepped forward, toward the adults.

"What's the story?" I asked Judy, in as professional and mature a voice as I could muster.

"Prancer has a broken bone in her foot." Judy held up the X ray and we all peered at it, though I for one couldn't make heads or tails of what I was seeing. "It's her pedal bone," Judy explained. "The fracture extends to the coffin joint. She's never going to race again."

"Oh, no!" Carole burst out. "What does . . ." She gulped, and her words trailed off.

"It means she can't race," Judy said quickly. "It doesn't mean she can't live. The bone will heal with proper care, but she'll always tend to favor it, and if she races again and favors her right foot, she'll run a great risk of breaking something more serious."

"What will you do with her?" Carole asked.

"I'm not sure," Mr. McLeod said. "I'll have to think about it. In a way it would be easier to take the insurance money, but Prancer's a gem, with the sweetest disposition I've ever seen. She should be with people, I think. For now, though, she's going back to Maskee Farms." He glanced around and spotted a groom. After a few words about preparing the van, he turned back to Carole. "You'd be the right one to load Prancer onto the van. Will you do it?"

Carole agreed, of course, and we helped her as she clipped a lead line to Prancer's halter and slowly, carefully, brought her out of the stall. Then we stepped aside as Carole coaxed her, step by step, up the ramp leading onto the van.

I glanced at Lisa and noticed a very odd expression on her face. "What's with you?" I asked her.

She hesitated, then smiled. "I just had an idea," she said. "Something Mr. McLeod said made me think of it. It's kind of crazy, but . . ."

"Spill it," I ordered. Then I listened carefully to what Lisa had in mind.

By the time she was finished, I was grinning. "There's only one way to find out if it will work," I said. I held up my hand and carefully crossed my fingers. Then I turned. "Oh, Judy!" I called. "We need to talk to you for a second. . . ."

191

Stevie Lake
47 Laurel Road
Willow Creek, VA

Dear Stevie,

It was great to hear your voice on the answering machine today—also a bit of a surprise! Not too many of my friends from back home call me here in England. It was wonderful to hear an American accent again. (Actually, I think it's these Brits who have the accent, but Nigel insists we Americans are the ones who talk funny!)

In any case, to answer your questions about the demonstration I did at Pine Hollow: To the best of my memory, I followed that second lead change with the counter-canter, and yes, there were a couple of pirouettes in the test, toward the end. Other than that, your description was pretty accurate. I can tell you must have really been paying attention! Good for you!

Sorry I couldn't call you back—would've loved to talk to you. But what with the time difference and my hectic schedule these days, I was afraid I wouldn't be able to catch you in time to help with the info you need for your school project. I figured it was better just to dash off this note and send it off—"post it straight away," as they might say here in merry old England.

Hope this helps. Good luck on your school project!

And please give my best to Max and the rest of the gang. (Including my dear old Topside, of course!)

Yours,
Dorothy

Welcome to My Life . . .

The day after our trip to the racetrack came another big event: Dorothy DeSoto's dressage exhibition at Pine Hollow. I had been looking forward to it from the second Max announced it, and now it was finally here!

Personality Background: Dorothy DeSoto

Miss Fenton, since I know you're not a big fan of equestrian events and stuff like that, I feel I should explain exactly who Dorothy is and how I know her. You see, years ago she was a student at Pine Hollow just like I am now. Actually, she was in some riding classes with Judy Barker, the vet I keep talking about. And Max was their instructor. Then Dorothy went off and became a big superstar in the show ring, thanks to Max's great teaching as well as her own natural talent and determination.

My friends and I met her right before the big show in New York City where she had a serious accident that injured her back and made her give up competitive riding. That's when she decided to send Topside to Pine Hollow, which is why I get to ride him now. Since the accident, Dorothy has spent most of her time at her training stable outside New York City. She has also been spending time in

England with her boyfriend, Nigel, who's a member of the British Equestrian Team.

Back to the story. A whole lot of people turned out to see Dorothy's demonstration. There would have been a big crowd in any case, since Max had advertised around town and it really was a big deal for anyone who knew anything about horses. But as I looked around at all the people packed onto the collapsible bleachers Max had set up, I couldn't help thinking that I had a little something to do with the great turnout, too. You see, I was in the process of putting my special plan into action, and I had been busy.

It wasn't turning out to be any trouble at all keeping it a secret. Carole was totally distracted worrying about Prancer, and Lisa had been spending all her extra time with Pepper, so they hadn't even suspected what I was up to. In fact, just about the only drawback was that all the planning hadn't left me much time for homework. But at the time I was certain it would be worth it when I saw the expressions of joy and gratitude on the faces of the people gathered at Pine Hollow that day. It was all falling into place. Soon the big moment would be here!

But before it would be time for that, I got to sit back and enjoy Dorothy's show. My friends and I arrived early to reserve seats in the front row. When Dorothy entered the ring, we waved at her cheerfully. She waved back, looking so happy to see us that we couldn't resist rushing over to say hello.

"I groomed Topside especially well for you," I told her proudly.

"He looks wonderful!" Dorothy said. "I can see you're taking good care of him all the time, not just for my visit. Thank you."

"Thank me?" I asked. "Thank *you* for selling him to Max. Topside's the greatest! I told him you were coming, by the way."

Dorothy smiled. "I thought so," she joked. "He didn't seem the least bit surprised to see me."

Then Max shooed us back to our seats. Before I went, he stopped me. "Stevie, are you all ready with—"

I couldn't believe it. He was about to give away my secret—right in front of Carole and Lisa! "Yes, Max," I said quickly, cutting him off. "I'm all ready." Then I turned and hurried toward the stands, carefully not making eye contact with either of my friends.

"What's that about?" Carole said suspiciously.

I was so excited about my plan that I was about to burst. But I knew I had to keep quiet just a little bit longer. It would be better if it was a surprise. So I didn't say a word.

"Think we can talk her out of it?" Lisa asked Carole.

I shook my head. "No way," I said. "Just wait, though. Just wait."

Then it was time for Dorothy's show to start. I suddenly remembered that I'd meant to bring a camera to record the event. I also remembered that my camera was sitting in the middle of the kitchen table, where I would be sure not to miss it—except that I'd been in such a rush to get to Pine Hollow that morning that I had just grabbed a couple of pieces of toast and rushed out without even sitting down, so I hadn't seen it there.

"Oh, well," I muttered. I dug into my pocket and found a scrap of paper. Actually, to be perfectly honest, it was the notes I'd taken the previous Friday in history class, which kind of explains a lot about my grade on the quiz we had the next Monday, since the notes kind of got written over and then crumpled up in my cubby at Pine Hollow . . . but I'm getting away from the subject. The point to remember here is, I'm so serious about dressage that I wanted to take a few notes. Dressage is kind of like homework that way, don't you think? Anyway, I thought it might be helpful to share my dressage notes with you now.

I can't promise they'll make a lot of sense to anyone who isn't familiar with my own private shorthand. But I thought it would be best to include them as they are (retyped for neatness, of course), with an explanation to follow.

Stevie Lake's Dressage Notes: A Transcript

SPCH:
- goal = Superhorse (ath.)
- part horse - !!!!!
- no rush—pat.

TEST:(T. looks AWESOME!!!!!!!!!!!!!!!!!!!!!!!!!!!)
- 4 L so we can . . .
- cnt. fl. lead cx-pir. -ctr-cntr. WOW!

Stevie Lake's Dressage Notes: A Translation

Ms. DeSoto began by giving a brief speech about the goals and traditions of the sport of dressage. Some of her major points were as follows:

- In dressage, a primary goal is to create a superior equine athlete.
- In dressage, a horse and its rider are partners. This is very important.
- Building this relationship between horse and rider takes time. The rider/trainer must have a lot of patience if s/he is to succeed in dressage.

Following her very interesting and informative speech, Ms. DeSoto entered the ring on Topside, who was in particularly fine form that day, perhaps owing to his pleasure in being reunited with his longtime trainer and partner.

Ms. DeSoto announced that she would be performing a Fourth Level dressage test that day. That's a few steps down from a Grand Prix test, which is what you would see in the Olympics (she's done that, since she was on the U.S. Olympic Team).

The rest of my notes simply indicate various interesting and impressive moves that Dorothy performed as part of the test, for instance, flying lead change at the canter, pirouettes, and counter-canters. Naturally, I was so busy watching and learning that I didn't have a whole lot of time to take extensive notes; hence the rather cryptic nature of what you see above. If you would like any further information or clarification on anything having to do with dressage, please feel free to ask me anytime. I'm always happy to talk about it, especially since it's a discipline—and I do stress the word "discipline"—that I take very seriously.

STEPHANIE,

I AM A LAWYER. ACCORDING TO THE LAW, EVERY CITIZEN IS INNOCENT UNTIL PROVEN GUILTY. THAT IS WHY I AM GIVING YOU A CHANCE TO EXPLAIN YOURSELF AND PROVIDE AN ALIBI—IF YOU HAVE ONE.

IN CASE YOU HAVEN'T FIGURED OUT WHAT I'M TALKING ABOUT, I HAVE ATTACHED A COPY OF OUR LATEST PHONE BILL. YOU WILL SEE SEVERAL EXTREMELY EXPENSIVE LONG-DISTANCE CALLS MARKED IN RED. ONE TO VERMONT. ONE TO LOS ANGELES. ONE TO LONDON.

DO YOU KNOW ANYTHING ABOUT THESE CALLS? IF YOU DO, I SUGGEST YOU THROW YOURSELF ON THE MERCY OF THE COURT AND CONFESS IMMEDIATELY OR JUSTICE WILL BE SWIFT AND SEVERE.

YOUR ALLOWANCE PROVIDER,
DAD

Welcome to My Life . . .

The dressage demonstration was fantastic, as expected. Dorothy was amazing, Topside was incredible, and the whole thing was so interesting that it probably even made me forget a little bit of what I'd learned in science class that week, which explains why I didn't do so well on the test I had a few days later.

I was so overwhelmed by the time the demonstration was over that I'd almost forgotten what was coming next. I remembered when Max walked into the ring and called for attention.

"We're not quite done yet this afternoon," he told the audience. "We have another treat in store for you, and it's something that will mean a great deal to a lot of the people here—to anybody who has ever ridden at Pine Hollow." He turned to me. "Ready?" he asked.

I grinned, nodded, and hopped up from my seat, not giving Carole and Lisa time to ask any questions. I raced into the stable as Max continued talking. Red O'Malley, the head stable hand at Pine Hollow, was waiting just inside the main doors. He was holding a lead line attached to a horse's halter. The horse was waiting patiently just behind him.

"Here he is," Red told me. "Ready to go."

"Not yet," I whispered, peeking out around the door. "I want us to make an entrance." In the ring, Max was still speaking. He was describing a certain horse his father had bought for Pine Hollow many years before. A horse that had failed as a competition horse, as a hunter, as a farm horse, and as a little girl's pony.

"This horse wasn't sleek enough or strong enough to compete successfully," Max explained. "He didn't like the loud distractions of a fox hunt. He wasn't strong enough to pull a plow, and frankly, one little girl just wasn't enough for him. Dad bought the horse whose name had been Clyde and renamed him . . . Pepper."

"Now?" Red whispered to me.

I shook my head. "Not yet."

Outside, Max went on. "Dad's instincts turned out to be one hundred percent correct," he said, speaking a little louder over the sounds of murmurs from the audience. "Pepper has been one of the most beloved horses at Pine Hollow. He has always been gentle enough for the newest rider and spirited enough for the most experienced. He's been just about perfect for us. But time has passed and Pepper has aged. He's no longer the strong young gelding Dad bought. He's not even the eager mature horse so many of us have loved. He's old; in horse years he's approaching ninety. At ninety even horses begin having dreams of retirement. We talked about a condominium in Florida for him. We also thought about a nice cruise around the world. When we asked Pepper about those things, all he did was look at the pasture out behind the stable at Pine Hollow. So, in thanks to him for all he's done for us—me and many of you—we're giving Pepper that pasture. But before we do that, we're giving him a little send-off, master-minded by one of our own riders, Ms. Stevie Lake. Stevie?"

As all eyes turned toward the stable door, I grabbed a very

special item I had stashed behind a bale of hay nearby. "Now," I told Red. "Give me a hand, will you?"

Seconds later, I was mounted on Pepper bareback. If the old horse was surprised, he didn't let on. He obediently walked forward out of the stable. I held the reins with one hand so I could hold on to that special item in the other.

As soon as everyone in the audience saw what it was that I was holding, they burst out laughing. I grinned—and held the giant gold watch a little higher. Okay, actually it wasn't a real watch. It was made of cardboard. But I had worked on it for hours the night before (which meant I didn't have quite enough time to finish the math problems I was supposed to do) and it looked really great.

"No retirement party is complete without a gold watch," Max announced.

"And no retirement party is complete without a sentimental farewell," I added.

"Ah, yes," Max agreed. "Most of the people here in the audience today have ridden at Pine Hollow at one time or another, right?" Heads nodded in agreement. "How many of you have ever ridden Pepper?"

I glanced around, raising my own hand high (after tucking the watch under my other arm). Hands were popping up all over the place. It was amazing. More than two-thirds of the people there had ridden Pepper at least once! And it wasn't just the kids—lots of adults raised their hands, too.

"Okay, let's give him a real send-off," Max said. "Stevie, you do the honors."

I was glad to. I slid down from Pepper's back and secured his lead line to the gate of the ring. Then I called out a few instructions to the crowd, getting everyone who had ever ridden Pepper to line up by age, with the youngest first.

"That way," I explained, "you can all have your chance to hug Pepper good-bye and wish him well in his retirement."

The first twenty or so riders were so young that Max had to lift them up so they could hug the horse. A bunch of parents even took pictures of their kids with Pepper. Then the older kids came—including Betsy Cavanaugh and Anna McWhirter and a whole bunch of other Fenton Hall students. When it was Carole's turn she stepped forward and gave Pepper the biggest hug yet.

"Good luck, old boy," she said, stepping back and wiping a tear from the corner of her eye. "We'll miss you. But you've earned it."

Then it was Lisa's turn. She was standing there, staring at Pepper with this misty look in her eyes.

"Next!" I prompted.

Lisa started, then stepped forward. She wrapped her arms around Pepper's gray neck and buried her face in his mane.

"I'll come visit you in the pasture," she promised. "I'll bring you some carrots, too."

That was all she said. But I knew that behind those simple words were a whole lot of emotions. And I knew that somehow Pepper knew it, too.

I smiled as Lisa moved away to let others have their turns. Then I turned my attention back to the line—the long,

long line of people waiting to make their farewells to a very special horse.

After everyone had taken a turn, Max stepped forward again. "And now," he said, "I invite you all to join me for a small reception in Pepper's new home."

I grinned and started to lead Pepper toward the back pasture. This was my favorite part of my plan.

"It's just a little party," Max continued. "But we do have refreshments. Stevie tells me that Pepper insisted on selecting the menu, so go help yourselves to carrot sticks, oatmeal cookies, sugar lumps, and apple juice!"

I grinned as my friends started to laugh. Soon the whole audience was laughing with them.

FROM: LAtwood
TO: Steviethegreat
SUBJECT: Here you go . . .
MESSAGE:

Hi! I just got your e-mail asking about my "Life" essay. Yes, you're remembering correctly—I did end up revising it after Pepper's retirement party. I liked it a lot better after that. And of course you can use it in your report if you want. It would be an honor.

I'm attaching the file to this e-mail. And don't worry, it was no trouble finding it. Actually, I had saved it on the hard drive of my computer, so I didn't even have to retype it. All I had to do was go into my "School Reports" file and call it up by title and date. Piece of cake!

LIFE
by Lisa Atwood
(edited slightly for length by S. Lake)

Pepper is Pine Hollow's gentlest, sweetest, kindest horse. He's every first rider's first choice. He is so attentive to his rider's needs that he makes riding seem easy. In fact, one time I was riding Pepper, unaware that we were in a field that housed a fierce bull. We were too far from the gate to get to safety, so Pepper did the only logical thing—he taught me to jump in one easy lesson! We both landed safely on the other side of the fence. I think I can say truly that I owe Pepper my life.

Now his life is coming to an end. His gray coat, once dark and dappled, is now white and dappled. His head, once held high with pride, often seems too heavy for his neck. His eyes, once sparkling and alert, are now rheumy and clouded with cataracts. His ears splay awkwardly, dulled to the familiar sounds around him. He is old.

I love him as he is, for that is how I have known him, but I like to think of him as he was.

Pepper was a champion, not because he got ribbons, though he surely did, but because he taught me and many other riders how to love horses—starting with him. And we do.

Pepper's life began in a barn in Willow Creek, Virginia. It will end in a pasture not far from that barn. That seems like a small accomplishment to some people, but Pepper's contribution to the many who have known and loved him cannot be measured by the yards he traveled from birth to death. They have to be measured by the lives he touched.

So now it's time for Pepper to take the final few steps of his journey and head for the pasture behind Pine Hollow. While I feel sad about the end of his days at the stable, I also feel a certain happiness. Pepper has earned the right to his rest because he hasn't just taught me and others about riding, or about aging, or about death. He's also taught us what's important about life. It doesn't matter how far you go. It matters what you do for others along the way.

Welcome to My Life . . .

There you have it, Miss Fenton. Lisa's essay. I only cut out some general stuff she wrote at the beginning about life. I think the essay kind of sums up how we all feel about Pepper, and I hope that helps explain how important it was for me to spend a lot of time planning that party.

By now you're probably wondering whatever happened to Prancer. Well, that's the next part of my story. You see, after Pepper's party, my friends and I walked back toward the stable with Dorothy, still carrying our cups of apple juice and some leftover treats from the refreshments table Red and I had set up that morning. We were just chatting with her—you know, catching up on her life and filling her in on ours. There was a lot to tell. For one thing, we told her all about Prancer and her accident the day before.

"Judy thinks she'll get better, but she's never going to race again," Carole explained. She looked sad when she said it.

I glanced over at Lisa. Her eyes were twinkling. I stifled a grin. We had worked pretty hard the day before to keep Carole from guessing what we had helped Judy decide to do.

Dorothy was chatting on about Prancer, but I hardly heard her. I was looking toward the driveway of Pine Hollow, watching for a certain vehicle to arrive.

Finally it came. "Hey, Judy's here," I said as casually as I could. I gestured to the light blue pickup truck that had just pulled into the driveway. I looked at Carole innocently. "Are you supposed to be making calls with her today?"

"No, I don't think so," Carole said. "I don't know why she's here."

There were still a lot of people hanging around outside from the demonstration and party. Judy stepped out of her truck and glanced around at the crowd, clearly looking for someone. She spotted us and kept looking. Then her gaze fell on Max. She walked briskly over to him and pulled him aside for a private conversation.

I smiled to myself. Then I turned back to Dorothy and Lisa. Lisa winked, then looked at Dorothy. "So, have you started training any interesting new horses lately?" she asked.

Dorothy answered, but I have to admit I wasn't paying much attention. I was keeping a close watch on Carole out of the corner of my eye. She was staring over at Max and Judy with a worried frown. I could tell she was afraid Judy had come bearing bad news about Prancer, and I was sorry to let her worry. But I knew it would all be worth it when she found out why Judy was really there.

After a moment, Max looked over at us. "Uh, Carole, could you come over here for a minute?" he called.

Carole gulped. Then she went.

I glanced at Lisa and giggled. She giggled back.

Dorothy looked at both of us, puzzled. "Okay, what am I missing here?" she demanded.

"Should we tell her?" Lisa asked.

"Of course!" I turned to Dorothy. "It's about Prancer. You see, Carole is terribly worried because she's afraid Prancer won't have anyplace to go now that she can't race anymore."

"But Stevie managed to convince Max and Judy to—well, to buy her," Lisa finished. She grinned. "Isn't it wonderful? Prancer is coming to Pine Hollow!"

Dorothy laughed. "That *is* wonderful!" she agreed.

"Max and Judy own her fifty-fifty," I explained. "Right about now, Judy's probably telling Carole about the part of the agreement where Carole—with our help, of course—will need to take care of Prancer while she's recovering from her injury."

I checked out Carole's face. From the expression of disbelief and joy on it, I was pretty sure I was right on target.

"She—Prancer, I mean—will be coming to Pine Hollow tomorrow," Lisa told Dorothy. "It's just too bad she couldn't come today so you could meet her."

"I'm sure I'll meet her on my next visit," Dorothy assured her. "In fact, I'll make a point of it."

I glanced over at Carole again. She was grinning from ear

to ear as she turned to run toward us. "Here she comes," I predicted happily, "to give us the good news."

A few days after Prancer came to stay at Pine Hollow, fox-hunt fever really started to take over the place. Max announced an organizing meeting for our mock hunt, and I invited Phil to come.

AND THEN WHEN HE GOT THERE WE STARTED SMOOCHING AND MAKING GOO-GOO EYES AT EACH OTHER. BECAUSE HE'S MY BIG STUDLY BOYFRIEND AND I'M A DORKY GIRLY-GIRL WHO THINKS ABOUT KISSING ALL THE TIME. I NEVER THINK ABOUT ANYTHING ELSE. AND

Grrrr! My idiot brothers are such total fatheads!!!!!!!! If they mess up my report one more time, I'm going to take each of their slimy little heads in my hands and hold them facedown in the manure pile at Pine Hollow until they beg for mercy. Then I'll tell all their friends they still wet their beds and suck their thumbs, and then I'll *really* start planning my revenge. . . .

Ah, aren't computers wonderful? Because now I can just delete this whole section (including my brothers' dorky contribution) and Miss Fenton will never know the difference!

FROM: HorseGal
TO: Steviethegreat
SUBJECT: Tallyho!
MESSAGE:

Glad to hear that you're about to get started on writing about the fox hunt. I just wanted to tell you one more time that I'd be happy to help you out if you're having trouble remembering all the stuff we learned about foxhunting terms and history and stuff. I have one really good book on the subject right upstairs in my room, and I've read a lot of other books and articles, too (you know how I'm always trying to learn everything I can about everything horse-related), so I think I have a pretty good handle on it. Plus I paid really close attention to everything Max and Mr. Baker told us, so I'm sure I remember every word in case you forgot some of it.

So if you want my input, or if you just want me to read over what you write and make sure it's accurate, give a holler. (Or maybe I should say "holloa!")

FROM: LAtwood
TO: Steviethegreat
SUBJECT: Foxhunting
MESSAGE:

I was thinking about how you told us today at the stable that you're ready to tackle the foxhunting portion of your assignment. If you want, I could help you remember all the info we learned about foxhunting in our meetings and on the hunts themselves. I realize you were a little distracted during both hunts, especially the mock hunt, so you might not have been able to keep track of all the important terms and stuff. By the way, I even still have that memo Max handed out with the permission slips, in case you want to include that.

Just give me a call if you want to talk about it or ask me any questions. I'll be here all night!

FROM: Steviethegreat
TO: DSlattVT
SUBJECT: AARGH!
MESSAGE:

Okay, I'm totally convinced that my two best friends think I'm completely scatterbrained. They both just wrote me these e-mails that make it perfectly clear that they think my head is filled with bran mash and my attention span is that of a gnat. They seem to think I couldn't possibly have learned a single thing during our entire foxhunting experience. Lisa even offered me this memo from Max that I had ALREADY PUT IN MY REPORT! SO THERE!!!!!

Sorry. It's just a little irritating sometimes when they think I'm too irresponsible to save anything or remember anything or know anything about anything. Just because I like to have fun and tell a joke or two once in a while

210

doesn't mean I don't pay attention to important stuff, too. I guess it's a good thing Miss Fenton didn't call them in as character witnesses before she gave me this assignment, or I'd probably be in summer school already, even though it's not even summer yet! Ha!

Okay, that's better. Thanks for listening. (Well, reading—you know what I mean.) I was just feeling a little annoyed, and I didn't want to take it out on my friends by writing back nasty e-mails or something, because I know they mean well (and they can be a little sensitive sometimes, especially Lisa). And I guess I might be a little on edge because my report is due in four days and my brothers are still driving me nuts and I don't know if I'm EVER going to finish this stupid assignment—or if Miss Fenton will even like it when (I mean *if*) I do.

But I'm not just writing to complain. I actually have some more news regarding the Mystery of the Suspicious Snob. Here goes: We had riding lessons today after school, and for like the third time in a row, Veronica didn't show up. And Max didn't even seem mad about it, which means he must have known she wasn't coming. I mean, you know Max. Since when does he EVER not get mad when someone skips a lesson without good reason?

So I was in the tack room after lessons when Betsy Cavanaugh and Anna McWhirter came in. I guess I said something kind of insulting about Veronica not showing up (you know, something along the lines of how I was glad to see she finally realized what a horrible rider she was and was giving up on lessons completely), and instead of ignoring me or in-

211

sulting me back, as I expected, Betsy said, "Poor Veronica," in this quavery voice and Anna started blinking really hard, like she was about to cry. Then they both turned around and ran out of the room!

It was totally weird. I still have no idea what's going on. But I'll find out, or my name's not Steven Lake!

Welcome to My Life . . .

A few days after Prancer came to stay at Pine Hollow, fox-hunt fever really started to take over. Max announced an organizing meeting for our mock hunt, and I invited Phil to come. Unfortunately, I also invited him to my house for dinner beforehand (I even finished at least half of my math word problems before he arrived). But even more unfortunately, all three of my low-life brothers were there.

They didn't leave us alone the entire time. Let me see if I can recall just some of the humiliating conversation over that dinner table.

Chad started it. As you know, Miss Fenton, he's the oldest. That means he thinks can say whatever he wants to the rest of us. It also means that Alex and Michael tend to follow his lead, especially when he's giving me a hard time. Which he always is.

"So, tell me, Stevie," he said in this fake-innocent voice. "Just where are you and Phil going tonight after dinner?"

I could already see where this was heading—straight downhill. Still, I did my best to answer politely. "We're going to an organizing meeting for the mock hunt."

"Oh, you hunt mocks?" my oh-so-humorous twin brother asked. "They've certainly been a menace to the local farmers."

Phil, being much more evolved than my brothers, answered patiently. "Not exactly, Alex," he said. "It's *mock* as in pretend. It's a pretend hunt being sponsored by Stevie's Pony Club to prepare all of us for the real fox hunt that's being held at my Pony Club."

Instead of shutting my brothers up, Phil's calm, intelligent words got them even more riled up. They started yelling "Tallyho!" and talking about drinking brandy from flasks and wondering if fox meat was any good to eat.

I have to admit, I was having kind of a hard time controlling myself. It was such a temptation to leap across the table and throttle them all. However, I knew my parents wouldn't exactly approve of that. Besides, I didn't want to fight with my brothers in front of Phil—which was exactly why I was so furious with them at that moment.

"For your information," I told them finally, after I'd gained enough control over my anger that I was pretty sure I wouldn't start yelling, "foxhunting is an old and honorable sport. In England, where there are lots of foxes, they're viewed as a pest and the farmers often really do want them to be caught as long as it's humane. Here in America, where there aren't so many foxes, they're rarely caught and even more rarely killed. In fact, most hunters would be disappointed if the hounds were to catch the fox. See, we want that same fox to be available to lead us on a merry chase the next time we go foxhunting."

As soon as that last sentence was out of my mouth, I cringed, knowing that I had just made a fatal mistake.

"A merry chase!" Chad howled. Alex and Michael joined in. Even my parents—traitors!—seemed to be having trouble keeping straight faces. I couldn't help blushing, which made me angrier than ever. I hate it when my brothers embarrass me. And I especially hate it when they embarrass me in front of Phil!

I was sort of speechless for a moment, trying to think of the most humiliating, horrible things I could announce to the table at large about each of my brothers. However, Phil spoke up before I could come up with anything good.

"There's a lot of misinformation out there about fox-hunting," he said. "We've been doing a lot of reading on the subject at Cross County, and one thing I thought was interesting was that only the huntsman, the master of the hounds, and the whippers-in are doing any actual hunting. The rest of us are just along for the ride."

"You mean you're not armed?" Chad's voice was so sarcastic that I glanced at my parents, expecting them to scold him. After all, we had a guest. But they were both busy with their food and didn't say a word.

So it looked as though I was the only one who could come to Phil's rescue. I took a deep breath to calm myself down. "Nobody on a fox hunt is armed," I said. "The hunt is just a good excuse for a cross-country ride with your friends over fences and through fields."

"Right," Phil agreed. "The exciting part is that you never

know where the hunt is going to go. It's not like going on a trail ride."

"It sounds very exciting to me," Alex said. He glanced over at Dad. "I don't know that we should allow Stevie to go on this thing. She's so excitable—"

"Ahem," my mom said. I grinned. It was a subtle signal, but an unmistakable one—a signal that my brothers were pushing it. Alex and Chad got it. Unfortunately, Michael didn't. I guess he's too young for such subtlety.

"Didn't you say the only reason Stevie wanted to do this was because Phil's doing it?" he said loudly.

I think I sort of lost consciousness for a few seconds after that. That happens sometimes when I get really mad at my brothers—I'm concentrating so hard on thoughts of revenge that everything else just sort of fades away. It's like I have no control.

I tuned back in just in time to hear another "Ahem," this one from my dad and a lot louder. "I think it's time to change the subject," he went on. "In fact, if we don't change the subject, I think I may disinvite certain family members to the circus, which is coming to town in two weeks."

I'm sure you remember the Emerson Circus, Miss Fenton. It was here in Willow Creek until just last weekend. My whole family loves going every year, so my dad's threat was quite effective in silencing all three of my brothers.

For the moment at least.

FROM: HorseGal

TO: Steviethegreat

SUBJECT: I'm not Carole

MESSAGE:

Hi, Stevie! This isn't Carole writing—it's me, Colonel Hanson. Carole let me use her e-mail account to send you a message. I thought you might be interested to know that I saw your headmistress, Miss Fenton, at the zoning board meeting I attended tonight. When she found out I knew you, she had quite a bit to say. It seems she thinks you're one of her brightest students, and that you have a lot of talent and creativity. (She also thinks I should send Carole to Fenton Hall instead of to public school, but that's another story. Ha ha!)

Anyway, I thought you would like to know how highly your headmistress thinks of you, especially since Carole tells me you're doing some kind of extra assignment for her now. You'll have to tell me all about it the next time you come over to the house for one of your Saddle Club sleepovers!

Bye!

Welcome to My Life . . .

After dinner, Phil and I left the house for the walk over to Pine Hollow. I was looking forward to the meeting, but I was also looking forward to that walk with Phil. Since he lives way over in Cross County, we don't get to spend nearly enough time together—especially time alone. It was a cool evening, and I slipped my hand into his right away and moved a little closer as we walked. He squeezed my hand back and looked down at me with those gorgeous green eyes of his. Sometimes I think I could look into those eyes forever. They've so deep, and compassionate, and understanding, just like Phil himself. And then there's the rest of his face. His cute smile, his hair . . .

AAAAAH!!!! What am I, crazy? There's no way I can let Miss Fenton read that. Or anyone! (Especially not my brothers—why did I type this on the typewriter instead of waiting till Mom was done with the computer, so I could just delete it? And why oh why don't Mom and Dad have a paper shredder? Oh, well—there's always the good old toilet.)

Welcome to My Life . . . (revised)

After dinner Phil and I walked briskly over to Pine Hollow. I was happy to spend time with him, but I was still thinking about my brothers. ~~I really, really, really wanted to murder them; no, torture them, nice and slow, with plenty of~~ I was very annoyed with them. ~~It made me want to rip their eyeballs out and stuff them down~~ But I put that out of my mind. I concentrated on the upcoming meeting instead. When Phil and I got to Pine Hollow, we found a crowd already gathered in Max's office. Practically all of Horse Wise was there, along with all of

217

Cross County, including their instructor, Mr. Baker. We quickly spotted Carole and Lisa and grabbed spots near them on the floor. The office was so full it was practically bursting at the seams—and I wasn't the slightest bit surprised. Nobody wanted to miss a word of this meeting.

Mr. Baker spoke first, explaining that the main purposes of a mock hunt were to have fun and learn about hunting. Riders would be assigned jobs. One would be the fox, another would be the master of the hounds, one would be the huntsman, several would be whippers-in, others would be hounds. Anybody who didn't get one of those jobs would be what Mr. Baker called the field. Then he went on to explain some fox-hunting terms, like "huntsman" and "whippers-in." Of course, I already knew what they all meant, since I had carefully studied the memo Max had handed out at Horse Wise earlier, just like the responsible and thirsty-for-knowledge person I am. But I listened to it all again, just to be polite.

"And now Max has a few words for you," Mr. Baker said at last, turning the meeting over to Max.

Max explained that we were all supposed to show up at Pine Hollow by seven-thirty on Saturday morning, that the mock hunt would begin at eight-thirty, and that we'd need every possible millisecond of that hour in between for tacking up and final organizing. He also told us how some of the roles would be chosen.

"The job of master will go to the person who has shown the most work on learning about fox hunts. We'll also choose a huntsman, a few whippers-in, and someone devious to be the fox," he said.

My ears kind of perked up at that. Devious? That sounded interesting.

Max continued. "There's one final thing I can't say too often, so I'm going to say it now, and I'll say it again and again until I'm sure you all understand. A fox hunt—even a mock one—is something we can do only with the permission of the landowners around Pine Hollow and Cross County. Mr. Baker and I have spent some time making arrangements with these people so our hunts aren't confined to our own land. We'll be riding on other people's property with their specific permission, and we must never forget that we're their guests. We will ride only where we are permitted, when we are permitted. We will leave all gates exactly as we found them and the land exactly as we found it. Anyone who violates these rules will be dismissed from the hunts immediately. There will be no exceptions. Am I making myself clear?"

Everybody nodded.

"Any questions?" Max asked.

Veronica diAngelo (you know her, Miss Fenton, so I'm not going to bother to describe her personality) raised her hand. "Isn't there traditionally a party after a hunt?" she asked.

Max nodded and explained that Horse Wise would be hosting a hunt breakfast after the mock hunt. That sounded nice and all, but I for one was a lot more excited about the mock hunt itself than some silly breakfast buffet. I couldn't wait. It was sure to be one of the most exciting things Horse Wise had ever done!

Still, before I could turn my full attention to looking forward to that, there was one other thing on my mind, one little thing I had to take care of— ~~revenge. There was no way I could let my brothers get away with their horrible behavior at dinner that evening.~~

~~There was one thing I had to take care of—settling the score with my brothers. They totally deserved it, don't you think? And I was pretty mad, mad enough to wreak horrible~~

~~There was one thing I had to take care of—getting even with my brothers. I know some people wouldn't understand if they don't have brothers of their own, but I couldn't let their unseemly behavior pass.~~

~~There was one thing I had to take care of—retaliation. It was only right. How could I let my brothers get away with~~

~~There was one thing I had to take care of—my brothers. The Bible states, "An eye for an eye and a tooth for a tooth." I looked it up just now, and it even says something about "a hand for a hand and a foot for a foot." So it wasn't like I was the first one who wanted to rip~~

STEPHANIE,

DO YOU BY ANY CHANCE KNOW WHY THE UPSTAIRS TOILET OVERFLOWED THIS MORNING? THERE SEEMED TO BE A LOT OF LITTLE BITS OF PAPER COMING UP FROM THE DRAIN, AND CALL ME CRAZY, BUT I WOULD SWEAR I SPOTTED THE NAME "PHIL" ON ONE OF

THEM. YOU HAVE THE RIGHT TO REMAIN
SILENT. BUT IF YOU DO, YOU WILL BE PROSE-
CUTED TO THE FULL EXTENT OF THE LAW.

MOM

FROM: Steviethegreat

TO: PhilmStar

SUBJECT: Moral dilemma

MESSAGE:

I'm running into some trouble with my paper, and I wasn't sure who else to ask about it. You see, it's kind of a moral dilemma. I'm just getting to the foxhunting stuff, which you would think would be a pretty easy section to write about since it just happened. And the actual foxhunting parts *are* pretty easy.

But this report is supposed to be about my whole life during that time. It really has to be so Miss Fenton can understand why all that homework couldn't possibly have gotten done. And part of what was happening during the time of the fox hunt was my little feud with my brothers. I was trying to write down how that all got started, and of course technically they started it by being such jerks that night you came to dinner. Remember?

So that part was easy. It's what happened next that's turning out to be a problem. I mean, you know and I know that what my brothers did was totally inexcusable—I *had* to get my revenge. No question. But I'm afraid Miss Fenton won't see it that way. She may think it's my fault because of the stuff I did to them next. (Especially since I don't think she ever found out about any of it, even though it mostly happened at school.) And then there's the stuff that happened a little later with Veronica. . . .

So basically I don't know if I can be totally honest about my motives after that dinner. If I tell the truth, the whole truth, and nothing but the truth, Miss Fenton may decide I'm a horrible person—she might not be able to handle it. But if I *don't* tell the truth about everything I was thinking and feeling, nothing that happens in the story will make much sense, and more importantly, she'll never be able to understand how completely caught up I was in the whole thing. And that means she definitely won't understand why I didn't have enough time to study for my big math test or finish my science lab report.

I'm especially worried because Carole's dad saw Miss Fenton at some meeting last night, and he said she kept talking about how bright and talented and creative I am. She actually used those words! So if she thinks I'm so great, this report had better be REALLY great, right? Or she'll decide I'm "not working up to my potential" (she's been telling my parents that for years) and send me to summer school. And then I can kiss Topside good-bye for the next three months.

But will she be more likely to think it's great if she thinks I'm a great person who would never stoop to something petty like revenge? Or will she think it's great if I tell the

truth, give her the full inside story, and really let her understand why I did the things I did?

FROM: PhilmStar
TO: Steviethegreat
SUBJECT: Re: Moral dilemma
MESSAGE:

I think you answered your own question. The whole purpose of this assignment is to make Miss Fenton understand
why your work didn't get done. And like you said, there's no
way she can get that unless she knows about everything that
happened and what you were thinking about it all.

I can understand why you're worried about it. I think the
whole sibling rivalry thing (my parents are ALWAYS talking about sibling rivalry!) is pretty hard for anyone to understand who hasn't been there. And you and your
brothers—well, let's just say you don't pull any punches.

But this is Miss Fenton we're talking about, remember? I
know you sometimes talk about her as if she's this frail, gen-
teel, little old lady. But I think she's tougher than that—after all, hasn't she dealt with you and your brothers up until
now? I mean, I don't even go to Fenton Hall and some of
the stories make *me* shudder! (Ha ha!) For instance, I seem
to remember hearing about the time a few years ago when
the four of you got in that huge water fight in the hall and
Miss Fenton ended up turning Alex upside down and phys-

ically carrying him off to break it up. Then there was the time in third grade when you and Dinah spent all your time pretending to be horses and "galloping" around the halls, and Miss Fenton brought a couple of bridles to school and threatened to make you wear them if you didn't stop. (And then she actually let you *wear* yours for a full week when you insisted you didn't mind, until she finally rubbed the bit with boiled carrots to convince you to stop.) And what about the story of how you and Veronica were fighting about something, and Miss Fenton figured out that you were the one who started that rumor about Veronica secretly being a dangerous forty-five-year-old mobster named Guido the Hun who was posing as a snobby schoolgirl as part of the Witness Protection Program . . .

Shall I go on? Or have I managed to convince you of what you should know already—namely, that your headmistress can handle anything you dish out in this report, and more?

Honesty Clause

(Miss Fenton: Please read this before opening this report)

The purpose of this assignment is to give you a firsthand report of my life for the past couple of months. Therefore, I am striving to be as completely honest as possible in all the facts I set down here. Honesty is an important factor in telling my story—even though some of the things I'm being honest about might not be the kinds of things I would normally tell anyone, let alone a headmistress who holds the power of life and detention over me. Not to mention summer school.

Therefore, Miss Fenton, I ask you to read my story with an open mind and an unjudging heart. And please understand my sincere hope that nothing I say here will be used against me, no matter how shocking, no matter how unexpected. Because it's all the truth, and the truth should set us free.

Welcome to My Life . . .

Before I could turn my full attention to looking forward to the mock hunt, there was one other thing on my mind, one little thing I had to take care of—revenge. There was no way I could let my brothers get away with their horrible behavior at dinner that evening. Revenge isn't always pretty, but sometimes it's necessary, at least where my brothers are concerned. So I spent quite a bit of time that weekend pondering exactly what to do to them.

One thing I was aiming for was a safe escape for myself. I was certain that vengeance was necessary in this case, but I wasn't sure that my parents (or, for that matter, *you*, Miss Fenton—I said I was going to be honest here, right?) would see it the same way. So my goal was to totally humiliate my brothers without letting them know—for sure—who was responsible. They *would* know, of course. Make no mistake about that. But they wouldn't be able to prove anything, and that would be the truly beautiful part.

My mind was brimming with plans that Monday morning when I got to school. The only problem was that my *ears* were brimming with the sound of Veronica diAngelo's voice. In case you didn't realize it, Miss Fenton, Veronica and I aren't exactly the closest of chums. So I have no idea why she decided to torture me with her chatter. I guess just because I was the first person she saw that day who also rode at Pine Hollow. In any case, she latched on to me almost the second I stepped through the school doors and followed me down the hall toward my locker, babbling on and on about what a good idea the fox hunt was because it was what all the "finest families" did. Veronica seems to think she belongs to one of the "finest families," though what she really means when she says that is one of the "richest families." And I, for one, don't think that being rich automatically makes you fine. Veronica is a perfect example of that.

Finally I'd had all I could take of her snobby bragging about "finest families."

"Finest families?" I said innocently. "Well, I guess that lets you out. After all, you just come from a tiny little family with one spoiled daughter. My family has four fine children. I guess that makes us a fine family, doesn't it?"

Veronica gave me a withering look, then walked faster to catch up to some girls walking ahead of us. That was just "fine" with me. It allowed me to go back to enjoying the start of what I was sure was going to be a perfectly wonderful day, despite the fact that I hadn't quite completed the reading assignment for English and really hadn't understood the math problems I was supposed to have done. But my mind was so filled with my extremely creative and talented plans for revenge that I didn't think much about that other stuff.

226

Ms. Milligan was out sick that particular day, so we had a study hall instead of English class. That gave me plenty of time to put the finishing touches on a few little signs. Then I asked to be excused to go to the girls' room.

When I got there, I pulled the first sign out of my backpack. I had typed them neatly on my family's computer the night before. (Mom thought I was working on my English assignment—although in my own defense, I never actually *told* her that. All I did was walk into the den carrying my copy of *Great Poems of the Nineteenth Century* and ask to use the computer. Can I help it if she jumped to conclusions?)

All the signs I made that day except one copy of this first one have, sadly, been destroyed. I have taken a great risk of losing this remaining precious memento of my cleverness by taking this sign out of deep hiding in order to copy it here:

ATTENTION ALL NINTH-GRADE GIRLS

Chad Lake has a new girlfriend. Her name is Valerie Ann Jones and she goes to Willow Creek High School. His previous girlfriend, as many of you know, was Virginia Ames. He carved Virginia's initials on his lacrosse stick. He's now added a "J" to that and has told Valerie that he *just* put her initials on his stick. Doesn't she deserve to know the truth? Call her at 555-3992 and tell her!

I also drew a picture of Chad's lacrosse stick, before and after, at the bottom of the page. The sign looked pretty good, if I do say so myself. I took some tape out of my backpack and posted the sign high on the mirror where everyone who came into the girls' room would be sure to see it. I was pretty confident that it would stay there all day long, since the teachers never go in there because they have their own bathroom.

The second sign involved Alex. As I said, it has been destroyed. In fact, I never saw it again after posting it on the mirror that day. But the basic gist of it was that Alexander Lake was having trouble deciding which of his classmates he liked better—Andrea or Martha. It also mentioned that he was currently leaning toward Andrea, but that he *might* ask Martha to the upcoming middle-school dance because he'd been talking about how great she'd looked doing jump shots in basketball the other day. (Which was totally true, by the way—*all* the stuff on my signs was true. That was what made them so great.)

Finally I pulled out the third and last sign. It was addressed to all the fourth-grade girls and stated that Michael Lake wore Spider-Man underwear. (Also true.)

I was zipping up my backpack and preparing to return to class when the door opened and Veronica walked in. I was curious to see what everyone's reaction would be to my signs, so I stuck around and pretended to wash my hands while she read them. (That doesn't make much sense, does it? Actually, I really did wash my hands. I just pretended they were dirty in the first place.)

Veronica finished reading and then turned to stare at me. "Girlfriends' initials? Spider-Man underwear? Is this what you meant by saying yours is a fine family?" She smirked in this really nasty way, the way she always does when she thinks she's just proven she's better than someone else. Then she brushed past me and left the room.

I was fuming. It was one thing for *me* to dump on my brothers and make fun of them and try to wreak revenge on them. It was another thing entirely for Veronica to put them down. After all, they're *my* brothers. Our family honor was at stake. That's why I decided I'd better extend my revenge plans to include Veronica. Someone needed to take her down a few pegs, and I've never been one to shirk my duties.

We had a special Horse Wise meeting the next day after school to prepare for the mock hunt. I was in a good mood when I got there. And as soon as I arrived, my mood got even better as people started rushing over to clap me on the back and tell me how great I was. I knew it was because of my signs—they had been a big hit at school the day before, and everyone was still talking about them. Everyone except my brothers, that is. I hadn't seen much of the three of them the evening before, since Lisa and I had been invited to Carole's house for dinner and we had stayed kind of late watching an old movie on TV with Carole and her father and then talking about the fox hunt.

However, I hadn't quite gotten around to telling Carole and Lisa about my revenge signs. They don't always approve of my little conflicts with my brothers, mostly because the two of them sometimes end up getting involved. And since they don't go to Fenton Hall, I figured I wouldn't burden them with it, at least not yet.

But they couldn't help noticing that something was going on. After Polly Giacomin patted me on the back and said, "Nice going," Carole and Lisa were starting to look really suspicious. They started muttering to each other, and I heard Carole say something like "We'd better look into this."

"Look into what?" I asked.

"Look into why everybody is clapping you on the back and congratulating you," Lisa said. "What have you done now?"

I decided since my friends already suspected something, I might as well tell them. Besides, I was still feeling kind of proud of myself. I was sure they would appreciate the clever and rather subtle method I had chosen to get back at my brothers. "Oh, it's just a touch of revenge," I said modestly. "Another ingenious plot by the famous, or should I say *infamous*, Stevie Lake."

"Big trouble," Lisa said to Carole, who nodded.

I wasn't sure what they meant by that, but I rushed to explain. "It has to do with my three troublesome brothers," I began. "See, when Phil came to dinner on Saturday, they were total pains, teasing us and making fun of foxhunting. I couldn't let them get away with that, could I? I just *had* to take steps."

"Steps, maybe," Carole agreed. "Leaps, definitely not. What did you do?"

I reached into my pocket and brought out a copy of each sign. Carole and Lisa scanned them quickly, then let out loud gasps.

"Aren't they wonderful?" I asked proudly. "I think I'll go into the Revenge Hall of Fame."

"If you live that long," Carole said rather darkly.

"What do you mean?" I suddenly realized that their gasps might not have been gasps of awe and admiration as I'd thought. When I took a closer look at them, they both seemed kind of horrified.

The two of them stared at each other for a moment. "You tell her," Carole said at last.

"We mean you're crazy!" Lisa said promptly.

Carole nodded. "A little teasing is one thing, but what you've done to your brothers is public humiliation. They aren't going to let you get away with that!"

"And there are *three* of them," Lisa added.

I didn't see why they were making such a big deal out of this. I figured it was probably because they didn't know what sibling rivalry was all about. I mean, Carole's an only child, and Lisa's brother is so much older that it's almost like she doesn't even have a brother at all. I shrugged. "Come off it," I told them. "You two just don't know how it goes between me and my brothers."

"Oh, yes we do," Carole said. "And it starts with a *T*, and that stands for Trouble. You haven't heard the last of this."

"It's no big deal," I assured her.

"If that's the case, why does everybody keep clapping you on the back?" Lisa asked.

I noticed that Carole had this really worried look on her face. Then I saw her lean over and mutter something to Lisa under her breath. Lisa muttered something back.

231

"What are you two whispering about?" I demanded.

"Nothing," they said at the same time.

I was about to insist they tell me when Max called the meeting to order. That made me forget all about my friends' silly concerns. Although, as it turned out, that was a serious error on my part. More about that later . . .

We decided to have a Saddle Club meeting at my house after the Horse Wise meeting. When we arrived, still talking excitedly about the mock hunt, we went into the kitchen to get a snack, pausing just long enough to call hello to my parents, who were watching TV in the den. Then we headed for the stairs.

"Where are your brothers?" Carole asked casually as we went.

That should have made me suspicious. But my mind was too full of other things, like fox hunts and revenge plots. "Who knows? Who cares?" I replied airily. "Chad's probably listening to that awful music he likes. Unless, of course, his ear is tired from all the phone calls he's had from his girlfriend yelling at him." I giggled at the thought. "Alex, on the other hand . . ." I continued to describe my brothers' individual plights as we walked upstairs to my room. I suppose to an outsider, my comments might have sounded a little heartless. But I knew my brothers deserved every bit of the humiliation they were suffering right then. It was only fair after the humiliation they'd put me through Saturday night.

As we walked down the upstairs hall toward my room, we could see that all my brothers' doors were closed. Heavy metal music was blaring from behind Chad's. Some electronic bleeps and bloops were emerging from Alex and Michael's room.

I looked at my friends and shrugged. "See? Nothing's happening. The three of them just know they got what they deserved. There's no trouble brewing here. Trust me."

They seemed to believe me. (Little did I know . . .) We started our Saddle Club meeting talking about our favorite subject—horses.

"How are you and Comanche doing?" I asked Lisa. She hadn't talked about him much since that first ride, and I was curious, especially since she seemed to be having a little trouble controlling him. I was starting to think she didn't quite understand his mischievous personality very well—probably because Lisa's own personality isn't mischievous at all.

"Only so-so," Lisa replied. "The last time I rode him, I spent an awful lot of time trying to get him to do what I wanted him to do instead of what *he* wanted to do."

"He's very headstrong," Carole agreed. "I always thought that was why he and Stevie got along so well."

I laughed. "We were quite a pair, weren't we? But now that I'm riding Topside, I realize that Comanche *could* be difficult."

"It may be that Comanche isn't a good horse for you," Carole told Lisa. "It's really important that a rider and a horse be matched carefully. Horses have personalities—"

"—just like people," Lisa finished for her. "See, I figured that since I like Stevie so much, I'd like a horse with a personality like hers." She sighed. "What I found, however, was

233

that *liking* Stevie and trying to tell her what to do are two different things."

It took me a second to work through that sentence again and figure out whether Lisa was insulting me or not. By the time I realized she was—and that it was pretty funny— Carole was already cracking up. I joined in. Lisa's a lot funnier than some people give her credit for, probably because a lot of her funniest comments are sort of subtle, like that one.

Anyway, we continued to discuss Lisa and Comanche, and in the end Carole advised her to ask Max if she could try riding Diablo instead.

"You think he'd let me ride Diablo?" Lisa asked.

Carole nodded, and I jumped in to agree. "Oh, he's a sweetie," I said. "And remember Max saying that he used to belong to someone who did a lot of hunting. I bet he'll be great in the field. It's important to have a horse with experience—one who won't bolt off when he hears the hounds barking and baying. Say, what *is* baying, anyway?"

That brought us into yet another discussion of the upcoming hunt, and that kept us busy for the rest of our meeting.

But my friends' comments about my brothers that day had made me think. I realized, kind of belatedly, I guess, that what I had done to them really was pretty humiliating. I mean, I know that was the goal, but still. Everybody at Fenton Hall—not to mention most of the remaining population of Willow Creek—seemed to be talking about what I'd done . . . *except* my brothers. It was kind of weird that they hadn't even reacted yet (except for Michael begging to stay home from school the day after the signs appeared).

That wasn't like them. Then again, I told myself, maybe they were finally maturing a little. Maybe they had realized I was just evening the score, paying them back for what they had done to me. Maybe they wouldn't retaliate at all!

But I couldn't quite believe that. No way. So as I headed off to school the next day, I kept one eye out for trouble. There was no telling when my brothers would strike. Or how. The only certainty was that they would do *something*.

Chad was the first one of them I saw when I got to school. "Hi, Stevie! I missed you this morning!" he called cheerfully as he dashed past in the hall.

I waved and smiled in return, not knowing what else to do. Chad doesn't usually bother to speak to me in the halls at all, let alone nicely like that.

Before I had a chance to worry about that, Alex tapped me on the shoulder. "Hey, I picked up your workbook by mistake. Sorry about that, but when I checked the work you'd done last night, I saw you'd made a few mistakes. I corrected them for you. Okay?" He shoved the book into my hands and took off.

Expecting the worst, I opened the workbook to see what he'd done. I almost fell over in shock as I realized he'd done exactly what he'd said—corrected my homework.

I ran into Michael a little later. He loaned me a quarter.

It was too weird. My brothers were being nice to me. Something was definitely up.

Meanwhile, although I didn't know it at the time, my two loyal best friends were plotting against me. Actually, to be fair, they thought they were trying to help me. They were worried that the battle with my brothers might somehow affect my riding privileges or something like that. They tend to worry more about things like that than I do, I think. But they mean well.

So they were spending a lot of time trying to figure out how to help me. That's our Saddle Club creed, as you know. So I guess they thought it was their duty.

Unfortunately, they're far too trusting and naive ever to hope to outwit my dastardly brothers. To begin with, they were working under the assumption that those three monsters are actually normal human beings. Poor, innocent Carole and Lisa . . . But more on that later.

I was having my own problems figuring out what my brothers were up to. Besides that, I still had to deal with everyday problems like Veronica diAngelo. She approached me in the cafeteria. I was a little distracted at the time, since my brothers had just offered to go and find me some lunch to replace mine, which I'd left at home that morning. I was trying to figure out whether they were more likely to pick some half-eaten food out of the garbage or find me something even more disgusting in the biology lab.

Veronica's arrival interrupted these thoughts. "Hi, Stevie!" she said sweetly. "Can I ask you a question?"

"You just did—and that's your limit," I snapped. I know that wasn't very polite, but I wasn't in a very polite mood just then.

236

Anyway, Veronica didn't take offense. Instead she laughed as if it were the funniest thing she'd ever heard. "You're so funny, Stevie!" she exclaimed.

I just stared at her in amazement, wondering if aliens had come down to earth and replaced her personality with a nice one.

She didn't notice my stare. "What I wanted to ask," she said, "is what happened between you and your brothers? I mean, you guys fight all the time, but what did they do to you that was so bad you decided to put those signs in the girls' room?"

"It's a family matter, Veronica," I said. There was no way I was going to tell her about that dinner with Phil.

Just then Lorraine Olsen (who also rides at Pine Hollow) sat down next to me. "What's up between you and your brothers?" she asked me.

I launched into a detailed answer to her question, explaining how my brothers had made fun of the fox hunt, Phil, and me. Meanwhile, I watched Veronica out of the corner of my eye, hoping she could appreciate the irony (another term I learned in English class, by the way) of my telling Lorraine what I had just refused to tell her.

I had just gotten to the part about the boys making fun of the mock hunt when Alex arrived. "Here you go, Stevie," he said, offering me a lunch bag.

I accepted it, mostly because I was curious to see exactly what hideous items he and the others had come up with. I peered into the bag as Alex hurried away and disappeared into the lunchtime crowd.

A sandwich was inside. Bologna and cheese on white. With mayo. Just the way I like it. I guessed that it had come from Michael's lunch, since that was his favorite sandwich, too. There was also some apple juice—Chad's drink. And an orange—Alex's favorite. I was confused. Each of my brothers had contributed something he really liked to my lunch. That was odd. Very odd.

I spent the rest of the lunch period pondering the situation. Could it be? Could my brothers really *not* be mad about what I'd done? Could they have accepted it and moved on?

It seemed impossible. But I was starting to wonder. . . .

I hadn't come any closer to figuring it out by the time Saturday rolled around. And brothers were the last thing on my mind as I arrived at Pine Hollow bright and early for the mock hunt. My friends and I—along with the other riders from Horse Wise and Cross County—were properly dressed in riding pants and boots, white shirts and ties, and jackets, as well as our usual hard hats. There were more than forty people participating in the hunt, so it was a pretty wild scene that morning, with everyone scrambling to get themselves and their horses ready on time.

But finally everyone was ready, and Max and Mr. Baker called for our attention.

"I am now ready to assign parts to all of you," Max announced. "Most of you will be in the field, but a few of you will have special jobs. First of all, we need a junior master of the hunt. This job is going to the person who has been the most serious student of foxhunting—the person who worked hardest at understanding all aspects of it."

Being junior master sounded like fun, but I was pretty sure Max would never pick me for the job. Like a few other people, Max has the mistaken impression that I could never be a serious student of anything, except maybe dressage or practical jokes. I wondered if he would give the job to Carole. I suspected he wouldn't, since she had started off knowing more about foxhunting than the rest of us and so hadn't worked that hard at learning about it lately. That left Lisa—the perfect choice.

Max was still speaking. ". . . and that person is Lisa Atwood."

I cheered loudly as Lisa grinned modestly and thanked Max.

Then Max went on to name a few of the other positions. Phil was chosen to be the huntsman. Carole was one of the five whippers-in. He also assigned six or seven riders to play the hounds.

"And now we come to the fox," Max said at last. "For this, we needed to find somebody who could be wily, clever, devious, cunning, sneaky, shrewd, sly, and deceitful." He paused, and I glanced around, trying to figure out who was left who would fit that description. I was surprised to find that absolutely everyone there was looking straight back at me!

Carole started giggling. So did Lisa. Within seconds, all forty riders were laughing.

I blushed. *"Moi?"* I asked, trying to sound innocent.

"If the shoe fits," Max remarked with a laugh. Then he started to tell us something about a map, when a loud, whiny voice interrupted him.

"Re-ed!" it shouted. "I need your help! Where are you?"

It was Veronica, of course. Late, of course. And, of course, she expected Red O'Malley to tack up her horse, Garnet, for her. Veronica never does any of her own stable chores if she can help it.

Red excused himself and went to tack up Garnet while Veronica joined the group of riders. I was sure Max would have made her go tack up Garnet herself, but he probably thought it was more important for her to hear what he had to say.

"As I was saying," he continued, "I have made up a map, which all riders should carry with them. There are a few farmers who have specifically asked us not to ride on their land, and we *must* respect their wishes. Do you all understand?"

Everybody nodded.

"Okay, then, I think it's about time for our fox to get going, so all you animals, come get your ears."

I was surprised when Max pulled out a bag full of headbands with fake ears sewn on. When I saw what the hounds were going to wear, I wrinkled my nose. They looked kind of silly.

My own ears, on the other hand, were a different matter. They were orange, and pointy, and furry—and absolutely adorable! I pulled them on proudly over my helmet. When Phil saw me, he let out a loud whistle.

"That's a wolf whistle," I joked. "Totally wrong for a fox."

"Well, let's see just how good a fox you are," he said. "I can promise you, you haven't got a chance against an awesome huntsman like me."

I grinned. I recognized a challenge when I heard one. "We'll see," I told him. "We'll just see!"

Then it was time for me to get started. Max explained that I had two jobs. The first was to try to avoid being captured. The second and even more important job was to lead everybody on a ride that would be fun.

"Fun is my middle name!" I told him.

"Sometimes I think it's your first and last names, too," Max said. I wasn't absolutely sure he meant it as a compliment, but I decided to take it as one.

Max told me I would have a ten-minute head start before the other riders came after me. He handed me a bag of confetti and told me it was "scent." I had to drop a handful of the confetti every five minutes so the "hounds" would have a trail to follow.

"Gotcha," I agreed, dropping my first handful of confetti right then and there. Then Topside and I headed for the woods at a brisk trot.

My mind was already racing with the possibilities. Max was counting on me to be the wiliest of foxes, and I wasn't going to disappoint him. I urged Topside through the woods quickly, dropping my confetti scent just as I was supposed to do.

A plan was already brewing in my mind. I planted some confetti on the trail leading into a wooded hillside where there were lots of caves and gullies and other hiding places.

241

I knew they were there, and I knew that Carole and Lisa (and probably most of the other Pine Hollow riders) knew they were there, too. I figured if they thought I was in there, they would spend a really long time searching every possible hiding spot. But they wouldn't find me in a single one.

I grinned. "Let's get going!" I told Topside, feeling very pleased with my deception. I followed the trail I had taken toward the hillside in reverse, being careful to drop my confetti on the exact same spots where I had dropped it on the way in. That way, the hounds and huntsman would see the confetti, but they wouldn't realize they were seeing a double dose.

The only tricky part was getting to the creek before I had to drop any more confetti. I meant to go into the creek and stay there, following it all the way back to the field. That way, when I dropped my handfuls of confetti, it would float downstream in the water and the other riders would never see it.

I almost laughed aloud when I thought of it. I had to be the cleverest fox any fox hunt had ever seen!

"Well, the cleverest human one, anyway," I told Topside, who didn't seem the least bit impressed.

The plan went perfectly. I reached the creek safely and was well on my way before I heard the distant sounds of the other riders approaching. I grinned and urged Topside forward a little faster through the shallow water.

Once we were a bit farther downstream, I allowed Topside to choose his own pace. There was no real hurry now—

my friends and the others would be occupied for quite some time on that hillside.

Eventually we reached the edge of the field. Actually, it was the first of several sizable open fields lying between me and Pine Hollow, a little less than a mile away. I had to make sure the area was empty before I entered it. I didn't want someone to spot me now, not after all my brilliant planning.

I scanned the fields carefully. There was no sign of any other riders. I clucked to Topside, and we moved forward.

"Okay, boy," I told my horse. "We don't want to blow this now. We're going to have to do this fast."

He snorted, and I took it as agreement. Reaching into my bag, I dropped one last handful of confetti. At almost the same time, I urged Topside forward.

Topside responded immediately, swinging into a trot that quickly turned into a canter and then a full-fledged gallop. *"Yeeee-ha!"* I whispered, not wanting to yell and risk attracting attention.

There was a fence separating the first field from the second. I aimed Topside straight toward it, and he jumped it cleanly and easily like the champion he is. A few seconds later, we approached another fence.

Suddenly I realized that we had a problem. "Oops," I said. "That's Mr. Andrews's land. We're not allowed to go that way."

I knew Topside couldn't hear me, let alone understand me. I was really talking more to myself. It was annoying to have to make a detour now, especially when I could almost taste my victory. But I knew I had no choice. Some people might think I have no trouble at all breaking rules, but all kidding aside, Max's rule about other people's land was sacred. I didn't even consider breaking it for a second.

I turned Topside sharply to the right and skirted Mr. Andrews's land, going clean around it. Then I turned again, once more aimed straight for the stable.

That was when I heard it.

"Help!"

I pulled Topside to a walk. Had it been my imagination?

"Help! Help!" the voice came again. A young girl's voice.

"Where are you?" I called. Following the sound of the girl's replies, I quickly spotted her. It was May Grover, one of the younger riders. She was sitting in the grass with tears streaming down her cheeks.

I hurried over and dismounted. "What happened?" I asked the little girl.

"My pony threw me," May said. "One of the big girls was supposed to look after me, but she just rode on. She didn't even notice."

I grimaced. I was pretty sure I knew who the "big girl" was—Veronica diAngelo. She's the only member of Horse Wise who would be that irresponsible.

I checked May over, and luckily she didn't seem to be seriously hurt. She was just upset at having been thrown. I comforted her as best I could, then helped her to her feet.

"I'll find your pony for you," I promised her.

"You'd do that for me?" May asked, looking surprised.

"Of course," I replied.

"But you're the fox!"

I had been so concerned about her that I'd almost forgotten about that. But her words gave me an idea. "You know foxes sometimes travel in pairs, right?" I said.

May nodded. "Max says two foxes are called a brace of foxes."

"You've been studying," I accused her.

May smiled proudly. "I wanted to know everything," she explained.

"Then you'll make a great partner for me," I said. I climbed back aboard Topside and hoisted May onto the saddle in front of me. Then we went looking for her pony.

It didn't take long to find him. He was nibbling on some grass behind a small stand of trees nearby. Since May seemed comfortable sitting in front of me, I left her there and led the pony beside Topside. All parties seemed perfectly happy with that arrangement.

Then we headed for Pine Hollow once again, May giggling as I carefully explained my foxy strategy to her. We had almost reached the paddock gate when something made me look back over my shoulder. It might have been a noise, or just a hunch. Either way, I spotted Veronica diAngelo waving wildly and screaming triumphantly as she rode toward us at breakneck speed.

"That's the girl who was supposed to take care of me," May said. "Now it looks like somebody ought to take care of her. What's wrong with her?"

"She just thinks she's so smart because she saw us first," I replied, my heart sinking as I realized it was true. She had spotted us. "That's why she's waving her arms."

"I didn't mean that part," May said. "What's wrong with her that she's riding across Mr. Andrews's field?"

I gasped as I realized she was absolutely right. It was the best news I'd had all day! I gave May a big hug. "You're quite a fox," I declared with a grin.

A little while later, all three of us were back at Pine Hollow. Actually, make that all six of us, including the horses. I was walking Topside around the indoor ring to cool him down after our ride. May was with me, walking her pony. We were being as quiet as possible because we were trying to hear every word that Max and Mr. Baker were saying to Veronica just outside.

"Veronica, you are very familiar with the rules," Max said in his sternest voice.

"But I saw Stevie," Veronica whined. "I had to catch up to her."

"It wasn't your job to catch up to her. That's the huntsman's job. It was your job to inform the huntsman that you'd seen her."

Veronica continued to protest, but the two men weren't having any of it. Finally she gave up.

"I'm sorry," she said. "It won't happen again." It sounded pretty insincere to me, and I figured Veronica was just tired of arguing.

What Mr. Baker said next surprised her, though—and me, too. "You're right about that," he told her. "And it certainly won't happen in any hunt that I have anything to do with.

246

As of now, Max is withdrawing his invitation to you to participate further in this mock hunt, and I'm formally disinviting you to the junior hunt at Cross County next week."

"You *what?*" Veronica exploded.

I could hardly believe it. It was a safe bet that nobody had ever disinvited Veronica to anything. This was better revenge than anything I could have come up with. "Isn't it great?" I whispered to May.

Soon our horses were ready to go back to their stalls, and May and I were ready to start digging into the hunt breakfast. But first I walked to the tack room to put away my tack. While I was there, I glanced out the window and saw Veronica standing by the road, obviously waiting for her ride.

Then something strange happened. My brother Chad rode past on his bike. Or rather, he *started* to ride past. Because Veronica spotted him and waved, and Chad stopped.

I rolled my eyes. Veronica may not be much in the personality department, but a lot of guys seem to think she's pretty. It looked as though Chad was no exception. I figured he was probably thrilled that a girl wanted to talk to him.

"You two deserve each other," I muttered in their general direction. Then I turned and hurried out of the room, forgetting all about what I'd seen—for the moment, at least.

May and I were into our second helpings of bagels and cream cheese when the first shouts came from outside the stable.

"Here's some more confetti!"

"It can't be! She must have dropped that on the way out!"

247

"No way!"

And so on. I grinned and winked at May as the voices came closer. Phil and Lisa were arguing about whether they should have checked more places on the hillside. Others were speculating on whether I could possibly have ridden into town for ice cream. The rest of the riders just sounded confused.

Then I heard someone let out a loud "Woof! Woof!"

"They must have just spotted Topside," I told May complacently. "It sounds like they're right outside his stall."

Sure enough, they had figured it out. A moment later they burst in, and May and I stood to toast them with our orange juice.

"Gotcha!" I cried. Everybody laughed, then cheered.

And by the end of the hunt breakfast, all the riders from the fox hunt—minus Veronica, of course—toasted May and me with their orange juice, bringing an end to one of the most enjoyable experiences of my whole life.

FROM:	HorseGal
TO:	Steviethegreat
SUBJECT:	Go to sleep!
MESSAGE:	

It's way too late to call, but I figured you'd probably still be up working on your report. My dad and I just got home from a double feature in town, and I couldn't wait until our

Horse Wise meeting tomorrow to tell you what happened on the way home from the theater.

I talked Dad into stopping by Pine Hollow on our way home, because I'd asked Judy to leave me a schedule of when she wanted me to work with her. Anyway, Dad waited in the car while I rushed in. Of course, after I picked up the note I decided to stop by for a quick good-night to Starlight. On my way to his stall, I spotted movement at the end of the hall. For a second I was kind of scared, thinking it was an intruder. I mean, it was pretty late, and there were only a few lights on. Then I decided I was being silly, that it was just Max or Red checking on one of the horses.

Still, I decided to play it safe. I stayed as quiet as a barn mouse as I crept forward, trying to see who it was.

When I reached the corner and peeped around, I got the shock of my life. It wasn't Max. It wasn't Red. It wasn't some ax murderer or escaped convict.

It was Veronica!

She was wandering around the section of the stable that's the bottom of the U—you know, the part where Rusty and Delilah and a few of the ponies are stabled. I was confused because she was nowhere near Garnet's stall. And she wasn't even paying attention to any of the horses, even though Rusty kept sticking his head out to snuffle at her as she walked by. She was just sort of pacing.

I was too surprised to say anything at first, and she didn't see me at all. After a second, she stopped pacing and hurried down the other aisle (the one I wasn't in) and disappeared. I came to my senses a moment later and raced around the corner to ask her what she was doing there—I was afraid maybe Garnet was sick or something—but she was nowhere in sight. I looked all around the stable, but there wasn't another human being to be seen anywhere (or Veronica either, hee hee!).

Anyway, it was so weird I just had to tell someone about it. Maybe Veronica has finally lost it! (Now if she'd just *get* lost . . . hee hee!)

See you bright and early tomorrow for Horse Wise!

Welcome to My Life . . .

Now, I didn't know about this next part of my story until Carole and Lisa told me later. But it seems they were still worrying about what my brothers might do to me. So they decided to get involved—directly. Really directly. They actually called up the three troublemakers and arranged a meeting.

Those poor girls never had a chance. Somehow, my brothers managed to get them talking about the hunt. I suspect that Carole did most of the talking, since as you've seen before in this report, Miss Fenton, she *really* loves to talk about anything horse-related. Apparently she told them all about how a hunt works, and how if there are no foxes around, the would-be hunters will make it a drag hunt. Basically, that means someone goes out with a bag of scent and drags it around to create a trail that the hounds can follow, just as if they were on the trail of a real live fox.

By the time Carole finished talking, my brothers probably knew almost as much about foxhunting as she did.

But as I said, at the time I didn't even suspect that anything like that was going on. However, I was still mighty suspicious of my brothers' behavior, which was still nice as pie. In fact, I spent so much time worrying about it that I completely forgot about one of my math assignments, and I only had time to finish half the chapter I was supposed to read in my history book. Okay, maybe it was more like a third. I was *really* worried.

That Monday was rainy, and I was in a pretty stormy mood myself as I headed for Pine Hollow. I had seen something that day that had totally freaked me out. It was one of those things that sort of make you think the entire universe has just shifted in some cosmic way that allows the unthinkable to happen. Or something like that.

Anyway, when I got to the stable, Red told me that Carole and Lisa were in the indoor ring. I let myself in. Lisa was over on one side working with Samson, a curious young foal who was born at Pine Hollow. Carole was aboard Starlight, working on gait changes. I just stood there for a minute or two, watching them work. Carole is such a good friend that sometimes it's easy for me to forget how truly impressive she is when she's working with a horse. I kind of take her talents for granted. But I was aware of them right then as I watched Starlight practically grow and learn in front of my eyes. Seeing that somehow put what I had seen that day in perspective and soothed me.

Eventually Carole and Lisa noticed me standing there and came over to say hi. After a few moments of chitchat, I got down to business.

"Something is definitely up," I told them.

"What makes you think so?" Lisa asked, looking worried as she stroked Samson's short black mane.

"It's Chad," I said. "He seems to have a new girlfriend."

Carole shrugged. "What's so strange about that? The average life span of a romance for Chad is about four days, right? So it's time for a switch."

I couldn't help smiling at that, since it was true. "I guess you're right," I admitted. "His lacrosse stick looks like a bowl of leftover alphabet soup! Anyway, what's funny isn't that he's got a new girlfriend, but who it is. Stand back, girls." I took a deep breath. "It's Veronica diAngelo."

They were stunned at that, of course. Almost as stunned as I had been.

"I saw them at school today," I went on. "They were giggling. The only time Chad ever giggles is with his girl-friends."

"Maybe it's just because he's been in love with every other girl at Fenton Hall and the only one left was Veronica," Lisa suggested.

That made sense to me. But it wasn't much comfort.

"And the good news is," Lisa continued, "it will only go on for another four days."

"Unless he marries her," Carole chimed in, "in which case, the whole Lake family can retire on her money."

It was meant to be a joke, but I couldn't help shudder-

252

ing at the very thought. It was so awful that I could hardly concentrate on anything else all week. Not even my science paper.

STEVIE,

OKAY, ENOUGH JOKING AROUND. WE'VE HAD ENOUGH OF YOUR LAME EXCUSES ABOUT HOMEWORK. WE WANT THIS COMPUTER.

<u>NOW!!!!</u>

IF YOU DON'T READ THIS AND SAVE YOUR REPORT IN THE NEXT HALF HOUR, WE WON'T BE RESPONSIBLE FOR JAWBONE'S ACTIONS. HE MAY JUST DECIDE TO DELETE THE WHOLE THING WITH A MONSTER CHOMP OF HIS MASSIVE JAWS. JUST A BROTHERLY WARNING . . .

CHOMPINGLY,
CHAD

DEAR CHOMPING CHAD,

YOU CAN TELL MR. JAWBONE THAT IF YOU AND YOUR BROTHERS DON'T LEAVE STEVIE ALONE AND LET HER FINISH HER REPORT, HE'LL BE CHOMPING HIS WAY BACK TO THE

COMPUTER STORE FIRST THING TOMOR-
ROW.
JUST A MOTHERLY WARNING . . .

MOM

FROM:	Steviethegreat
TO:	DSlattVT
SUBJECT:	Brothers and snobs
MESSAGE:	

Guess what? My brothers just got busted! They've been leaving these snotty little notes stuck to the front of the computer all week, and Mom finally caught them at it. They haven't so much as poked their faces into the den since.

But that's not really why I'm writing. I have another update on the Veronica saga. It's a pretty annoying update, too, if you ask me. You see, this morning at Horse Wise I overheard some of the other girls talking about Veronica (who was late, as usual). Betsy said something about how she was so happy to run into Veronica at the mall yesterday after school, and how Veronica had about a million shopping bags stuffed full of things that she'd bought. Then Lorraine pipes up with some story about how she and Veronica went for a long bike ride a couple of days ago. And Meg Durham was acting all thrilled because it was warm enough this week for her and Veronica to hang out at Veronica's pool all afternoon for two days in a row.

Normally, none of that would be the least bit surprising. But this week it is. Because this week, as you will recall from my previous e-mails, Veronica is supposed to be spending all her spare time writing a report for Miss Fenton, just like I am!

Part of me is really ticked off that's she's lounging around having fun while I'm killing myself working on my report. Another part is actually kind of glad about it, since it should mean that my report is guaranteed to be a million times better than hers.

However, as you know, with Veronica there are no guarantees. Knowing her, she's probably paying someone to write her report for her or something. Ha ha!

Welcome to My Life . . .

The day of the fox hunt came at last. My brothers still hadn't made their move, but I figured I was safe for one day at least, since I'd be all the way over at Cross County. The hunt was promising to be quite dramatic. And in the spirit of that idea, I now present . . .

OUTFOXED!

A Thrilling, Action-Packed Movie Script by S. Lake

FADE IN
INTERIOR Cross County Stables, a little past seven in the morning.

CLOSE-UP on STEVIE, an astoundingly good-looking girl in flawless hunt attire, as she hurries down the hallway. PULL BACK to reveal other riders bustling around. Stevie approaches CAROLE and LISA. They are both similarly attired. All three girls look a bit sleepy but excited.

> STEVIE
> (cheerful but a bit perplexed)
> Tallyho, girls! Did you see what I just saw?

> LISA
> What?

> STEVIE
> Veronica diAngelo.

> CAROLE
> (scoffing)
> No way! Even Veronica wouldn't have the poor judgment to try to get in on the hunt at the last minute—not after she was so officially disinvited a week ago. Are you sure it was her?

Stevie rubs her forehead and shakes her head in confusion.

> STEVIE
> It's early and I could be wrong. But I don't know another chauffeur-driven Mercedes in this area, and I know I saw one. It was

256

pulling out of a parking lot not far from here.
It was heading back toward Willow Creek
when I saw it.

CAROLE
I'm sure it was all in your imagination.

CUT TO
EXTERIOR Just outside the stable. A large truck is pulling
into the driveway. A terrible din comes from the back of
it—barking and baying. Students, including Stevie, Carole,
Lisa, and PHIL, pour out of the building to see.
PAN TO
CLOSE-UP on Phil, who is smiling gleefully. The three
girls are standing near him.

PHIL
Methinks the hounds have arrived!

CUT TO

STEVIE
(whispering to herself in happy disbelief)
This is real! The hunt is really real!

FADE OUT
FADE IN ON
EXTERIOR Cross County Stables. It's a short time later—
the sun is a bit higher—and the Pine Hollow horses have
been unloaded from vans and the students are in the process

of saddling them. Everyone is rushing around getting ready or helping others get ready. Stevie is helping a cute little girl, MAY, tighten the girth on her pony's saddle.

> STEVIE
> . . . and that's why it's so important to always do your homework, May.

Stevie gives a last pull on the girth, then steps back and brushes off her hands.

> STEVIE
> (kindly)
> That should do it. Wait here, okay? I'm going to go get Topside. We can start out together in the hunt if you want.

> MAY
> (thrilled)
> That would be great! You're the coolest, Stevie. And thanks for all the tips about doing my best in school. You're a true inspiration.

Stevie smiles and walks across the crowded stable yard. On the way, she passes a small paddock where the HOUNDS are milling around, making a lot of noise. The hounds' owner, CHESTER, is standing nearby talking to MAX, who looks slightly worried. Stevie pauses nearby, sensing that something is going on, and listens.

258

MAX
Why are they making so much noise?

CHESTER
The fox must have been right through here. They've picked up a scent for sure, and they're ready to go. If they're this excited, the fox must be nearby. This may be a short hunt.

Stevie frowns at that. Then she moves on toward TOPSIDE.

FADE OUT
FADE IN ON
EXTERIOR Same location a little while later. All the RIDERS are mounted and gathered in one area. Max is walking around inspecting them. MR. BAKER is also present, as are Chester and his hounds.

CHESTER
(addressing the riders and indicating his hounds)
These guys are ready to go. Are you?

The young hunters all nod and/or cheer.

CHESTER
Then let's be off!

PAN TO Max. He pulls a short brass horn out of a bag, raises it to his lips, and blows a rapid one-note call. As he finishes, Chester releases the hounds. The hunt begins. The hounds leap forward dramatically. However, they soon pull up and start retracing their steps. Soon all the hounds are running around in circles in the stable yard, yipping and barking and howling, dashing beneath the horses, and generally going crazy. Stevie approaches Chester, who is riding near her.

STEVIE
What's the matter?

CHESTER
(looking confused)
It's the hounds. They should be following the scent, and Mr. Baker was sure it would head over to the east.

PAN TO
CLOSE-UP on one particular hound. He puts his nose to the ground, takes a few tentative steps forward, and begins a new kind of bark.
CUT TO

CHESTER
(excited)
He's got something! It's a find!

CUT TO the hounds. They are all beginning to follow the first hound's lead. They all follow their new trail—right into the barn!

CUT TO the astonished faces of Mr. Baker and Chester.

MR. BAKER
(indignant)
No way was a fox in there!

CHESTER
(a bit irritated)
Something was in there.

PAN OUT to WIDE-ANGLE SHOT of the barn.
In a FAST-MOTION ACTION SEQUENCE, all the riders urge their horses forward and follow the hounds into the barn. For a moment, they disappear from view. Then we see the hounds emerging from the far end of the barn, with forty riders just a few steps behind them. The camera PANS to follow the action as the hounds next lead the riders up onto the front porch of a nearby house, stopping just short of going inside, and dashing off the far end of the porch. Then they dash around the rear of the house, through a flower garden and under a clothesline full of flapping white sheets. The riders follow, accidentally crushing most of the flowers and trampling the sheets in the mud, as MRS. BAKER emerges from the house and shakes her fist at them. The hounds are still running, scurrying under a swing set and through a vegetable patch. The riders follow, dodging the swings and most of the vegetables.
CAMERA returns to NORMAL SPEED and
PANS to CLOSE-UP on Chester's confused face.

CHESTER
Something's definitely wrong.

PAN OUT to show entire scene again as the hounds run toward the road. They stop dead at the roadside and begin sniffing around aimlessly. Then one hound crosses the road and howls. He has picked up the scent again. The hounds follow it along the edge of the road for about a hundred yards as the riders follow. The hounds stop again.
CUT TO
CLOSE-UP on Stevie.

STEVIE
Let's see if it picks up on the other side of the road.

Another FAST-MOTION ACTION SEQUENCE. The hounds follow the track as it zigzags, jumping back and forth from one side of the road to the other. This goes on for about half a dozen jumps. The riders look more and more perplexed as it continues.
Return to NORMAL CAMERA SPEED
PAN TO Chester.

CHESTER
This is weird. Smells don't leap across roads.
Something's fishy.

CUT TO Stevie's face. She looks a bit suspicious, and a bit unhappy. She is wondering exactly what is going on.

FADE OUT
FADE IN on
EXTERIOR Near Cross County. Actually, just a little way down the road from previous scene. The hounds are sniffing about, still following the bizarre trail near the road. The adults in the group (Max, Mr. Baker, Chester) all look very perplexed and disgruntled. Stevie still looks slightly nervous and confused. All the other young riders look happy—they are having fun, joking and racing back and forth after the hounds. It is evident from their frequent glances at the adults that they are amused at the adults' obvious confusion.
CLOSE-UP on Stevie.

STEVIE
(muttering)
This has been going on for half an hour. I have a bad feeling about this. . . .

PAN TO

CHESTER
The hounds have the scent again!

PULL OUT to reveal the hounds. They are racing in a straight line, dashing along the edge of the road. The forty riders follow, looking gleeful (except for the adults and Stevie, who still look perplexed). The hounds run along the road for a minute, then take a sharp right turn into a park-

263

ing lot. The only vehicles parked in the lot are a bunch of trucks and trailers labeled EMERSON CIRCUS.

CLOSE-UP on Stevie bringing Topside to a halt on the edge of the lot and looking around.

> STEVIE
> (muttering)
> This is the same parking lot where I saw that dastardly Veronica diAngelo's Mercedes this morning.
> (looks at the circus trucks and gulps)
> What if the hounds wreck the circus like they did Mr. Baker's garden?

PAN TO the hounds. They are not going anywhere near the circus trucks. Instead, they are dashing wildly up to a lamppost in the center of the lot. Then they stop.

PAN TO the riders, with Max near the front.

> MAX
> (sarcastically)
> Are we to assume the fox climbed the lamppost?

> CHESTER
> (unapologetically)
> They just follow their noses, Mr. Regnery. Their noses tell them something stopped here.

MR. BAKER
(also sarcastic)
If the fox went to ground here, we've got a
new burrowing and digging tool that the
construction industry is going to want to
know about.

CLOSE-UP on Stevie, who is beside Carole and Lisa. She
is listening to every word the men say, clearly very uncomfortable and anxious about what is happening. Her great
sense of responsibility is telling her that she may, somehow,
have had something to do with what is happening.
Lisa leans over to whisper to both her friends.

LISA
(amused)
Boy, this fox is cleverer than you were, Stevie!

Carole laughs. Stevie doesn't.

STEVIE
(with a gulp)
It's not a fox.

CAROLE
(confused)
If it's not a fox, what is it?

STEVIE
(grimly)

It's my brothers and Veronica. I don't know what they've done, but it's something. This whole thing just smells of trouble, and I'm the cause of it.

LISA
(dismayed and disbelieving)
No way. They promised!

Stevie turns to give her a sharp, suspicious look.

STEVIE
What do you mean, "They promised"?

Carole gasps, looking guilty. Lisa looks guilty, too. She gulps.

LISA
(slowly and reluctantly)
Carole and I were worried about them. We met them and asked if they were plotting revenge.

STEVIE
(with disbelief and dismay)
You talked to my conniving brothers?

CAROLE
(naive and earnest)
Yes, we did. We wanted to be sure they wouldn't do anything to ruin the fox hunt. They said they weren't mad at you. They

promised they wouldn't do anything. In fact, they were really interested to learn about the hunt. They asked us all kinds of questions.

CLOSE-UP on Stevie. We should be able to see her heart sink, almost literally, as she realizes the huge mistake her trusting friends have made.

> STEVIE
> Exactly what did you tell them?

> LISA
> Everything. We explained the differences among a mock hunt and a real hunt and a drag hunt—you know, that kind of thing.

Understanding dawns on Stevie's face. Then guilt and dismay as she realizes that she has ruined the fox hunt for everybody just because of her silly feud with her idiot brothers.

> STEVIE
> I have to go talk to the adults. It's the responsible thing to do.

She leaves her confused friends behind and rides toward Max, Mr. Baker, and Chester, who are still arguing and look quite angry.

STEVIE
(interrupting)
I know what's happening here.

The three men fall silent and turn to look at Stevie. She looks nervous but brave. The light of responsibility is burning in her eyes.

STEVIE
It's all my fault. My brothers and Veronica are angry with me, and this is their way of getting revenge. You see, my brothers know all about drag hunts. And I saw Veronica's family's car in this parking lot early this morning. I'm sure what she did was to take a bag of something that would draw the hounds and pull it behind her, on foot or maybe by bicycle. Can't you just see her laying the trail across Mr. Baker's porch and under the clothesline?

MAX
(nods slowly)
I guess I can.

He turns to Chester, looking apologetic.

MAX
And I guess we owe you an apology. Your hounds weren't the problem here after all.

CHESTER

I knew there was something fishy about it all.
These hounds will always follow a good
line—unless something distracts them, like a
fresh drag.

Mr. Baker turns toward Stevie with a serious look on his
face. Stevie gulps, then looks sad, suspecting she is about to
be formally disinvited from the rest of the hunt.

MAX

Would you excuse us for a moment, Stevie?
We need to talk.

Stevie turns Topside and rides away from the adults and all
the other riders. She looks very sad. Aimlessly she watches
the activity going on near the circus trucks.

STEVIE
(softly, to herself)

I guess I might as well see what I can of the
circus right now. Because once Mom and
Dad hear about what happened, none of us
will get to go.

She sighs sadly.
PAN TO an area in Stevie's line of sight, just behind one of
the larger trucks. An animal handler is guiding a big old
BULL ELEPHANT as it works to set up a tent. First the elephant picks up a long pole and carries it to the center of the

parking lot, where the circus's roustabouts are waiting to set it upright.

PAN BACK TO Stevie, who is watching the whole thing with a smile on her face, enjoying the sight. Then, a moment later, her nose suddenly wrinkles. She leans forward to pat Topside, addressing the following comment to the horse.

> STEVIE
> It's a good thing I like to ride horses instead
> of elephants. Imagine what it would be like
> to muck out an elephant's stall!

Stevie laughs and holds her nose.

> MAX (offscreen)
> Stevie, could you come over here?

Stevie suddenly looks nervous and guilty again. She rides back to rejoin the men.

> MAX
> We've had a little talk. We agree with you
> that this has come about because of your ac-
> tions, and you know we have talked in the
> past about the problems with practical jokes.

He pauses to glare at Stevie. However, his glare isn't totally convincing. One corner of his mouth keeps twitching as if he's fighting not to smile.

MAX

One thing we know about you, Stevie—
aside from your intense dedication to your
academic studies, that is—is that if there's
a tricky problem, you're always more likely
than anyone else to come up with a tricky
solution. That's why we're giving you a
shot here. Can you think of a way to sal-
vage this situation? To get the hounds back
to Cross County and off the scent of the
drag so they can pick up the line of a fox?
You have one chance to save yourself, Stevie. This is it.

CLOSE-UP on Stevie. She nods and looks around thought-
fully. The hounds are still barking wildly by the lamppost.
Her friends and some of the other riders are watching her
curiously. Then Stevie's gaze shifts back to the circus trucks.
The tent poles are all in place now, and the elephant is being led back toward a large pen nearby. Suddenly a "Eu-
reka!" expression crosses Stevie's face. She has just had a
great idea.

STEVIE
(to Chester; still staring at the elephant)
What if we mask the scent of the drag with a
stronger, more frightening, and unpleasant
smell?

Chester and the other men follow Stevie's gaze to the elephant.

> CHESTER
> Ingenious.

> MR. BAKER
> Ah, yes!

> MAX
> (to the other men)
> Would you excuse us, please? Stevie and I
> have some fast talking to do.

FADE OUT on Stevie and Max riding eagerly toward the elephant trainer.

And now, Miss Fenton, I think an article from *The Cross County Courier* can explain what happened next better than I can.

PACHYDERM JOINS PONY CLUB

A local fox hunt seemed to be in big trouble last Saturday—until the circus came to town.

The trouble all began when the hunters, consisting of young Pony Club members from Cross County and Pine Hollow Stables (the latter hailing from nearby Willow Creek) discovered that unknown parties had left a trail of scent that completely distracted the foxhounds and bamboozled the riders.

That was when the Emerson Circus (which will be performing on Fairville Road through the end of next week) came to the rescue, thanks to a brainstorm by one of the young riders, Stephanie "Johnny" Lake of Willow Creek.

Young Johnny quickly realized that the troublesome scent could only be masked by a much stronger scent. Quickly spying—and smelling—an elephant named Jumbo, one of the stars of the Emerson Circus, which was setting up nearby, Johnny realized that her hunt's salvation was at hand. She convinced Jumbo's trainer to ride the ponderous pachyderm over the offending area, thus eradicating the aroma that had drawn the dogs, and leaving them free to sniff out the fox they were bred to pursue. Local resident Wilbur Whiteside described the following scene: "There was this dang enormous elephant," he said. "It trundled on down the road, and a big old bunch of dogs and kids on horses followed right along with it. It was the strangest sight I've seen on this Earth these seventy years. Definitely the strangest. "Clearly, this impromptu pachyderm-puppy-and-pony parade will be remembered by onlookers for a long time. Johnny Lake's ingenious plan to save the hunt will surely be remembered just as long by the grateful members of two Pony Clubs.

Hi, Stevie,

Sorry I missed you today at the stable. But I got your message from Carole, and of course I'd be happy to

273

contribute an essay to your report. I was starting to get jealous because Carole wrote that big essay on leg injuries, and so far I hadn't gotten to do anything! (Except my "Life" essay, which doesn't count because I wrote it weeks ago.) Anyway, Carole said you wanted me to comment on the fox hunt and your role in . . . well, you know.

My mom said we could drop this off at your house on our way to the mall. So here it is. Hope it helps!

Lisa

THE BLAME GAME
An Essay by Lisa Atwood

Blame. It's a short word with a seemingly simple definition. But once we take a closer look at the whole concept of blame, it becomes much more complicated. It can sometimes be deceptively easy to point fingers of blame about things. But things are rarely that simple.

For example, my Pony Club recently joined another Pony Club for a fox hunt. Many people blamed my friend Stevie Lake for certain unplanned things that happened during that hunt. However, is she really completely to blame? I think not.

First of all, Stevie herself had nothing to do with creating the drag line that distracted the hounds. She never touched the scent that created it. She never told anyone else to create it. All she did was become enmeshed in a feud with certain parties, through little fault of her own, aside from feelings of vengefulness and anger.

And who among us has not been angry? Stevie was only revealing her all-too-human weaknesses when she completely humiliated her three brothers in front of everyone they know. She was merely expressing these same weaknesses when she insulted Veronica diAngelo.

Of course, one might argue that these same brothers and Veronica were only responding out of their own human weaknesses. In which case blame becomes muddy once again. But the worst anyone could say about Stevie then is that she was just one cog in the wheel of blame.

Stevie has suffered this same problem in the past. For instance, when a fully populated anthill turned up in a certain Pine Hollow rider's cubbyhole, everyone immediately pointed the finger of blame at Stevie, never stopping to think that perhaps she was simply teaching a fellow rider tolerance for *all* living things, great or small. For even if that wasn't exactly Stevie's conscious intent, mightn't it have been a happy side effect of the incident? And finally, when Stevie stole all the chalk from the classrooms and supply closets of her school and donated it to a local thrift store, most people might have assumed that she did it to play a prank on her teachers or to get out of some work. But why couldn't it have been that she was truly worried about the plight of the chalkless poor?

Stevie is not perfect. As her friend, I accept that—and love her nonetheless. I know that she sometimes gets too caught up in the moment and loses track of the consequences of her actions. But that isn't so unusual. And you can't really blame Stevie for what she *is*, only for what she *does*. Admittedly, what she does isn't always totally blameless. But everyone makes mistakes.

Stevie is a good person. Isn't that worth something here?

FROM: Steviethegreat

TO: LAtwood

SUBJECT: Gee, thanks

MESSAGE:

Okay, I know you tried. But let's be honest here. Do you really think this essay is going to help my cause?

Please don't take this the wrong way. I mean, the essay was really well written, of course, but maybe not exactly what I had in mind.

Still, I really am to BLAME for this one. (Ha ha!) After all, I know you too well. I know you're too honest to write an essay that isn't totally truthful. So I hope you'll appreciate my honesty when I tell you there's NO WAY I can include your essay in my report, no matter how truthful it is. I mean, honesty is one thing—but I don't want to get myself expelled! (And by the way, Miss Fenton still doesn't know who took that chalk.)

But I'll tell you this—I'll definitely keep your essay in my scrapbook for future reference. Maybe it will actually keep

me from getting myself into this same kind of scrape someday. HA HA! :-)

FROM: LAtwood
TO: Steviethegreat
SUBJECT: Re: Gee, thanks
MESSAGE:

I'm so glad you're not mad about the stuff I said in my essay. After I finished it, I realized it might not make you sound
quite as innocent as I meant it to. But sometimes it's hard to
explain exactly how things happen, you know? I mean, I
know you never meant to cause trouble for the hunt (or the
ants—though your teachers are another story—ha ha!). But
I guess you really had to be there to appreciate that, so maybe
there's no way Miss Fenton could ever really understand that
particular part of the story. Although I'm sure you can make
her understand if anyone can! (After all, you were persuasive
enough to convince that elephant trainer to go along with
your wacky plan against his better judgment, right?)

Not to change the subject, but I just saw something I
thought you'd be interested to hear. Remember how you
were telling Carole and me the other day about how you'd
heard Veronica has been goofing off instead of writing her
report? Well, guess what—you're right (at least regarding
today).

See, I just got back from a trip to the mall with my mother (ugh—don't ask!) and I saw Veronica there. I don't think she saw me—she seemed kind of distracted. Mom had dragged me into Maxwell's, that snooty boutique where Veronica likes to shop. And when we walked in, there she was at the counter, buying some scarf that looked like it cost about a zillion dollars. It would have matched the outfit she was wearing just fine, too—Veronica was dressed up so much she could have headed over to the White House for dinner with the President and made him feel underdressed! She did look nice, I'll admit, though it was hardly the outfit I would have chosen for a day at the mall. (Let alone a day in my room or at the library slaving over an incredibly important school report, which was where she should have been.) Anyway, thought you might be interested. . . .

I'd better sign off now. I don't want to distract you too much. I know your report is due the day after tomorrow, so you're probably crazed right about now.

Just one more thing, though. Seeing Veronica today made me think more than ever about how hard you've been working on this report. In case I haven't said it before, I'm really proud of you for all the effort you're putting into it. You should be proud of yourself, too, no matter what Miss Fenton says—though I'm one hundred percent sure she'll love it!

Anyway, I was thinking that after it's finished you'll really be ready to relax a little. How about we plan a nice, long Saddle Club trail ride for Monday afternoon? And we don't have to talk about school or reports or anything like that unless you want to. How does that sound? I'm going to e-mail Carole about it right now and make sure she's free.

So get back to work!

FROM: HorseGal
TO: Steviethegreat
CC: LAtwood
SUBJECT: Trail ride
MESSAGE:

Thanks for your e-mail about the trail ride, Lisa. I think it's a fantastic idea! For one thing, Stevie, it will remind you exactly what you've been working so hard to save. Plus it will be great to spend some quality time together, just the three of us. We've missed you, Stevie!

But don't think about that right now. Just concentrate on your report. Because you're almost there—and I know it's going to be the most incredible school assignment Miss Fenton (or anyone else) has ever seen!

Welcome to My Life . . .

After masking the drag trail (and hauling up Mrs. Baker's laundry poles), Jumbo returned to the circus, and the rest of us returned to the hunt. Chester led us into a field behind the stable, far enough so the hounds wouldn't be confused

279

by any of the strange scents floating around there. Then he turned them loose. And the *real* hunt was on!

This time everything was very different. The hounds circled eagerly and soon picked up the scent they were looking for. They raced across hill and dale at top speed, following the scent of the fox. We followed the hounds, urging our horses to canter and gallop to keep up. It was so much fun! We jumped a whole bunch of fences and gates and even a huge fallen log.

There were a lot of wonderful things about that hunt. One of them was that Lisa discovered what a fantastic jumper Diablo is and totally fell in love with him (and jumping). Carole decided she had to add foxhunter to her list of possible careers (though I'm not sure there's much money in it). And I started to forgive myself for putting the whole hunt in jeopardy earlier.

After a while, the hounds lost the scent in the middle of a wide, smooth field. While they were sniffing around, trying to pick it up again, I pulled Topside alongside my friends. We chatted for a few minutes about how wonderful it all was. And then, suddenly, I spotted some motion in the grass about a quarter of a mile ahead.

I squinted and shaded my eyes. I couldn't help wondering if the bright sunshine was playing tricks with my vision.

It wasn't. The movement came again, and this time I was sure. I caught a glimpse of a long, furry tail.

"It's a . . . a . . . Did you see . . . ," I sputtered. I was so excited I could barely talk. So I just pointed.

"Strange to see Stevie speechless," Phil remarked. "Usually we can't shut her up."

Carole and Lisa laughed. They didn't even seem to realize that I was trying to tell them something important.

"Look . . ." I tried again. "It's a . . ." But the words still wouldn't come.

"There she goes again," Lisa joked.

Finally Max glanced over at me from where he was riding nearby. I guess he noticed my frantic pointing and figured out what I was trying to tell someone. Because he started waving wildly at Mr. Baker and Chester. "The fox!" he shouted. "Stevie spotted the fox!"

"Master! Huntsman! Whippers-in!" Mr. Baker called. "We have to get the hounds on the line again!"

It took some organizing, but in a very short time the whippers-in and the huntsman managed to head the hounds in the direction I was pointing. As soon as the hounds were turned around, one of them picked up the scent and began giving tongue. The other hounds quickly took the hint, and soon they were all baying at the tops of their lungs. The noise was incredible—and the excitement, among both hound and human members of the hunt, was so strong you could practically smell it.

The hunt had been fun up until that point. But as the hounds dashed across the field in hot pursuit of the fox, it got even better. My heart was pounding with excitement, practically drowning out the pounding of Topside's hooves as he thundered across the field after the hounds. It was positively thrilling!

The hounds led us across the field, into the woods, and through a glen. We had to leap over fallen trees, dodge around rocks, splash across creeks, and duck under branches. With every step, the hounds howled loudly, each pushing to get to the front of the pack and be the first to catch the wily fox.

And then it stopped as suddenly as it had started. The hounds fell silent. They still sniffed eagerly, but now they were just circling around in this grassy, open area surrounded by thick underbrush.

"He's gone to ground," Lisa commented, sounding a little breathless from our wild ride across the countryside.

I nodded. What Lisa meant was that the fox had found a burrow or hole to hide in underground. That meant the fox was probably safe and the hunt was probably over.

"We'll wait a little while," Chester said. "Sometimes foxes make mistakes."

So we waited. But after twenty minutes, it was clear that the fox had outfoxed us.

"Maybe the fox went back to Cross County for the hunt breakfast," Lisa suggested. "Certain other foxes have been known to do that."

Chester looked confused. Everybody else laughed, including me. Then we headed back to the stable for a well-earned meal.

But even though the hunt was over, the memory of it has stayed with me ever since. In fact, I found the whole thing so inspiring that, once again, I am forced to express my feelings in verse.

THE CHARGE OF THE FOX BRIGADE
A poem by S. Lake
(with appreciation to Alfred, Lord Tennyson)

Half a mile, half a mile,
Half a mile onward,
All in the valley of Cross County
   Rode the forty riders.
"Forward after the fox!
Follow that fox!" Max cried.
Into the valley of Cross County
   Rode the forty riders.

"Forward, Pony Clubbers!"
Did any among us blubber?
No, for we knew to catch
   That fox, we had to burn rubber.
Ours not to stare into space,
Ours not to make a face,
Ours but to ride and chase.
Into the valley of Cross County
   Rode the forty riders.

Fences to the right of us,
Fences to the left of us,
Fences in front of us.
   Galloping and jumping.
Led all over hill and dell,
Boldly we rode and well,

After the wily fox
None of us even fell!
    We forty riders.

When can our glory fade?
O what a wild ride we made!
    We'll remember it forever.
Honor the ride we made!
Honor the Fox Brigade!
Noble forty riders!

That just about sums up how I felt after the hunt was over. (And how I feel about the wonderful art of poetry, thanks to my many fine English teachers over the years.) Of course, I still had a little business to take care of afterward. Now that the thrilling chase was over, I remembered what my brothers and Veronica had done.

Still, I had learned a little something from this whole experience. I had learned that sometimes silence can be the strongest weapon of all. Phil and I discussed it on our way back to Willow Creek. He was coming to dinner at my house again, and neither of us wanted anything like a repeat of his last dinner there. So by the time we arrived at the table, we had agreed upon a plan.

Chad was the first to bring up the hunt. "So, Stevie and Phil, tell me," he said in his most fake-casual voice. "How was the fox hunt today? Anything interesting happen?"

As if he doesn't know! I thought. But I kept the thought to myself.

"Oh, it was great," Phil said. "We went all over the woods by Cross County. Stevie even spotted the fox once."

"A real fox?" Alex asked, looking surprised. "Are you sure?"

"I definitely saw its tail," I said. "And the hounds followed it all over the place. It was something."

"It was great," Phil added. "You can't imagine the adventure foxhunting is."

"Hmmm," Alex said.

"I don't get it," Michael added.

I smiled at them innocently. "I've never had a ride like that," I said.

Chad glanced at the other two with an odd look on his face. I almost couldn't stop myself from smirking. It was great! We were driving my brothers crazy.

"Well, did you catch the fox?" Chad asked after a moment.

"Of course not," I replied. "We never wanted to do that. I told you that. It's not about catching foxes. It's really just a fun kind of riding."

"The *most* fun," Phil put in.

"But didn't anything unusual happen?" Alex asked, sounding a little desperate.

"Ahem," my mother said. I was pretty sure she had no idea what was going on. But I was even more certain that she could tell that *something* was going on.

Michael didn't notice her stern look. "So, like, didn't you spend a lot of time on the road?" he asked.

I pasted my most innocent expression on my face. "Road? What road?"

By now my father had smelled a rat, too. "Boys, what's going on here?" he demanded.

"Nothing," all three of them answered at once.

I smiled at them sweetly. They stared back in total confusion. It was wonderful. I knew they would find out the truth eventually, but for now the joke was on them. And that was all I really wanted.

Phil and I discussed it after dinner when we had a few minutes alone.

"Your parents are going to find out about this," Phil predicted.

I nodded. "They're going to be pretty angry about it, I'm sure. We'll probably all get grounded, and if I know Dad he'll make good on his threat not to take us to the circus this year." As a responsible person, I knew it was only what my brothers and I deserved for all the trouble we'd caused. "I'll be sorry about that," I went on, "but otherwise, the whole thing has turned out wonderfully. And the circus will be back next year. I can wait until then."

When I looked at Phil, I noticed that he had a mischievous sparkle in his green eyes.

"What is it?" I asked. "Why are you smiling like that?"

"Like what?" he replied innocently.

"Like the cat that swallowed the canary."

"Not a canary, exactly." He reached into his pocket. "More like an elephant."

I still didn't get it. "What are you doing?" I demanded.

"I just wanted to see if I had anything interesting in my

pocket here." He pulled something out. "Oh, what's this?" he asked, obviously trying to sound surprised. "Oh, my, my."

I recognized what he was holding immediately. "Tickets?" My mind raced. It could mean only one thing. "To the circus?"

Phil nodded. "Jumbo's trainer seemed to think that being on a fox hunt was the most fun he'd had all day. He was looking for a way to thank you for letting him join in. I just made a suggestion, that's all. Are you free next Friday night?"

I grinned at him, hardly believing my good fortune. "You bet I am!"

Welcome to My Life: Conclusion

So you see, Miss Fenton, my life has been pretty busy for the past couple of months. I was forced to make some choices: To learn all about making maple syrup and help my friend Dinah instead of reading *To Kill a Mockingbird* and studying fractions. To pay tribute to a wonderful old Pine Hollow friend at his retirement and support Carole at the racetrack instead of reading my history assignment and finishing my science project. To throw myself into the excitement of the fox hunt instead of completing my word problems and writing my English essay.

I wish I could say that I wanted to go back and do it all again—that I would be willing to change my actions and choose homework over life. But I promised to be honest in this assignment, and I'm not going to stop now. So I must admit that I wouldn't change a thing.

However, I can promise you this: I've learned a lot from my experiences. And one of the things I learned is that I can sometimes get a little bit carried away. That is a valuable lesson, and one I'll always remember.

I can also promise you that I'll do my very best not to let myself get so far behind on my schoolwork in the future. I know learning is important.

And I ask you, Miss Fenton, what better lesson could I have learned from my recent studies in the School of Life?

FROM: Steviethegreat
TO: DSlattVT
SUBJECT: Whew!
MESSAGE:

Well, I did it! It's Tuesday evening as I write this. I just finished dinner, and it's my brothers' turn to wash up. So this is the first time I've been able to use the computer since I finished my report—the three of them have been Jawboning it up nonstop.

Anyway, you'll never believe how everything turned out. First of all, I left my report on Miss Fenton's desk the second I got to school on Monday. She wasn't in her office at the time, and I was just as glad about that. (Although her secretary looked kind of shocked when she saw how long the report was—it filled up an entire three-ring binder.)

288

I wasn't really looking forward to hearing Miss Fenton's comments on my report. I mean, I'd worked my brains out for two weeks straight, but that didn't mean she was guaranteed to like it. So I was pretty nervous all through homeroom, and I hardly heard a word my teachers said in my morning classes.

Then, just before the lunch bell rang, Miss Fenton called me to her office. I walked as slowly as I could on my way there, since I was certain I was walking to my doom. If she had something to say to me this soon, it could only be bad news.

But I was wrong! Miss Fenton was all smiles when I entered.

"Congratulations, Stephanie," she said, putting me out of my suspense right away. "I've spent all morning reading your report. It's wonderful!"

I was so relieved that my knees actually went weak. I plopped down in the chair across from her and just stared. I guess I didn't quite believe my ears.

I think she sort of understood that. She went on. "Your report was one of the most creative and interesting I have ever had the pleasure to read. And your teachers tell me you've done satisfactory makeup work for them as well. So let me be the first to assure you that your average is now up to a solid B."

"Thanks, Miss Fenton," I said, finding my voice at last. "Thanks a million!" Visions of myself riding through the woods behind Pine Hollow flashed through my mind. My summer was safe!

"But that's not all, Stephanie," Miss Fenton went on. "As you know, I've been busy myself this week. I'm supposed to announce the winner of the school essay contest tomorrow morning."

Essay contest? For a second, I had no idea what she was talking about. Then, vaguely, it started to come back. I remembered hearing something on the morning announcements last week about how each teacher was allowed to submit their favorite student essay or writing assignment of the year. Miss Fenton was supposed to read them all and pick a winner—the best of the best, I think she'd called it.

Anyway, even after I remembered all that, I still had no idea why she was telling me about it.

Luckily, she explained. "I know I'm not technically a teacher, but it *is* my contest. So I figured if I wanted to submit a favorite student writing assignment of my own, well, who was going to stop me? I'm the headmistress, after all."

By now I was starting to get an inkling of what she was getting at. "Do you mean— Did you—"

She smiled. "Yes, Stephanie. I chose to submit your 'Welcome to My Life' paper in the writing contest." She paused and winked conspiratorially at me. "And I probably shouldn't be telling you this, but I suspect you ought to spend a little time working on another writing assignment this evening."

"Huh?" I said, lost once again.

This time her smile was more like a grin. "That's right. You're going to want to have a victory speech ready when I announce the winner tomorrow."

I grinned back at her, a little amazed at how well this had

290

all turned out. Just think—I hadn't even been sure she would appreciate or understand or like my report at all. And now here she was telling me she was actually giving me an *award* for it! Just wait until my brothers hear about that. Not to mention Veronica . . .

Who knew Miss Fenton was so cool?

So by the time I met Carole and Lisa at Pine Hollow after school, I was really in a celebrating mood. I was glad they'd suggested our special trail ride. Naturally, I told them my good news right away, hardly making them squirm at all first. Then we tacked up our horses and headed off toward our favorite wooded trail. The weather was perfect, my mood was perfect, and of course my friends were perfect as always. It was so great to just relax and hang out with them again. After two weeks of hardly seeing them, I had almost forgotten what they're like!

But that's not all I have to tell you. I'd better write fast, because my brothers could burst in any minute. The main reason I'm writing is to tell you what I finally found out about Veronica. Prepare yourself—it's pretty shocking. In fact, it's so shocking that I could never, ever, in a million years, tell anybody in Willow Creek about it, not even Carole and Lisa.

You see, while I was in Miss Fenton's office hearing about my prize-winning report, I happened to notice another report lying on the end of her desk. You'll be glad to know that all those afternoons you and I spent teaching ourselves to read upside down came in handy. I was able to scan the entire first page of the report.

It was Veronica's extra-credit assignment, of course. The title was *Why the Homework It Is Necessary*, and the first few lines went something like this:

I, Miss Veronica, am very smart and intelligent. I always my homework am doing, and it is well. My grades, they suffer for reasons that are no my fault, and I explain the ones here. You understand, my family it is very wealthy, and . . .

I don't remember the rest of it, but you get the picture. As difficult as it was to believe, I was positive that she'd gotten her maid, Luisa, to write it for her. The poor woman hardly speaks English, but since when has Veronica ever taken no for an answer? (Even though you say no the same way in English *and* Spanish, ha ha!) Besides, she probably offered Luisa some huge bonus to knock off five pages of excuses.

I couldn't help gloating a little over that. And I couldn't help saying something to Miss Fenton about it. "So," I said casually, wanting to be subtle. "Does this mean my report was better than, say, any other special assignments you've read lately? Say, today?"

I guess I wasn't quite subtle enough. She must have followed my gaze to Veronica's paper and figured out what I was driving at. But instead of getting mad or stern or something, she just looked sort of sad. Or sympathetic, maybe.

"It's *really* too bad," she murmured. At first I thought she was mad at me for peeking. Then I realized she seemed to be talking mostly to herself. When she noticed I was listening, she seemed to come to some sort of decision. She hemmed and hawed a little, but finally, after swearing me to secrecy, she told me about Veronica.

After the first few seconds I was so shocked and stunned by what I was hearing that I don't remember exactly how Miss Fenton explained it all. But the upshot is that Veronica's grandmother has been pretty sick lately. In fact, until just this past weekend they were pretty sure she wasn't going to make it.

But that's not all. Apparently Veronica and her grandma are really, really close. So that's why Veronica has been having so much trouble in school lately—and why she's been acting so weird. She was worried about her poor sick granny!

I can imagine what you're thinking as you read this, Dinah. Like me, your first thought is probably that Veronica just invented some fake granny to weasel her way out of trouble. But after nosing around a bit during the rest of the day, I found out that it's the truth! Veronica has been spending all her free time visiting her grandma in the hospital over near Cross County. She's been giving her extravagant gifts (like this really expensive scarf that Lisa saw her buying), calling her twenty times a day (including a few times from Pine Hollow), and generally moping around alone and being miserable (instead of making everyone else's lives miserable like usual). The more I found out, the more the pieces fell into place. It explained why she had been missing a lot of school and Pony Club meetings. And all her other weird behavior, too.

So here's the million-dollar question: Could Veronica

diAngelo, the snob we both know and despise, actually have a human side to her personality? A soft, sympathetic, and (shudder) *likable* side that actually cares so deeply about a sick relative? It hardly seems possible, and yet . . .

I managed to push the whole topic out of my mind during the trail ride with my friends, but I've spent most of the last twenty-four hours thinking about it. Two days ago I couldn't have imagined feeling the slightest bit of sympathy for Veronica, ever. But now I'm not so sure.

Luckily, Veronica's granny is on the mend. I checked on it by calling the hospital and pretending to be Veronica (though I had to hang up fast when the nurse tried to put me through to the patient's room). So at least the sympathy is unnecessary now.

Still, it makes me feel kind of weird—almost queasy, actually—to think about what this all means. So I've decided not to think about it ever again after I finish writing this e-mail. And I've vowed never to breathe a word of it to anyone in Willow Creek, even my best friends. Actually, make that *especially* my best friends. They're already much quicker to forgive or ignore Veronica's rotten behavior than I am. If they knew she might actually be human, they'd probably never go along with one of my brilliant practical jokes on her again.

And then how would I manage to have any fun at all?

ABOUT THE AUTHOR

Bonnie Bryant is the author of more than a hundred books about horses, including The Saddle Club series, Saddle Club Super Editions, the Pony Tails series, and Pine Hollow, which follows the Saddle Club girls into their teens. She has also written novels and movie novelizations under her married name, B. B. Hiller.

Ms. Bryant began writing The Saddle Club in 1986. Although she had done some riding before that, she intensified her studies then and found herself learning right along with her characters Stevie, Carole, and Lisa. She claims that they are all much better riders than she is.

Ms. Bryant was born and raised in New York City. She still lives there, in Greenwich Village, with her two sons.

Don't miss the next exciting
Saddle Club adventure . . .

SECRET HORSE
The Saddle Club #86

Stevie Lake, Carole Hanson, and Lisa Atwood are
hoping to compete in a prestigious horse show. To that
end, they're doing everything they can to stay on stable owner Max Regnery's good side—including doing
extra chores around Pine Hollow, such as helping to
exercise the horses.

Veronica diAngelo is sure she'll be making the trip
to the horse show—just as she's sure she'll bring home
a blue ribbon. And of course Veronica has no inten-
tion of lifting a finger to help anyone.

The Saddle Club would love to beat Veronica, but
how? She and her horse are tough competition. Then
Lisa takes one of the horses over a jump, and he's a natural. Now The Saddle Club has to keep their secret
weapon under wraps and teach Veronica a lesson she
won't forget!

This story concludes in *Show Jumper*, The Saddle
Club #87.